THE PORTRAIT OF

Mrs. Charbuque

JEFFREY FORD

TOR

First published 2002 by William Morrow
an imprint of HarperCollins Publishers, New York

First published in Great Britain 2003 by Tor
an imprint of Pan Macmillan Ltd
Pan Macmillan, 20 New Wharf Road, London N1 9RR
Basingstoke and Oxford
Associated companies throughout the world
www.panmacmillan.com
www.toruk.com

ISBN 1 4050 0659 5

1 3 5 7 9 8 6 4 2

A CIP catalogue record for this book is available from
the British Library.

Printed and bound in Great Britain by
Mackays of Chatham plc, Chatham, Kent

For Lynn,
singular, mysterious, and beautiful

THE PORTRAIT OF
Mrs. Charbuque

A NICE BIT OF WORK

*M*UCH TO my unease, Mrs. Reed positioned herself, all evening, beneath or immediately to either side of her new portrait. She had, for this occasion, worn the same black gown and diamond necklace I had requested she wear when posing for me. Given the situation, comparisons between God's work and my own were unavoidable. I daresay the Almighty's original was found somewhat wanting in the face of my painterly revision. Whereas, in His unquestionable wisdom, He had gone for the grandiose in the formation of her nose and saw fit to leave a prominent gap between the front teeth, I had closed ranks and reduced to beautiful normalcy those aspects of her features that made her *her*. By using a faint shade of rose and sparing the chiaroscuro, I had added a certain youthful radiance to the tone and elasticity of her flesh, turning back the clock to but a few minutes after that earlier hour when these corresponding changes would have seemed ludicrous.

Perhaps Mrs. Reed was wholly unaware of these discrepancies or, being aware of them, believed that by standing as close to her fairer double as possible she would permanently confuse artifice and reality in the minds of her friends and family. Perhaps she was hoping for some supernatural transmutation between flesh and paint, as was the plot of Wilde's recent novel, *The Portrait of Dorian Gray*. Whatever the case, she appeared to be beaming with joy. As for the rest of us in attendance, we were all uneasy conspirators in a plot to ignore the truth. Thankfully, her husband had spent a small fortune on good champagne for the unveiling and encouraged all to drink freely.

Many of the fifty or so guests felt compelled to approach me and offer praise for my work, which if not for the alcohol would have left my expression a permanent wince.

"Piambo, the rendering of the goldfish in the bowl on the table next to Mrs. Reed is spectacular. I can count the very scales from here."

"The barely wilting nasturtiums in that Chinese vase behind her are so lifelike."

"No one can capture the fold of a gown as you can, and my, how the diamonds sparkle."

I politely thanked them all, knowing that in the coming year I would be doing for some of them precisely what I had done for Mrs. Reed. When I thought I was finally to be left alone, Shenz, my colleague in the fine art of portraiture, sidled up next to me. A short fellow, sporting one of those close-trimmed beards that come to a point, he was well known for an adherence to the tenets of the Pre-Raphaelites and his portraits of the lesser luminaries of the Vanderbilt clan. Hiding his impish grin behind a large cigar, he stared across the spacious parlor at the portrait.

"A nice bit of work, Piambo," he said, and then slightly turned his head and shifted his eyes to look up at me.

"Have some more champagne," I whispered to him, and he quietly laughed.

"*Salubrious* is the word I would use," he said. "Yes, quite salubrious."

"I'm keeping a running tally," I told him, "as to whether people appreciate the goldfish or the nasturtiums more."

"Put me down for the nose," he said. "A truly ingenious economy of paint."

"I think that was Reed's favorite also. He paid me exorbitantly for this one."

"And well he should," said Shenz. "I think your magic has enchanted his wife into completely forgetting his indiscretion with that young salesgirl from Macy's. Forget about all that new money his ready-made shoe mills have pumped out; only your abilities could have saved his marriage and respectability."

"Lord knows there is much more to it than simply painting," I said. "Who is *your* next victim?"

"I've picked up a commission just this evening to immortalize the Hatstells' corpulent offspring. A pair of overfed little monsters I am contemplating drugging with laudanum to make them sit still for me." Before departing, he raised his champagne glass and offered a toast. "To art," he said as the rims of fine crystal touched.

After Shenz left me, I took a seat in the corner next to a potted fern and lit my own cigar, sending up a smoke screen behind which I could hide. By then I had had too many glasses of champagne, and my head whirled. The light reflecting off the ornate chandelier hanging in the center of the room, combined with the flash of jewelry bedecking the better halves of New York society's nouveau riche couples, nearly blinded me. Snatches of conversation occasionally leaped out of the oceanic rumblings of the assembled guests, and in a matter of minutes I had heard pieces of discussions concerning everything from the opening of the Columbian Exhibition in Chicago to the latest antics of that nightshirted child who inhabited "Down Hogan's Alley," the *World*'s new cartoon.

In my daze it came to me that I not only wanted but *needed* to be elsewhere. I realized that of late I had been spending more time in chandeliered parlors, drinking myself to the verge of a stupor, than I did in front of the easel. At that moment the sea of partygoers shifted, my eyes focused, and I caught a glimpse of Mrs.

Reed standing now by herself, staring up at her portrait. My view of her was from the back, but I saw her slowly lift one arm and touch her hand to her face. She then turned quickly and walked away. An instant later my view was again obscured by a woman wearing a green silk gown, the color of which reminded me that I was feeling a twinge of nausea. I stubbed out the cigar in the potted fern and then rose unsteadily. Luckily, without having to venture too far into the thick of the merriment, I was able to find the maid and request my coat and hat.

My plan had been to beat a hasty, unnoticed retreat, but as I made for the stairs that led down to the front door, Reed intercepted me.

"Piambo," he called, "you can't be leaving."

I turned around and saw him standing there, weaving slightly, his eyelids at half-mast. He was smiling his patented close-lipped Reed smile, which for all but those with a portraitist's keen ability to analyze physical effects would seem a manifestation of goodwill itself. The man was handsome in a modern way, with sideburns and mustache and features that appeared chiseled into existence by Saint-Gaudens. He was also lucky beyond measure, that was a certainty, but I tell you, what I saw when I studied him was a mechanized mill of insincerity.

"You are the guest of honor," he said, approaching me and putting his hand on my shoulder.

"Forgive me, Reed," I whispered, "but I am guilty of trying to consume all of that wonderful champagne myself. My head is spinning so, I need to get some air."

He laughed out loud, and his racket turned the heads of nearby guests. I glanced momentarily at the crowd in my embarrassment, and among all those faces, not knowing the cause of Reed's joke but laughing along with him at my expense, I also saw Shenz shake his head and glance at the ceiling as a secret signal to me that, yes, Reed was an overbearing ass.

"Before you go, let me fetch the missus. I'm sure she would want to thank you and bid you good-bye."

"Very well," I said. Reed disappeared, and I stood staring down the long flight of steps toward the portal of escape. A few moments later he returned with his wife in tow.

"Piambo has pressing business across town, dear," he said to her. "He must, reluctantly, be on his way. I thought you would want to thank him for the portrait."

Mrs. Reed smiled, and I fixated on that gap between her teeth. In the days that I'd spent in her presence, she had seemed almost devoid of personality. She had been an obedient model and not unpleasant, but I had never tried to get at her true essence, because it had been indicated to me in not so many words, by her husband, that inner spirit was not to be the point of the portrait.

She stepped forward in a manner to indicate that she was going to kiss my cheek. In that instant, as she came toward me, I caught a fleeting glimpse of something more than the dull affect to which I had grown accustomed. Then her lips grazed my face, and before she pulled back I heard her whisper in a voice no louder than the sound of a wet brush gliding across canvas, "I hope you die." When she was again standing before me so that I could see her entire countenance, she was smiling.

"Thank you, Piambo," she now said. Reed put his arm around her, and they stood together as if posing for a work meant to depict marital bliss. The facility of vision I had trained for so many years to see into the souls of those who sat for me, yet had ignored of late in an effort to render instead what Shenz had termed the *salubrious,* suddenly engaged, and I beheld a pale, mortally weary woman in the clutches of a vampire. I turned and fled, stumbling slightly on the stairs, dogged by the feeling that might attend the abandoning of a child fallen into an icy river.

THE MESSENGER

I PASSED UP the hansom cabs that Reed had waiting to ferry his guests home. Turning to my left, I set off south down Fifth Avenue, my head still spinning from the alcohol and Mrs. Reed's whispered desire. I pulled the collar of my coat up and the brim of my hat down, for it was as if summer had quietly expired at some point during the party. A stiff breeze blew down the avenue at my back, carrying past my left shoulder a sheet of yellowing newsprint that flapped and flew beneath the gas lamps like the fleeing ghost of that warm season. It was late, and I had many blocks to walk to my home on Gramercy Park, but I needed more than anything the air, the motion, the night, as an antidote to the staleness of the crowded parlor and the false, fractured light of that damnable chandelier.

The city streets were far from safe at that bleak hour, but it was a certainty that no matter how vicious an assailant I might meet, he could never be quite as insidiously dangerous as Reed. I shook my head at the thought of what his poor wife had been made to endure and how I had been a willing, albeit a somewhat unwitting, participant in her torture. What was evident to me now was that she had known all along what the game was. Most likely for the sake of her children, but also for her own survival, she had pretended to be enchanted by Reed's pretense. If this was the first time, I doubted it would be the last, but now, with each future assault on her dignity, the charming, ageless beauty in my painting would forever bear witness to the increasing ugliness of her marriage and her life. That visage that was almost her, but not quite, was undoubtedly the woman her husband wanted. In truth, the real Mrs. Reed had more in common with the goldfish trapped in the bowl and the cut flowers left to wither in the ornate Chinese vase. I did not realize when I chose those props how telling they would prove to be.

"Piambo, what have you become?" I said to myself, and then realized I had spoken aloud. I looked to see if any passersby had heard me. But no, the few others out and about at that late hour continued on, wrapped in their own desires and admonitions. During the day the city carried on like a hell-bent millionaire genius, pursuing the future with a frenetic energy that would someday allow it to overcome its quarry, but at night, while it dreamed, its streets were like the specter-haunted thoroughfares of a deep-sea kingdom.

Even the streetcars moved at a more languorous pace, like great serpents swimming through a darkness made thick by the cast-off regrets of the day. I forestalled answering my own question by stopping at the corner of Thirty-third Street to peer across the avenue at the moonlit remains of what once had been the mansion of John Jacob Astor. I had read in the newspaper that his son, to spite the mother, was going to raze the old building and erect a fine hotel. There it sat, half dismantled, like the rotting carcass of some behemoth washed ashore in a painting by Vedder. Here was a testament to the corrosive power of the city's new wealth. Even the old gods and their legacies were not protected from its onslaught. The new deity was fortune, and there was an army of Reeds willing to adjust their moral barometers in order to join the priesthood. Its catechism trickled down from the upper reaches of Manhattan Island all the way to the Lower East Side, where immigrant families chased the insubstantial spirit of what they could not readily grasp.

In the face of such a pervasive societal mania, how was I, a mere painter, not also to be changed by it? There had been a time not too long ago when photography established itself on the scene, and those of my profession gasped and held their breath in trepidation, envisioning a future of poverty. But once the well-to-do realized that now it was possible for even a peon to have a cheap copy of his likeness, the practice of commissioning portraits by accomplished painters exploded among the blue bloods and the self-made elite. After all, a photograph yellowed and cracked within a generation or two, but an oil painting would carry its exalted subjects intact into the distant future. Then the blizzard of bills began to fall, obscuring my view of what it was I had initially sought to accomplish with my art. That is when I came under the whip of that aspect of portraiture that John Sargent called the *tyranny of vanity*—all the machinations and intricate webs of intrigue perpetrated by its patrons.

Since Sargent was the reigning king of portraiture, my own style had slowly metamorphosed into a slightly less resilient copy of his slick realism. I should say I had a better take on it than most of my contemporaries who were following suit, but still, there was only one Sargent, and I was not he. The money and a certain fame came along all the same, though, and I had, almost without realizing it, done for myself what I had recently done for Mrs. Reed. With much less to lose than she, I also had opted for the definite but invisible boundary of the goldfish bowl and so was also withering inside like those cut flowers ensconced in the ornate vase that was my life.

As I walked on, the fresh air doing its job, it became clear to me that the important question was not "What have I become?" but more "What am I now to do?" How was I to return to myself and paint something of worth before I grew too old to care, too weak to try? I turned and looked at my shadowed self passing in the glass of a shop window, and it was at that moment I remembered a painting I had seen at the National Academy of Design a year or so earlier. That work was titled *The Race Track* or *The Reverse* and had been painted by the enigmatic Albert Pinkham Ryder, originally of New Bedford. He now resided at an undistinguished address on East Eleventh Street and worked in a cramped, run-down attic studio on Fifteenth. I had met him briefly through Richard Gilder, the editor of *Century Magazine,* who was a neighbor of mine in Gramercy.

The painting was harrowing in its imagery of the figure of skeletal Death wielding a scythe while riding atop a horse racing alone clockwise around a track. In the foreground was a writhing serpent and in the background a lowering sky rendered in shades of ochre, burnt sienna, and some indistinguishable but lurking scarlet that, together, perfectly captured the somber stillness preceding a storm. The piece projected the raw emotion of dread, and anyone brave enough to have purchased it and hung it in a parlor would have been inviting a nightmare into their home. That picture had truths to tell and was the opposite of the technically perfect, stylistically safe work of Sargent's that was so popular with the moneyed class.

Gilder had told me that Ryder painted it after hearing the story of a waiter who had worked in his brother's hotel. The poor fellow had scrupulously saved five thousand dollars and then lost it in one fell swoop on a single race at Hanover. Following his loss he committed suicide. This then was Ryder's eulogy for him.

Ryder sold his work when there were buyers, but he worked regardless of money, toiling to capture those things in paint that could not be expressed in words. By all accounts he was a strange fellow, somewhat shy and retiring, who used anything at hand on his paintings—alcohol, candle wax, varnish, oil. When his brushes failed him, he supposedly used the palette knife to spread thick gobs of paint. When the knife failed him, he used his hands, and when the varnish did not bring forth the quality he desired, it was said he used his own spit. He would paint a picture and, before it dried, paint another over it. I would not say he was naive, but when I met him I sensed a palpable innocence about him. With his calm demeanor, his large stature and full beard, he struck me as being like a biblical prophet.

I remembered encountering one of his seascapes when I was a young apprentice to my mentor, M. Sabott. It was of a small boat in a wild ocean, and it radiated the overwhelming power of Nature and the courage of the insignificant sailor in the prow. Sabott, who stood next to me, labeled it *a muddle*. "This fellow is like a baby painting with his own shit upon the nursery wall. The sign of a master is restraint," he said, and for some time that assessment stuck with me when I would happen upon one of his canvases at Cottier & Co., his gallery, or at one of the juried shows. Sabott may have had a point, but oh, to be that baby once again and revel in that singular vision, ignoring the Reeds of the world and their wealth.

An acquaintance of Ryder's had once quoted to me something the painter had written to him in a letter. It went like this: "Have you ever seen an inchworm crawl up a leaf or twig, and then, clinging to the very end, revolve for a moment in the air, feeling for something, to reach something? That's like me. I am trying to find something out there beyond the place on which I have a footing."

I made a left at Twenty-first Street and headed toward my address, realizing that this was precisely what I needed. The trick was to reach *beyond* the safety of my present existence and rediscover myself as an artist. My only fear was that in reaching out, I might grasp nothing. I had already surmounted the crest of my years and begun on the denouement. Or let us say, I could feel the quickening wind in my thinning hair. What if I were to fail and on top of it lose my position as one of the most sought after portraitists in New York? I thought again of Ryder's painting of Death on horseback, and then of the fool who had saved and squandered everything at once. After all my serious contemplation I was more confused than ever. The pursuit of wealth and safety and the pursuit of a kind of moral truth had ingeniously changed horses, so to speak, in midstream. My longing to be other than what I was had risen to the surface, fraught with good intention, and then burst like a bubble in champagne. I shook my head, laughing aloud at my predicament, and that is when I felt something lightly strike my left shin.

I looked up to see a man leaning against the wall, and it gave me quite a start. I composed myself and said, "Excuse me, sir," not without an air of irritation. He withdrew the black walking stick with which he had accosted me, and stepped forward. He was quite large but old, with a short white beard and a ring of white hair forming a perimeter to his otherwise bald scalp. His three-piece suit was pale violet, given interesting undertones of green by the glow of the street lamp near the curb. This unusual play of light took my attention for a moment until I looked him in the face and was startled by the discovery that his eyes had lost the distinction of pupil and iris and clouded to a uniform whiteness.

"I believe you are the one who signs his paintings *Piambo*," he said.

Anything ill to do with the eyes truly upsets me, and it took me a few moments to recover from the sight of his. "Yes," I said.

"Watkin is the name," he said.

"And?" I asked, expecting him to put the touch on me for some change.

"My employer would like to commission you to paint her portrait," he said in a soft voice that held a hint of menace in its precision.

"I'm afraid I'm engaged for months to come," I said, wanting to be on my way.

"It must be now," he said. "She will have no other but you."

"I admire the good woman's taste, but I'm afraid I have given my word on these other projects."

"This is a job like no other," he said. "You can name your price. Take all the other commissions you have given your word on, tally the amount you would have received, and she will triple it."

"Who is your employer?" I asked.

He reached into the pocket of his jacket and retrieved a rose-colored envelope. The manner in which he proffered it, not so much to me but to the universe at large, assured me now that he was blind.

I hesitated, sensing that I did not want to become involved with this Mr. Watkin, but there was something in the way he had said "a job like no other" that made me finally reach out and take it.

"I will consider it," I said.

"Good enough, good enough," he said, smiling.

"How did you know to find me here?" I asked.

"Intuition," he said. With this, he angled the walking stick out in front of him, turned to face west, and brushed past me. He intermittently tapped the tip of the stick against the building facades as he went.

"How did you know it was me?" I called after him.

Before he disappeared into the night, I heard him say, "The smell of self-satisfaction; a pervasive aroma of nutmeg and mold."

FIRST WIND OF AUTUMN

ACCORDING TO my pocket watch it was 2:05 A.M. by the time I finally arrived home. The creak of the door closing behind me echoed faintly through the still rooms. I immediately turned on all the lamps in the parlor and the front hallway (electricity had recently come to Gramercy) and set about building a fire in the main fireplace to offset the sudden appearance of autumn. I threw an extra log on as if to cure the chill that had spread through me from the inside out upon hearing that damn Watkin's closing remarks. The *mold* part of his assessment I had a vague understanding of, like a ghost creaking floorboards in the attic of my conscience, but *nutmeg*? "What in hell does nutmeg have to do with anything?" I said aloud, and shook my head.

I knew that no matter how late the hour, sleep would not readily come. A nervous tension resulting from the incident at Reed's and my subsequent crackpot ruminations had left me wide awake, with no recourse but another visit with the demon rum. I picked up a glass, the bottle of whisky, and my cigarettes and retired to my studio, where I always did my best thinking. That vast space was also wired for electricity, but I chose to leave the lamps off and instead light a single candle, hoping the shadows might lull me into weariness.

The studio, which was attached to the back of my house, was nearly as large as the living quarters. Ironically, it was the wealth that resulted from those portraits I had spent all night disparaging that enabled me to design and have the studio built to my exact specifications. I had included a fireplace to allow me to work there in any season. Three large tables topped with expensive teakwood, which was hard enough to resist the insults of pen nibs, razors, and pallet knives, were positioned around the room. One held my painting equipment; another, the materials I sometimes used to make wax models as studies; and the last, which I did not bother with much anymore, the stones and various inks and solutions for lithographs.

My drafting board, its surface composed of the same hardwood as the tabletops, was an outlandishly ornate piece of furniture with lion paws for feet and alternating cherub and demon faces decorating the legs. During one of his frequent visits, Shenz had said, "I don't believe I could muster the presumption to create upon *that* altar."

The most remarkable aspect of the studio was the system of pulleys and gears that operated the overhead skylight. By merely turning a crank handle, I could draw back the ceiling and allow the fresh light of morning to flood the room. When lit by the sun, what with all the materials, the paintings lining the walls, the drips and puddles of bright color everywhere, the place appeared to be a kind of wonderland of art. That night, though, as I sat there sipping my whisky in the dim glow of the single taper, it showed quite another side. If it were possible to peer through the eye of a madman into the chamber of his mind, it might resemble the shadowed, cluttered mess I now beheld.

The failed and refused portraits that hung on all four walls of the studio made up the family I had only recently so longed for in my midlife loneliness—a dozen or so of kin, framed, suspended by tacks and wire, glazed into stasis, and composed not of flesh but of dried pigment. The blood of my line was linseed oil and turpentine. It had never before struck me with so much force how poor a substitute they were for the real thing. My own dogged pursuit of fortune had brought me many fine things, but now they all seemed less substantial than the trail of smoke rising from my cigarette. My gaze followed its spiraling upward course, while my mind drew me back and back, rummaging through my memories of earlier days. I sought to recall the precise moment when those seeds were planted that would latently germinate and blossom into the present flower of my discontent.

My family had come to America from Florence sometime back in the early 1830s and settled on the North Fork of Long Island, which at the time was little more than pasture and wood. The name Piambotto, my full surname, was well known as far back as the Renaissance as belonging to a line of artisans and artists. There is mention in Vasari of a certain Piambotto who had been a famous painter. Although my grandfather had been forced to take up farming when arriving in the New World, he had continued to paint gorgeous landscapes every bit as accomplished as those of Cole or Constable. Until but a few years ago, I would still see his work from time to time at auction or hanging in a gallery. He, of course, retained the name Piambotto, as did my father. It was I, now living in this whirlwind age of truncated moments with an emphasis on brevity, who shortened it. I signed my work Piambo, and to one and all I was Piambo. I don't believe even my intimate friend, Samantha Rying, knew I had spent my early years speaking Italian and that my first name was really Piero.

My family moved from the wilds of eastern Long Island to Brooklyn during the building boom that prompted some to think that eventually Manhattan would become merely an addendum to its neighboring borough. My father was an interesting fellow, reminiscent of the ancient Greek Daedalus in that he was a supreme artificer. He was a remarkable draftsman and an equally accomplished inventor who had the ability to give physical form to the varied products of his imagination. I was too young at the time to remember exactly how things transpired, but during the Civil War, because of his renown as a machinist and engineer (he was completely self-taught in both fields), he was solicited by the powers in Washington to create weapons of war for the Union army. In addition to making some parts to, of all things, a submarine, he also designed and built a weapon called the Dragon. It was a kind of cannon that used compressed nitrogen to shoot a stream of oil that was ignited as it spewed forth. It could hurl flames at advancing troops from a distance of twenty yards. I remember having seen it tested and can tell you it was aptly named. This strange piece of artillery was used just once, at the battle of Chinochik Creek, and its results were so horrific that the Union commander given responsibility for its first deployment refused to use it again. He returned it to Washington accompanied by a letter describing the ungodly scene of rebel soldiers "running, screaming, consumed in flames. Human beings melted to skeletons before my eyes, and the stink that hung in the air that day still follows me no matter how far I travel from Chinochik." He confessed that the conflagration had been as demoralizing to his own troops as it had been to those of the enemy.

As a result of his invention of the Dragon, my father was invited to New York to receive a medal of honor, as well as his payment, from the military. I, his only child, made this trip with him. It was the first time I was ever in the city, and my head swam with the sights and sounds of the exotic metropolis. We went to a huge building with grand Roman arches, which I have never since been able to find again, and he was given a bag of gold and a medal by a group of mustached men in ribbon-bedecked uniforms. Once the ceremony was over and we were again on the street, he lifted me up and hugged me to him.

"Come with me, Piero," he said, and set me down. Taking my hand, he led me swiftly down crowded streets to another building.

We entered and passed down long marble corridors lined with paintings. I was dizzy from looking up at them. I begged him to stop and let me examine them more closely, but he pulled me along by the hand, saying, "That is nothing. Come, I will show you."

We entered an alcove, and at its center was a fountain that by way of some magical plumbing produced a mournful music. With the fine spray at our backs, he pointed up at M. Sabott's newly painted masterpiece, *The Madonna of the Manticores*. The figure of the fair Madonna, whose placid outward gaze evoked a sense of utter calm in me, had no equal for beauty, and every single strand of hair, row of ivory teeth, luminous red eye, and fatal stinger of the weird tripartite beasts prowling at her feet was brimming with the energy of aberrant nature held tenuously in check.

"*Here* is something," he said.

I was enchanted, and while I stood there with my mouth agape and my eyes wide, he whispered urgently into my ear, "I began life wanting to create something as beautiful as this, but all my time and energy, all my talent, has gone to waste. Now I can only build machines of death for money. I have won battles and in the process lost my soul. Create, Piero," he told me, clutching me by the shoulders. "Create something beautiful, or life is meaningless."

He was to die the following year, when I was eight, cut to ribbons by a weapon he was developing called the Way Down, a self-propelled tornado of shining blades. I had been helping him in his shop that day and was unable to save him. I have erased the horrible imagery of that moment from my mind. Soon after he was buried, I began to draw, trying to capture his likeness so as not to forget it. As a result, I discovered I had inherited my father's creative ability. My mother encouraged me in this direction as a tribute to the husband she had loved.

I believe his spirit has somehow followed me through life, because years later, by a strange coincidence, I was to become the apprentice of M. Sabott, artist of *The Madonna of the Manticores*, as I am sure my father would have wished. Perhaps it was not the Reeds and their pitiful situation or the champagne or chandelier or even Watkin that had set me on this course of thought, but my father, from the night's plutonian shore, sending me a message imbued with such importance that it succeeded in leaping the chasm between life and death and traveling to me on the first wind of autumn.

My evening finally ended with the bottle half empty. I was bleary-eyed and my head hurt, but I remembered to blow out the guttering candle. I went to my bedroom, undressed, and lay down. The birds had begun to sing across the street in the park, and for a few moments I studied an interesting pattern on the wall projected by the moon shining through lace curtains.

In my sleep I had a most disturbing dream of watching my father being rent to pieces by M. Sabott's manticores. It was so vivid, so immediate, I woke with a scream to the light of the sun now streaming through the lace. My mouth was dry and my head thick from the alcohol and cigarettes. I felt nauseated, but it did not stop me from scrabbling out of bed. I went directly into the parlor and found the jacket I had worn the previous night. Digging into the pocket, I retrieved the rose-colored envelope Watkin had handed me. I tore it open and pulled out a sheet of paper of the same rose color. On it, written in a looping style, was an address. I recalled the old man telling me "a job like no other" and in that instant decided I would take it.

MY PATRON

I

IF I had gone about things intelligently, I would have waited to meet my mysterious new patron before severing the agreements I had made with those already in line for my services. This was a bold move on my part; bolder than I had at first given myself credit for. With each missive I penned, gracefully disengaging myself from my promises, a new and stronger wave of doubt passed through me, and my hand quaked slightly as I signed the last of them. All I could picture was that hapless hotel waiter at the betting window, placing all his money on an oat-burning nag incapable of winning any race but the one to the glue factory. Still, there was a certain thrill that also came along with the act, and although I felt disaster hard upon my heels, the future swept open like a door before me. As I stepped through into a nebulous world of light, that which had a moment before been an entrance suddenly became the solitary exit. It slammed shut behind me, and all my nervous agitation was instantly replaced by a sense of calm, as though I were now floating among the clouds like a kite.

My tether, as it were, was my plan, if you could call it that. I would take Mr. Watkin's employer's commission, do the work to

the best of my ability, craft any portrait the sitter required, and then collect the promised enormous payment. With the promised amount—triple what I had expected to receive over the next year—I would be free to pursue my muse without want for quite a long time. The prospect of overthrowing the tyranny of vanity, of actually painting something other than a face trembling with the exertion of proving itself worthy to future centuries, buoyed me up. I tell you, it even reduced the effects of my hangover. I daydreamed of traveling to an exotic location and taking my easel outdoors to capture the ageless visage of Nature or, more important, journeying within myself to find and release those images I had so long ignored.

After washing, shaving, and dressing in my best gray suit, I put on my topcoat and set out toward Seventh Avenue to catch the streetcar uptown. The address on the sheet of rose-colored paper undoubtedly belonged to one of those new monstrosities constructed in the last decade way up past where the city's sprawl had by then extended. Designed and raised by the architectural firm of McKim, Mead, and White, the residences of the upper reaches of Manhattan were a hodgepodge of classical styles melded with the novelty of a contemporary New York look—Byzantine meets Broadway, so to speak. Constructed with the finest imported marble and limestone, they were some of the most opulent monoliths in the country. I had visited quite a few by way of attending parties and in fulfillment of commissions. The address was a comfort in that it indicated my patron would certainly have the means to back up the outlandish deal Watkin had set before me.

Although the day had begun with sunshine, it was now growing overcast, and the cold wind that had blown into town the previous night seemed determined to stay. Scraps of paper and dead leaves scuttled along the sidewalk, and my breath came as steam. Others I passed were bundled up for the weather in scarves and mittens, and I had to check my memory to recall what had become of *my* summer. I relished the fact that painting was not like factory or office work with set periods of labor steadily reminding one of the disintegration of precious hours, but it usually left me with only a vague sense of what day it was. Most of July and all of August and September had been swallowed whole by what was to become the dissatisfaction of Mrs. Reed, leaving me only a faint impression of their suffocating heat. Prior to that, April, May, and early June, the delicate months of spring, were represented by the besotted Colonel Onslow Mardeeling, whose nose, with its eruptions and crevices had been a true study in lunar geography. All of my mature years presented themselves as a gallery of the faces and figures of others. I had to ask myself, "Where was I in all of this?"

It was well past noon when I finally arrived at my destination, a two-story edifice with marble columns, looking more like a downtown financial institution than a residence. In its white weight of stone it exuded the solemnity of a mausoleum. The amethyst skies had opened the moment I left the streetcar, and it was now raining rather fiercely. A huge maple tree standing before the house was losing its orange five-pointed leaves to the downpour, the brisk wind scattering them across the small lawn and the path that led to the front door. I stopped for a moment to double-check the house number. Then came a flash of lightning, and this prompted me to move.

I had barely withdrawn my hand from the brass knocker when the door opened inward. There before me stood Mr. Watkin, his head with its milky-white eyes shifting rapidly from side to side.

"May I help you?" he asked.

I did not speak immediately, waiting to see if the old man could again place me by my scent.

Just when I thought I had caught him off guard, he sniffed the air delicately and said, "Ah, Mr. Piambo. Good choice, sir. Please, come in out of the storm."

I remained silent, wanting to give him no satisfaction.

He ushered me into an antechamber off the foyer and instructed me to wait there while he announced my arrival to the lady of the house. To my amazement, what was hanging over the divan on the wall facing me but an original Sabott. I recognized the piece immediately as one I had worked on while an apprentice in my mentor's studio. It was called *At Sea*—a fanciful portrait of Mr. Jonathan Monlash, a well-known ship's captain of the seventies with a famous predilection for the effects derived from smoking hashish. I had been no more than twenty at the time the work was done, and I could still recall the old sailor's high spirits and unfailing sense of humor. If I remembered correctly, I had painted some of the demons dancing in a dizzying whirl around the head of the long-faced subject. At Monlash's insistence, Sabott had rendered him with the nozzle of the hookah between his lips. Though made of pigment, the billows of gray-blue smoke issuing from the side of his mouth were so airy they seemed to be rolling and rising. I shook my head at the sight of this long-lost friend, knowing the piece must now be worth a small fortune. So distracted was I by the discovery of the portrait, I forgot where I was and did not notice Watkin's return.

"This way, Mr. Piambo," he said.

"Where is your violet suit today, Watkin?" I asked as I followed him out of the chamber and down a dark hallway.

"Violet?" he said. "I don't recall owning a violet suit. Perhaps you are thinking of the puce."

He led me through a sumptuously decorated dining room with crystal lamp fixtures whose reflections sparkled in the mirrorlike gloss of a long table. The walls were hung with paintings I recognized as originals by renowned artists, old masters as well as contemporaries of mine. We passed through a study lined with floor-to-ceiling bookshelves filled with leather-bound volumes, and then down a hallway paneled with aromatic cedar, no doubt from Lebanon.

Finally we came to a room at the very back of the house. My guide opened the door and stepped aside, motioning with his hand for me to enter. As I did, it struck me that Watkin had navigated the entire journey through the heavily furnished rooms without a hitch. I didn't remember so much as one of his fingers touching a wall to find his place.

I found myself alone in a large, nearly empty space. There were no adornments here, and there was hardly any furniture to speak of. The ceilings were at least fifteen feet high, and there were two arched windows on either of the side walls. The left-hand view was of a fading rose garden in the rain, a few pale yellow petals still clinging to stems. The opposite view showed a piece of the neighboring house, its architecture silhouetted against the drab sky. To the very left at the back, there was an open door, revealing a shadowed stairway leading up. The floor was magnificent, of a pale maple inlaid with arabesques of a darker wood and waxed to a high sheen. The walls were papered with a green and gold floral design on a cream background. At the very center of the room there stood a screen, five feet tall, consisting of three panels in hinged cherrywood frames. On these panels, the color of old parchment, was depicted a scene of falling brown leaves.

Positioned in front of the screen was a simple wooden chair with a short back and wide armrests. Watkin, who had stepped into the room behind me and shut the door, said, "You are to sit in the chair. My employer will be with you momentarily." I walked forward, my steps echoing as I went, and did as I was told. The moment I sat down, I heard the door open and close again.

I was excited at the prospect of finally meeting my patron, and concentrated on gaining a modicum of composure so as to better represent myself when she appeared. The item I focused on in order to effect this was the subject of what price I would ask for the commission. If Watkin had spoken truthfully, she was willing to part with an extraordinary amount of money. I smiled at the great sums that slithered through my thoughts like eels, and practiced whispering one to see if I could speak it in a voice that would not betray my awareness of how ridiculous it was. The first sounded convincing enough, but when I tried a number a few digits higher, I was startled by a vague noise from behind the screen in front of me.

"Hello?" I said.

There was no response, and I was beginning to think that the insubstantial sound of someone clearing his throat had come from my own conscience, directed at my plan of artistic piracy. As I was about to return to my prices, the sound came again.

"Hello, Mr. Piambo," said a soft, female voice.

I froze for a moment and then spoke loudly enough to indicate my embarrassment. "I didn't know anyone was there."

"Yes. Well." She paused slightly, and I leaned forward. "You may call me Mrs. Charbuque," she said.

THE ONLY STIPULATION

I TRIED TO recall if I had ever heard the name before, but nothing came to mind. "Very well then," I said. "A pleasure to make your acquaintance."

"Watkin tells me that you have agreed to paint my portrait," she said, the panels of the screen lightly vibrating the sound of her words.

"If we can make the appropriate arrangement, I am quite interested," I said.

Then she mentioned a sum that was far beyond even the most dazzling I had dared to consider.

I couldn't help myself. Taking a deep breath, I said, "That *is* a lot of money."

"Yes," she said.

"I don't want to seem impertinent, Mrs. Charbuque, but may I ask why we are speaking with this screen between us?"

"Because you may not see me, Mr. Piambo," she said.

"How then am I to paint you if I cannot see you?" I asked, laughing.

"Did you think I would offer you such a great amount of

money for an ordinary portrait? Money I have, sir, but I am not a fool with it."

"Forgive me," I said. "I don't understand."

"Surely you do, Mr. Piambo. You must paint me without seeing me," she said.

I laughed again, this time louder, in ratio to my growing confusion. "I would think Mr. Watkin, who navigates the complexity of the city without benefit of sight, would be better suited to the task."

"Watkin has his abilities, but painting is not one of them," she said.

"Can you give me an idea of how this might work?" I asked.

"Certainly. You will visit me here, sit before my screen, and ask me questions about myself. From the information I give, my voice and my stories, you will construct in your mind an image of me, which you will then render on canvas."

"Excuse me, but I'm afraid that sounds impossible," I said.

"*Impossible,* Mr. Piambo, is a word I have found carries little meaning. I agree that it is *difficult,* but I have my reasons for making such an odd request. All you need do is paint a fine portrait, which I know you are more than capable of. If, though, you should succeed in capturing my exact likeness, I will double what I have already offered. There is no possibility of failure for you, and there is a chance that you will walk away from this commission extremely wealthy."

As she spoke, I tried to form a picture of her from the sonorous voice that seemed now to issue from every point in the room. In my mind's eye I caught a glimpse of chestnut locks gathered up in a bun, but as soon as she began to speak again, that knot of hair came loose and tumbled down into a whirl of perplexity.

"The only stipulation is that you cannot see me. If for some reason you should not be able to contain your curiosity and try to gaze upon me, the commission will be immediately canceled and you will be severely punished for your impertinence. Is that understood?"

"Punished?" I said.

"I will not be had by your eyes. Should you force the situation, I warn you that Watkin, who has certain—how shall I say it—*skills*, will deal with you. Don't be so foolish as to underestimate his proficiency," she said.

"Please, Mrs. Charbuque, I'm a gentleman. I can assure you that will not be necessary."

"For my part," she said, "I will answer no questions as to my physical appearance, but other than these, you may ask me anything, and I will be completely forthcoming in my answers."

"And the why of it?" I asked.

"That is not for you to concern yourself with," she said.

A brief image of sparkling green eyes flashed in my mind.

"Do we have a deal?" she asked. "Don't feel badly if you decide to decline my offer. I have chosen another if you should disappoint me. There is a very fine painter, a Mr. Oskar Hulet, who I believe might do a wonderful job. Do you know of him?"

"You must be aware that I do," I said. She no doubt knew as well as I did that Hulet was still in Europe.

"Perhaps," she whispered, and I thought I heard her laugh.

Those eyes turned blue and then hazel as I tried to decide. I envisioned myself engaged in a struggle to the death with Watkin, followed by an image of Hulet at work on a masterpiece, which melted into a recollection of M. Sabott brought low in his twilight years, raving like a madman in the street.

"Yes, a deal," I said hastily, feeling equal parts of regret and exhilaration rush through me.

"Very well. I will be at your disposal between the hours of two and three, every day of the week save Saturday and Sunday, for the next month. You need only come as much as is helpful to you. Perhaps you know enough already to attempt the portrait. At the end of that time, during the second week of November, you must present me with a painting."

"Agreed," I said. "I will return tomorrow and we will begin."

"As you wish," she said.

Before getting up, I remembered the portrait of Monlash and asked, "Mrs. Charbuque, the painting in the small room off the foyer, the one of the sea captain smoking the pipe, where did you acquire it?"

"Watkin purchased it somewhere. I also have one of your grandfather Piambotto's landscapes upstairs. Something with cattle in a meadow drenched in morning light."

"You know a few things about me," I said, not sure I liked the idea of it.

"I'm a thorough woman, Mr. Piambo. I know everything about you."

IT WAS only that evening, while I sat in the balcony of Palmer's Theatre watching Samantha perform in a newly written version of the old tale of *A Ghost's Amnesia,* that the absurdity of what I had earlier agreed to do struck me with all its import. I smiled, realizing that a healthy sense of humor would advance me further with this commission than any other quality. "And what was that business about Watkin punishing me?" I wondered. Mrs. Charbuque was willing to have me dealt grave damage rather than have me see her? I wanted to contemplate this aspect of things a bit more, but my thoughts were shattered when, up on the stage, a masked Samantha suddenly screamed at the touch of an invisible entity that had long forgotten the beauty of life.

Later on that evening, I lay in bed next to my love. A scented candle she had given me as a gift that night burned in its holder on the dresser. We had gone to Delmonico's for drinks after the performance. The wine we had consumed and a lazy round of lovemaking finally helped me shake off the pervasive sense of uneasiness that my meeting with Mrs. Charbuque had engendered. I found security in the fact that Samantha was as direct a woman as my patron was mysterious. It was not that Samantha didn't possess her share of female mystique, but she was also unwaveringly practical and forthright—very much her own person. These traits no doubt had allowed our relationship to continue over many years without her demanding that we marry. If truth be told, she was as devoted to her stagecraft as I was to painting, and this was perhaps the thing I loved most about her.

"How did you like the show this evening?" she asked.

"Marvelous," I said. "You were wonderful."

"The aging actress isn't a part that took much preparation," she said. "But I thought the ghost was terrible. Who ever heard of a fat ghost?"

"He was more like a butcher who had fallen into a sack of flour. No Edwin Booth, to be sure. He recited his lines like a dunce learning to read."

She laughed. "That is the theater owner's nephew," she said. "Derim Lourde is his name. The writer wanted to strangle him when the show was over."

"Well," I said, "his character *was* supposed to have forgotten about life."

"The only problem," said Samantha, "is that he never quite convinces one that he has ever lived at all."

"I don't think the audience cared," I told her. "They applauded thunderously, especially for you."

"Piambo, you are my favorite critic," she said, and leaned over to kiss me. "And now, what of your day?"

I was hesitant at first to divulge the details of my meeting with Mrs. Charbuque, but eventually I decided I would have to tell someone. This was not the type of thing I was capable of keeping a secret until its closure. I gave her the entire story, from my meeting with Watkin to that afternoon's interview.

She laughed when I was finished, and said, "There is more

insanity in this city than in the entire rest of the world. How are you supposed to accomplish that?"

"I don't know," I said, "but I thought you might give me some questions to ask that would lay bare her likeness to me through her words."

Samantha was quiet for a time and then said, "Why are you bothering with this parlor game?"

"It is a challenge," I said, "and besides, with what I earn from it, I will be able to escape the economics of portraiture and paint something unique."

"So, you are in blind pursuit of wealth in order to avoid pursuing wealth?" she asked.

"Something like that," I said.

"I understand," she said. "I've been getting too many parts lately where I am asked to play the aging actress, the middle-aged wife, the older . . . whatever. Last month I played a hundred-year-old witch. It would be absurd for them to cast me now as the lead and love interest, but I would relish the challenge to see if I could still bring it off."

"So, what shall I ask?" I said.

She was silent again.

"I thought maybe I would inquire about her childhood," I said.

"That would be a start," she said, nodding, "but after that, ask her about these four things: her lovers, her greatest fear, her greatest desire, and the worst day of her life."

I thought about Samantha's list, and just briefly contemplating those questions caused the figure of a woman to cohere in my thoughts. She stood on a flat rock that elevated her above the surf, and the wind was blowing her blue dress, the ringlets of her hair.

"Good?" she asked.

I nodded, trying to focus harder on the image, but was momentarily distracted when Samantha got out of bed. In the candlelight, her body looked nearly as young as when she had first come to pose for me twelve years earlier. I watched as she bent above the flame and blew it out. Once in darkness, I could see only a fading image of her smooth back and long legs. She returned to bed and rolled over to put her arm across my chest.

"That's a disturbing commission," she said sleepily. "Somewhere between foolish and mysterious."

I agreed, now picturing the falling leaves that adorned the screen of Mrs. Charbuque. It came to me that even that static scene of autumn must be a clue. "What type of woman would choose that object?" I wondered.

Samantha's breathing grew shallower, and I knew she was on the verge of sleep.

"What is the scent of that candle?" I wondered aloud.

"Do you like it?"

"It seems familiar; very peaceful," I said. "Is it cinnamon?"

"No," she said, drifting off, "it's nutmeg."

CRYSTALOGOGISTICS

ATKIN CLOSED the door behind him, and I took my seat.

"Are you there, Mrs. Charbuque?" I asked.

"I am here, Piambo," she said, sounding younger, her voice lighter than it had the previous day.

"I must confess I've pictured you as at least a hundred different women since yesterday," I told her.

"The imagination is a cornucopia," she said.

"Very true," I agreed. "But for the artist it can at times also seem a vast, frustrating Sahara."

"And which is yours today?" she asked.

"Neither," I said. "A blank slate, waiting for your words to make the first mark."

She laughed, a sound both joyful and demure, the sophisticated nature of which thoroughly enchanted me. I said nothing for a brief time, caught up as I was by the absolute serenity of that high-ceilinged room. Although I had but a few minutes before been out on a thoroughfare where newsboys yelled, streetcars clanged, and humanity surged, drawn on by a million individual desires and pursued by as many tragedies, inside this quiet, cleanly space it was as if I had been transported to a distant mountain retreat. Whereas the day before there had been a distinct urgency about our meeting, now Time itself yawned and closed its eyes.

"I was wondering if today you could tell me something of your childhood," I finally said. "I'm not so interested in a general history, but I was hoping you could relate to me the precise event that comes in all children's lives when you first realized that you would not remain a child forever. Do you understand?"

I saw a vague shadow move on the screen and tried to read the figure, but there was not enough light coming in the windows for the projection to reveal anything specific.

"I do," she said.

"Please," I said, "tell me in as much detail as possible."

"I will. Let me think for a minute."

That morning as I had ridden uptown I had formulated a method by which to proceed. I had recalled that during my tutelage under M. Sabott, he had once had me practice a certain technique. Set up on one of the tables in his studio was a still life composed of a human skull, a vase of wilted flowers, and a lit candle. I was to draw the scene by indicating only those places where the lines of the three objects and the lines of the background images intersected with each other.

"I forbid you to draw any entire object," he had told me. When M. Sabott forbade something, it was unwise to go against his wishes.

All I created that day was a sizable hill of crumpled paper. Many times, just when I thought things were going well, my mentor would walk by and say, "Begin again. You have botched it." To say I loathed the exercise was putting it mildly. Three days later, the flowers having lost all their petals, the candle now a guttering nub, I finally grasped the technique. Sabott leaned over my shoulder and said, "You see, it is possible to define a figure by its relation to those things that surround it."

Now I crossed my right leg over my left, positioning the sketch-book upon my thigh, and then brought the charcoal pencil down to hover over the blank page. If the details offered by Mrs. Char-buque were keen enough, I hoped to expose her by those elements of the story that were *not* her. Luckily I had a strong memory of M. Sabott. He lurked in the back of my mind, eager to tell me even now if I botched it.

The wind, muted by the marble architecture, whipped around outside the house, and I noticed through the window that the last yellow rose petals had flown. That is when I became aware of the light respirations of Mrs. Charbuque. Her slow, steady breathing was like a whispered chant that inculcated itself into my con-sciousness and regulated my own respiration in accordance with hers.

"You," she said, and the word startled me, "must be familiar with the name Malcolm Ossiak."

"Certainly," I said. "The man who had it all and lost it all."

"At one point he was as wealthy as Vanderbilt. His influence was felt in nearly any industry one could imagine. His mills turned out everything from textiles to hydraulic pens. He had in-terests in railroads, shipping, real estate, and armaments. Some be-lieve that for a time he was the wisest businessman this country had ever seen, as there are those who will tell you he was a com-plete fool. Be that as it may, he was a very singular man in that he sought advice not only from his stockholders, managers, accoun-tants, and salesmen but also from a legion of diviners. He had on his payroll astrologers, card readers, interpreters of dreams, and even a band of old hunters who read the entrails of beasts killed upon the grounds of his western estate."

"I had no idea," I said.

"His belief," she said, "was that to remain the preeminent man of the present, he had to have an edge on the future. He hoped that through these metaphysical disciplines he could circumvent the drudgery of waiting for the natural passage of time. When he was questioned about it by reporters, his only response was, 'For every raised eyebrow and mocking laugh of the doubters, I have made a thousand dollars on my investments. My wealth runs into the tens of millions, while the cynics scrabble for crumbs.' "

"You are related to Ossiak?" I asked, hoping for a tangible clue to Mrs. Charbuque's lineage.

"No, but my father was one of his diviners, who coaxed hidden meaning from Nature's processes. Unlike the others, though, my father's expertise was in a field so unique, he was its only practitioner. I don't believe my father thought of himself as part of the group of metaphysical investigators, because his pursuit employed mathematics as much as it did intuition and an understanding of arcane lore. He thought astrologers to be charlatans, and dream interpreters he referred to as *'ringmasters of nightly befuddlement.'* On the other hand, he would proudly tell anyone who asked that he was a crystalogogist."

"A what?" I asked, hearing the word but not registering its meaning.

"It has a tendency to tie the tongue in a knot," she said. "A crystalogogist—*crystal* referring to the *crystalline form* and *logos* being *the word*."

"Very interesting," I said, "but could it mean that he listened to the discourse of salt?"

She laughed. "No, he decoded the hieroglyphics of the sky. He searched for import in the formations of snowflakes."

"No doubt he had incredible vision and the ability to read very rapidly," I said.

"Nothing of the sort," she told me, "but his work did require that we live half of each year in a remote location high in the Catskill Mountains. From October to March, we were like castaways. It was of the utmost importance that we be present to read the first and last snowfalls of each cycle of the seasons. Up there at a great altitude, at the edge of an old-growth forest only a few hundred feet below the tree line, the flakes were unsullied by the soot from mills and the warmth of civilization. Back in those days that area was the stuff of fairy tales—wolves, dark days, crested drifts as tall as a man, a startling silence in which the only thing louder than your thoughts was the wind, and a seamless, unchanging solitude.

"We had a large old house near a lake next to which sat my father's laboratory. The house, of course, was well heated, but the laboratory was colder inside than it was out. It was a rather solitary and bleak existence for a child. I had no brothers or sisters, and there were no playmates for hundreds of miles. When I finally reached the age where I could be of some use to my father, out of equal parts devotion to him and the sheer boredom of the situation, I became his assistant.

"We would work together as he had done with his own father, wrapped in cumbersome clothing, out in the frozen laboratory constructed from sheets of tin. Every inch of both the exterior and interior was covered by a film of frost throughout the days of winter. The mechanisms, the instruments, all had icicles hanging from them. Before each reading we would have to chip the buildup off the knobs that focused the huge optical magnifier through which he would gaze at the snowflakes. We had to be very cautious with the glass lenses for that device because, in the constant cold, the slightest tap would shatter them into pieces no bigger than the crystals we were studying.

"It seemed the snow fell constantly, but of course that is merely a child's impression. In actuality, it probably did snow a number of times each week, usually at least flurries and sometimes great blizzards that lasted for days on end. When the conditions were right for taking a sample, the wind velocity not too high and the precipitation at the precise temperature to fashion the spindled, star-shaped formations that carried the most important information, my father would stand outside, holding up to the open skies a flat piece of wood wrapped in black velvet. As soon as his board's collection resembled an abundance of stars in a clear night sky, he would whisk it away inside the laboratory.

"He would then place the board onto the stage of the optical magnifier; a tall black machine with a ladder that led up to a chair situated so that the occupant could stare into a lens no bigger than a circling of the index finger and thumb. While he took his position in the investigator's seat, I would place around the edges of the viewing stage clumps of a type of seaweed that gave off its own luminescence. It was important that he have enough light with which to see, but we could not use candles or lamps because their heat would melt our specimens.

"At the perimeter of the laboratory there were lamps, three to be precise, but even when they stayed lit, the light they gave was weak. The glow from the seaweed was a yellow green. This, mixed with the overall blue of the cold, imbued the laboratory with a strange underwater ambience. 'Lu, more seaweed,' he would call down to me as he sat peering into the eyepiece at his end of the long cylinder. As the barrel of the device proceeded toward the viewing stage it flanged out, and at the bottom, where it held the huge lens that was like a circle cut from the frozen lake, it was wide enough to encompass the entire board."

"Lu?" I asked, interrupting the flow of her story.

THE TWINS

UCIERE," SHE said. "I was named after my mother."

"Forgive me," I said. "Please continue."

"My father would gently turn the knobs of the huge machine, and the gears would lift and lower the long barrel holding the lenses. As he did this, I would hear him grumble and hum. His favorite saying when he would discover one of the certain flakes we were searching for was 'Eureka.' You must understand that, although he took his work seriously, he was not beyond a sense of humor about himself and his profession. As for my part, I would applaud to encourage his efforts.

"Once he sighted a worthy specimen, he would descend from the chair. Fitting a jeweler's loupe into his eye and taking out one of the toothpicks he kept handy in his shirt pocket, he would lean over the black velvet. This was my sign to run and fetch the atomizer filled with a precise mixture of clear plant resins. This noxious mixture had to be prepared in the house, each batch cooked for two hours on the stove so that it would remain in a liquid state for the course of that day's investigations.

"With the care of a surgeon, he would single out the flake in question and then, after licking the end of the toothpick, very carefully touch its tip to the very center of the frail and minuscule six-pointed star. Once he had it on the point of wood, he would lift it away from the board and hold it up in the air for me to spray. Usually he had singled out more than one for preservation. Since the black velvet absorbed heat that would alter the forms of the crystals after a brief period, we could not leave the flakes on the material for too long a time. In answer to this problem, my father had perfected the ability to hold up, at one time, as many as twenty toothpicks between his thumbs and forefingers. This was a delicate process, and I had to pump the atomizer ball with just the right amount of force so that the mist would cover the samples completely but not blow them away. It was a point of pride for me that I was expert at this technique. Every time I successfully lacquered another crystal, my father would praise me to the heavens. When I failed, he would shrug and say, 'There are more where that came from.'

"The flakes were then cast in the coating of resin, which dried quickly in the cold air. What was left was a perfect, unmelting replica of the flake. Have you ever seen the skin shed by a snake and how that skin is exactly the form of the snake? This was how precise our models were. Once in this form, he would not have to rely on his memory or his questionable abilities as a sketch artist but could take them into the house to his study and begin to decipher their meaning.

"Father's study was at the back of the house. It had a large window that offered a view of the lake, and its own fireplace that was always stoked and roaring. What with the smoke from his pipe, the scent of burning logs, and the ever-present smell of the resin, the place had a very distinctive aroma. In the corner was a comfortable old couch with broken springs and stuffing peering from tears in its fabric. Many an afternoon I'd come in from a long time out in the cold and the warmth of the room would overcome me, and I'd drift off to sleep on the couch. My father sat in his chair, much like the one you are now sitting in, at his desk, surrounded by cabinets overflowing with tiny boxes that held our manufactured fossils of snow.

"In addition to all this there were the books, handwritten tomes holding the charts and formulas necessary for translating the idiosyncrasies of each flake into a meaningful unit of knowledge. While at his desk, he would examine specimens through a magnifying glass, all the time flipping through the reference works penned by his grandfather. Upon locating the appropriate principle, he would lift his pencil and jot down a long string of numbers. An abracadabra of addition, division, and multiplication would follow, capped off by the subtraction of the digit one hundred forty-four, the numerical constant for human error. He would never tell me what the final verdict was for any of the flakes but would record his findings with neat penmanship in black ink in a leather-bound journal.

"All snowflakes have the same basic form—six points emanating from a design of either greater or lesser complexity at the center. The first rule I learned from him about crystalogogistics was that no two snowflakes were exactly alike. Either the center pattern exhibited an extra concentric device or the spindles were burred with fewer pegs or the tips were barbed or flat, but each one came from above a unique creation. I did pick up a few hints about how to read them from the times he would let slip a word or two that would betray his knowledge. For instance, I knew that a spiderweb design in the center portended treachery, and a rounded tip a time of plenty. So this was my life when I was nine years old."

"And what of your mother?" I asked.

"Mother had nothing to do with our work. She had no understanding of its importance, and I could tell even then that she considered my father a fool. I think she stayed on with us simply because she had come from a poor family and Ossiak saw to it that we wanted for nothing. She also relished the opportunity to move amid society's elite when in April we traveled back to the city to confer with father's employer on our findings. Then she would come alive with a sense of self-importance. I would not say she was a mean person, but as a child, when I came to her with some hurt or fear, instead of warmth or comfort, all that her cold demeanor inspired in me was an unsettling sense of awe. I never did hear the story of how they came together in their younger days."

She was silent for a moment, and I pictured her, strangely enough, as myself, floundering in one of those brief periods of confusion that result from my thinking too much. "I believe you were going to tell me about some change that had taken place in your life," I said.

"Yes," she said. "I hadn't thought of all this for some time, save for in bits and pieces. Each remembered image tugs at me, wants me to follow it off in another direction."

"I understand," I said.

"Now that I have set the scene for you, I can address your question," she said. "It was soon after Ossiak's men had come with sleds hitched to mules, which was the only viable means of moving stores up through the difficult passes of the mountains. They came each midwinter to replenish our stock of firewood and to bring other supplies. For a few nights previous there had been strange lights in the sky, not the aurora, which we sometimes saw and were used to, but a kind of pulsating brightness. The captain of the supply team mentioned it to my father and asked him what it might be. Father admitted that he was equally bewildered by it. That night it became a moot point, because the clouds had moved in and it was obvious a great storm was brewing. The supply team set off without waiting until morning, hoping to make it down the mountain before a blizzard struck.

"When the snows started, although it was late, my father insisted that we take a sample. This we did with great difficulty, since the wind was high and the temperature more bitter than I had ever felt it. Inside the laboratory we went through the usual routine, setting up and lighting the viewing stage, my father ascending the ladder to his seat. I stood looking up at him, awaiting pronouncement of the word that meant we had been successful, but it never came. Rarely did we not garner at least one spindled star. I thought perhaps this was due to the severity of the weather. Instead, he seemed very agitated by what he saw through the eyepiece.

"Without humming or grumbling, he finally came down the ladder and took out two toothpicks. As he positioned the loupe in his eye, I noticed the most incredible thing, which prevented me from running for the atomizer. He was sweating. 'Hurry, Lu,' he shouted, not in his usual good humor. I came to and jumped at his command. When I returned, he had the two picks out in front of him. He saw that he had made me nervous, and said, 'All right, girl, take a deep breath and be your best.'

"I lacquered the two perfectly at once with a single pump of the ball. 'You're a genius,' he told me, and I smiled, but it became clear to me that he was not joking. As soon as the specimens had dried we went inside.

"At his desk, he did not bother to scribble but simply held up the two flakes we had transfixed, and stared at them through the magnifying glass. I sat on the couch watching him, noticing that he still seemed nervous. After quite a while, he put them down and got up out of his chair. He crossed the room to the window and stood in silence with his hands joined behind his back, peering through the darkness into the blinding storm that now raged. Only then did I register the ferocity of the wind, like the wailing of ghostly children.

"When he finally went back to his desk, he called me over to him. He held up the two new samples and positioned the magnifying glass before them. 'Tell me, Lu, what do you see here?' he asked. I was concerned by his behavior, but at the same time I felt something akin to pride, since he was asking my opinion. I peered through the glass and immediately noticed the most astonishing thing.

" 'They're identical,' I said.

" 'Impossible but true,' he said.

"I looked at him, and his face was a mask of worry. There was also something about his eyes, a peculiar lack of light that could only be described as hopelessness. In that moment I had a premonition, like a sudden bright flash in my mind, of the supply team trapped in the blizzard on their way down the mountain. A few days later, the Twins, as my father and I had come to call the identical crystals, began to exhibit their strange qualities."

Mrs. Charbuque fell silent then, and for the first time since her story had begun, I looked down at my sketchbook and saw that I had drawn nothing. The page was as white as a blizzard.

"The Twins—," I said to her, but had no chance to finish my question, for as I spoke the door behind me opened and Watkin said, "Your time is up, Mr. Piambo."

Dazed, I rose and slowly left the room.

THE VIZIER'S COURT

FTER LEAVING Mrs. Charbuque's, I walked over to Central Park and entered at Seventy-ninth Street. As it was a weekday and bitterly cold, the place was fairly deserted. I headed south, toward the lake, on a path lined with barren poplars and strewn with yellow leaves. Once there, I sat on a bench at its eastern shore and gave myself up to considering all she had told me. The wind rippled the water, and the late-afternoon sunlight slanted through the bare branches, adding a golden patina to the empty boathouse and esplanade.

My first question was, of course, whether or not she was to be believed. "Crystalogogist," I said to myself, and smiled. It sounded almost too bizarre to be fiction. She had spoken with the facility and authority of truth, and I had clearly seen in my imagination, plain as day, her father's thick muttonchops, his riotous eyebrows and kindly smile. I had felt the bitter cold of the laboratory and peered through the glacial undersea glow. My mind was a whirl of imagery—snowflakes, lists of numbers, iced machinery, toothpicks, black velvet, the frozen lake, and reflected in it the drawn, dour face of the mother.

When I again noticed the water before me, I was smoking a cig-arette and reasoning that if Mrs. Charbuque had lived some part of her early life during the heyday of Malcolm Ossiak, she was most likely close to my own age. This did little to help, for what I really wanted was a glimpse of the face of that little girl, living out half her childhood in a frozen wasteland. All I could conjure of her was that she wore her hair in pigtails and that her eyelashes were long and beautiful.

I smoked another cigarette and noticed that it was getting late. The orange sun had now dipped behind the trees, and the sky at the horizon was a splash of pink, darkening to purple and then to night above. I had sat too long in the cold and was shivering. Adopting a brisk pace, I hoped to reach the Fifth Avenue entrance just north of the unsightly, ramshackle zoo before night fell in earnest. As I hurried along, I entertained the idea that perhaps Mrs. Charbuque, though she sounded sane enough, was truly un-hinged. And then as quickly, I asked myself, "Would it really be of any great consequence to my portrait?" I realized I was lending a great weight of importance to her personal history, whereas in re-ality the mere cadence of her words, the gentle tone of her voice, and even the lies she might be telling me were every bit as alive with clues to her face and figure as was the reality of her days. The whole affair was like trying to reassemble the pieces of a convo-luted dream shattered by waking.

I should have gone home and at least tried to work out some of the figures of her story on paper, but I was still too caught up in the mystery of my new commission to concentrate at the draw-ing board. Besides, I feared that waiting for me would be responses to those letters of disengagement I had sent to my erstwhile pa-trons, and wanted to forestall facing their thinly veiled unpleas-antries and innuendos hinting at my lack of professionalism. Samantha, I knew, would be busy propping up the insubstantial performance of the amnesiac ghost, so there was no possibility of spending time with her. I decided to head down to the seamy side of town and harass Shenz for a spell. Out on the avenue, I caught a hansom cab easily enough and directed the driver to my friend's address.

Shenz lived on Eighth Avenue on the outskirts of that area known as Hell's Kitchen, a nightmarish territory marked by stock-yards, warehouses, and tenements, where a gumbo of humanity's destitute scratched out a grim existence that in its inadequacy staggered the imagination. The closest I wished to get to it was Shenz's place. Of course, being the liberal-minded fellow I was, I had read enough of the recent crop of publications exposing society's ills to be sympathetic to the plight of these poor people, but in reality my mission was not to effect change. Instead, my efforts went selfishly toward avoiding, geographically and philosophically, the whole unsightly mess.

Shenz was interesting in that respect. As he had told me, he liked to live close enough to these cataracts of chaos to feel the raw energy of life they contained. He said it did something for his painting. "At times, Piambo," he had said to me, "it is a good thing to leap the garden wall and join the living. That society we move in for our work is too often so delicately moribund."

Back before they had cleaned up the Tenderloin, scattering the vermin who squatted there like scorpions under rocks, and turned it into an area of commerce, Shenz had an address perilously close to the illicit action. Once, when I made some disparaging remark about what they did with their women and children, he retorted that I would most likely think it only good fun to attend one of Stanford White's soirées where each distinguished gentleman was given his own naked female as a party favor. That's what I admired most about Shenz—he could move through any stratum of society and adopt its customs, but he never lost sight of the truth. It was precisely this quality that I now sought out in relation to the conundrum that was Mrs. Charbuque.

Stepping from the streets of the West Side into Shenz's rooms involved a disconcerting transition. At one moment you were out in the dark on the hard cobblestone, a thuggish figure moving toward you through the shadows, the ill aroma of the slaughter-houses wafting around you on a breeze from the Hudson. The next you were transported into a Turkish vizier's court. In his painting and his taste, Shenz was a Romantic, a Pre-Raphaelite with a great belief in the pertinence of the mythological and a strong allegiance to the exotic. Jasmine incense smoldered in the gaping mouth of a brass dragon. Thick Persian carpets covered the floors like flowering beds of mandalas, and the tapestries that hung upon the walls pictured beasts and birds and Eastern beauties ca-vorting through forests of trees whose crisscrossing branches made a design as intricate as lace. The furniture, with overstuffed cush-ions, appeared to have no legs at all but to float a few inches above the floor.

We sat facing each other in exceedingly low, wide chairs that required one to sit cross-legged like a swami. Shenz took a puff of his opium-laced cigarette, its blue fog mixing with the brass dragon's exhalations and causing my eyes to water. With his pointed beard and trim mustache, those eyebrows that curled up in points at the ends, and a paisley satin robe, he looked for all the world like a modern-day Mephistopheles about to broker a deal.

"The last I saw of you, Piambo, was your back as you fled from Reed's," he said, smiling.

"I had cause for alarm," I said. "The missus, as she mimicked kissing my cheek, whispered to me that she wished for me to die."

He laughed out loud. "True?" he asked.

I nodded.

"Good God, my boy, another satisfied customer."

"Shenz," I said, "I can't believe you haven't been robbed yet. Don't your neighbors know that you are living here like Mani in his pleasure garden?"

"Certainly," he said, "but my house is protected, and I have free passage in Hell's Kitchen."

"Do they fear your palette knife?" I asked.

"Precisely," he said. "Do you know the name Dutch Heinrichs?"

"I've read it in the newspapers," I said. "He's the head hooligan, isn't he?"

"He controls the most powerful gang in the area, if not the city. Back in the seventies, I did a portrait of him. He had begun fantasizing about his significance in the scheme of things and decided that a record of his features would be an important artifact for future historians. Burne-Jones himself would be proud of the job I did. I depicted the seasoned criminal as a glowing saint in an ultramarine and mauve cityscape, a transcendent martyr of the mean streets."

"And he actually paid you?" I asked.

"Certainly, he paid me in protection. He was a bit irascible as a subject, often intoxicated, couldn't sit still for too long. But I tell you, when his fellows saw what I could do with a brush, they were in awe. Art, you would think, might be the last thing that could impress them, but it did. They came to think of me as some sort of magician. Last winter I did a nice little portrait of the wife of the boss of the Dead Rabbits gang."

"You're pulling my leg," I said.

"Not at all," said Shenz. "Do I look like a man who fears for his safety?"

I shook my head and sighed in exasperation.

"There's no difference between this world and the world of Fifth Avenue," he said. "Life is full of blackguards. Some wear fine suits and bilk great masses of humanity; some have shoes with gaping holes and break into warehouses. Just remind yourself of the scurrilous thieves of Tammany Hall. The only difference between there and here is that their crimes were publicly sanctioned and the ones on this side of town have been deemed reprehensible."

"There is less murder on Fifth Avenue," I said.

"Think of all those poor bastards and their living deaths laboring away in one of Reed's shoe mills. It's all a matter of perspective."

"I'm still not sure I believe you," I said.

"As you like," he said, and chuckled.

"But now *I* have something to tell that you will certainly doubt the veracity of," I said.

"Do your worst."

"I met a blind man, a Mr. Watkin, on the way home from Reed's the other night . . . ," I began, and then proceeded to tell him the whole thing, including Mrs. Charbuque's fairy tale of snow and solitude.

SALVATION

I LOOKED AT Shenz and saw that his eyes were closed and he was leaning back in his chair. I thought for a moment that he had succumbed to his cigarette and was now off in some other land where haloed maidens sported with lambs and the armored chestplates of knights pressed the nubile breasts of water nymphs, but then he spoke, one word.

"Salvation," he said in a groggy voice, and leaned forward wearily to train his glassy eyes upon me.

"Salvation?" I asked.

"Yes, yours," he said, and smiled.

"What do you mean?" I asked.

"You say you are playing this game of hide-and-seek for the money, a perfectly mercenary approach and one befitting a man of your time, but then you go further and say that this money will allow you to extricate yourself from society, give you the precious space you need to discover your abilities and paint something worthy of your skill and training. The bit about Albert Ryder I'm not quite clear on. The man seems bent on producing mud puddles, but so be it, if he is your inspiration. Nevertheless, this woman's inane proposition could be a two-edged sword of salvation for you."

"I wasn't aware that I was in need of salvation, exactly," I said.

"Well, you are. First," he said, "you need to do this to honor the memory of M. Sabott. You know as well as I do how shoddily you treated him near the end of his days. No . . . let's not have any looks of wounded pride. You cut him loose like a dangling thread on a new suit of clothes when he became a burden to your grow-ing reputation. Now is your opportunity to fulfill the promise he saw in you and repay all he did on your behalf."

"Sabott had gone mad," I said in my defense.

"Mad or merely in search of what you yourself are searching for now? Don't forget, I was with you that day at Madison Square when those fine gentlemen were offering you impressive sums of money to execute their portraits. Then who should wander along but old Sabott, ranting at the sky. Do you remem-ber, he worked himself into such a lather that he fell over in the gutter? I did not know you then, but I thought you had been or were his student, and I said, 'Piambo, is that not an acquaintance of yours?' You denied you knew him, and we walked on and left him there."

"All right, Shenz, all right," I said. "You've made your point."

"I make it not to distress you but to show you that this is a debt that still needs to be settled. Not for Sabott—it's not going to do him any good—but for you. Your betrayal still weighs heavily upon you."

"And what is the connection between that and Mrs. Char-buque?" I asked.

"The other side of the sword. Piambo, you are the finest painter I know. You are wasting your talent on rendering the features of the banal, trading opportunity for status and wealth."

"The finest?" I said with a short sharp chuckle.

"This is not a joke," said Shenz. "You have seen my work. What do you think of the brush strokes?"

"Varied and effective," I said.

"Yes, all well and good, but the other night, after you left Reed's, I took a moment to step up close to the portrait of his wife and study your brushwork. Do you know what I saw?"

"What?" I asked.

"Nothing. I saw nothing. Now there are ways to disguise brushwork, but these methods, you know yourself, are as evident as if the direction of the application were obvious. After staring for some time, I realized that each time you touched the canvas, the effect was like a small explosion of color. I've seen you paint, and you approach the work with great energy, great vitality. It comes from inside you, in here," he said, and brought his clenched fist slowly to his chest. "All this truth put in the service of lying about what you see and feel." I said nothing. Where I had at first been irritated with him for mentioning the incident with Sabott, I was now feeling nothing but gratitude. He had just corroborated everything I knew to be true in my heart.

"If I were you," said Shenz, "I would paint this Mrs. Charbuque with a mind toward getting as much money out of her as possible. If this is how you feel you can free yourself, then take all you can get from her."

"All I need do is come up with a competent portrait," I said.

"No, you must capture her likeness precisely," he said.

"How, though?" I asked. "I'm in doubt about whether her words are meant to help or lead me astray."

"Yes," said Shenz, laughing, "that business with the science of reading snowflakes is rather preposterous. But there are methods of finding your way through that squall."

"Such as?"

"Cheat," he said. "I'm sure we can find out what she looks like. There is no woman I know of with that much money who does not have a past. If there are no photographs, she must exist in someone's memory. A little research should undoubtedly reveal her."

"I never thought of that," I said. "It seems dishonest."

"Unlike the portrait of Mrs. Reed?" said Shenz. "I will even help you."

"I don't know," I said.

"Think of the time free of worry or constraint the ultimate sum will buy you," he said.

After our discussion he brought me into his studio and showed me the first rounded sketches he had made of the Hatstell children. "These are not youngsters," he told me, "they are doughnuts on legs." By the time I took my leave, he had me in stitches, describing his feckless attempts to have his new subjects remain still for more than five minutes at a time. "Tomorrow I will bring either a whip or a bag of chocolates," he said. As we parted at the door, he shook my hand and said, as a reminder of his earlier offer, "She is out there somewhere. We can find her."

I breathed a sigh of relief once I crossed Seventh Avenue and was heading back toward civilization. It was very close to midnight, and the streets were uncharacteristically empty owing to the cold. My head was in a bit of a fog from having imbibed, secondhand from Shenz, the blue opium mist, which had calmed me but also made me exceedingly weary.

Although my thoughts were slippery, I tried to decide how to proceed with Mrs. Charbuque the next morning. The question I posed to myself was whether I should let her lead me on with her narrative, or force her through a series of rapid inquiries to divulge bits of information she had not intended to part with. I thought it highly suspicious that the first installment of her story had reached a climax at precisely the moment my time had expired. I suppose because I had just visited Shenz, it reminded me of the Arabian Nights entertainment, with Mrs. Charbuque in the role of Scheherazade. As much as I felt I was being led by the nose, I did very much want to know what had become of the child she had brought to life in my mind. Upon reaching Twenty-first and Broadway, I decided that I must take control and turn the tables on her. I would eschew the story about crystalogogistics for a grocery list of simple questions.

I was no more than two blocks from my home when I looked up and saw some commotion beneath a street lamp across the way. From their uniforms and their hats, I could identify two of the three men as officers of the law. Even in the poor light, I recognized the man in civilian clothes—a derby and topcoat—as John Sills, a Sunday painter, a miniaturist, whom I had been on friendly terms with for a number of years. In addition to being an artist, he was also a detective on the New York City police force. They were gathered around what appeared to be a body on the sidewalk.

I crossed the street and came up behind the trio. As I drew closer, one of the men moved slightly to the side and I had a brief glimpse of a horrific sight. With the light from the lamp above, I was now able to see that they were all standing in a pool of blood. The young woman was not lying horizontally on the curb but was propped up against the base of the streetlight. The bodice of her white dress was soaked bright red; crimson red streaked down her even whiter face. It gathered on her lips and dripped off her chin. I thought at first that she must be dead, but then I saw her move her head slightly from side to side. She was trying to whisper something, and the thick liquid at her mouth bubbled. As the officer who had initially moved aside and given me my view turned and noticed I was there, I realized that the stream of gore was issuing from her eyes as if she were weeping her own blood.

"Mind your business," said the man, and he raised his club with all intention of striking me.

By that time John had turned and, seeing it was me, caught the other fellow's arm in midswing. "I'll take care of this, Hark," he said. He came forward quickly, put his arm around my shoulders, and turned me away from the scene. Pushing me along, he herded me back across the street.

"Get out of here, Piambo, or we will have to arrest you," he said.

"Go and don't tell anyone what you saw." He shoved me on my way. Before turning back to the incredible scene beneath the street lamp, he warned me again, his voice loud, "Not a word."

I said nothing, thought nothing, but broke into a run. When I reached my home, I was winded and nauseated. I drank whiskey until I regained my normal pulse. Then I stumbled into my studio, sat down, and lit a cigarette with shaking hands. All I could picture was that poor woman's bloody eyes, and through some twisted association with the day's events, I thought of them as the Twins.

GOD IS FALLIBLE

MY FATHER put them in an old silver locket that had been his sister's and latched its chain around my neck. He told me I must never open it but always to remember that they were there, hiding. Then he swore me to secrecy, telling me the Twins were a secret that must never be revealed. When I asked him why, he shook his head and got down on one knee to face me. 'Because it proves that God is fallible,' he said, 'and the world neither needs nor wants to know that.'

"I was not sure what the word *fallible* meant, but what I was certain of was a growing sense of pride at being chosen to bear this important talisman. Because he had told me never to mention them, they became an increasing obsession for me. I felt as if they were alive inside that tiny silver chamber, like the germ of life inside a seed. There seemed to be a thrum of energy pulsating through my breast at the point where the pendant touched my flesh. The chain tingled against the skin of my neck. Not too long afterward I began to have strange dreams at night, colors and vibrations in my skull, wild images so abundant it was as if I were dreaming for three. The nights were not long enough to give vent to them, and they began to seep into my waking hours. I did not tell my father, fearing that he would take back the locket.

"Then one day, when the snows had abated for an entire week, and I was out in the forest of tall pines playing at being an adventurer to the North Pole, I heard them whisper to me. It was an odd communication because, although I knew they were speaking words, I registered their message as an image in my mind. What I saw was a shooting star moving through the heavens, throwing off sparks like a July Fourth rocket. This vision lasted only seconds, but in the time I beheld it, it was crystal clear.

"The experience was both frightening and exciting, and when it was over I stood still among the trees for a long while. Of course, as a child I had no way of defining the feeling this experience gave me, but now, thinking back on it, I believe it can best be described as a sense that Nature and, beyond that, the very cosmos was alive. God was watching me, so I ran back to the house to hide.

"By that afternoon, after playing with my dolls and helping my mother with the laundry, I had forgotten about the incident. When I was finished with my chores, I went to visit my father in his study. He was at his desk with the magnifying glass, studying a specimen and jotting notes in his journal. I sat on the couch, and when he heard the broken springs shift, he turned around and smiled at me. A few minutes later, he asked me to fetch him a book from the bookcase. He turned in his chair and pointed to a large blue-bound volume on the second shelf. 'That one there, Lu,' he said. '*The Crystal Will* by Scarfinati.'

"As I pulled the book off the shelf, the one beside it shifted and fell open on the floor. After carrying the volume he wanted to my father, I returned to pick up the one that had fallen. I saw that the book had opened to a full-page illustration of a shooting star, much like the one the Twins had whispered to me that morning."

"Mrs. Charbuque—" I said, but she interrupted me.

"Please, Mr. Piambo, allow me to finish," she said.

"Very well," I told her, sketching madly. The day was bright, and the sun coming in the windows was projecting a faint but somewhat definable shadow on the screen. I had been filling pages with quick, crude drawings, my hand moving over the paper as I kept my eye trained on the scene of falling leaves.

"I did not mention the remarkable happenstance to my father but kept it inside me and, whenever I turned my attention to the thought of it, felt a genuine thrill. It was as if God were sending me a secret message, for me alone to see. I was filled with a strange sense of expectation for the remainder of the day. That is why I nearly leaped out of my skin when, that night as we sat by the fire, my mother and father reading in the glow of the gas lamps, there came a pounding on our door.

"Naturally my parents exchanged worried looks, for who would be calling so late at night at the top of a mountain? Warily my father got up and went to see who it was. His look of concern alarmed me, and I followed him to make sure he would be all right. There on the doorstep stood a large man, wearing a fur coat and a broad-brimmed hat, carrying a large pack and a rifle. My father seemed to know him. The man also worked for Ossiak as a tracker. He had come to search for the body of one of the fellows from the supply team. On the way down the mountain in the storm, one of the men had lagged behind and apparently lost his way. He was believed to have succumbed to the storm and died of exposure. My father stepped aside and let him in. As he showed the man to a seat by the fireplace, he called back to me, 'Lu, close the door, please.' The three-quarter moon drew my attention as I swung the door, and then something suddenly streaked across the star-filled sky, leaving sparks in its path.

"The visitor's name was Amory, and he told us that he had come up the mountain that day looking for the corpse but had not found it. He asked to stay the night. He planned to leave early in the morning and descend the mountain, giving the dead man one more chance to be found. My father said he felt somewhat responsible for the tragedy, and told Mr. Amory that he would accompany him halfway. Then mother and father questioned Amory about what was going on in the world down the mountain. Soon afterward I was sent to bed.

"I woke in the middle of the night to the sound of a whispered gasp. At first I thought it was the Twins trying to tell me something, but then realized that it was coming from the parlor. I don't know what time it was, but it felt very late, like those bleak hours of the very early morning. It was cold, but I crept out of bed and tiptoed down the hall to the parlor entrance. Since the moon was shining that night, there was a very dim glow coming through the parlor window. I heard another gasp like the one that had awoken me, and I saw my mother, sitting astride the tracker with her nightgown pulled up, revealing her bare legs. His large hands were rubbing her breasts through the thin material.

"I apologize for being so forthright about this, Mr. Piambo, but I am trying to be accurate. My mother was rocking forward and back, her eyes closed, breathing heavily. I was astounded at this strange display and had no idea what was happening, but something in the back of my mind told me I should not be witnessing it. I was about to turn and go back to my room when my mother suddenly opened her eyes and saw me. She did not stop, nor did she say a word, but just stared at me with a look of great hatred. I ran back to my room and climbed into bed, shutting tight my eyes and putting my hands over my ears.

"The next morning I awoke worried that I would be in trouble, but nothing was said when I set to helping my mother in the kitchen. As my father and Mr. Amory ate breakfast, the Twins spoke to me again. I saw their words as a picture in my mind, and what they showed me this time was horrible—a man, stiff as a statue, covered in frost. His mouth was gaping, a round dark hole, and his eyes staring so fiercely I knew he must be dead. It was the corpse of the man from the supply team, and I saw where he was. He lay in a meadow off the main trail about a quarter of the way down the mountain. I knew the spot because we stopped there each year for a picnic at our end-of-summer ascent.

"This vision, again, only lasted moments, but as I came to, I saw that my father and Amory were making ready to leave. I was torn between revealing my knowledge and keeping it and the power of the Twins a secret. When they opened the door to take their leave, I sprang forward and begged my father for a kiss. When he leaned down, I whispered in his ear, 'In the picnic meadow.' I wasn't sure if he had heard me. He simply patted me on the head and said, 'Yes, Lu.' Then they were gone.

"The second they were out of sight, my mother was at me, grabbing my shoulders and shaking me. 'What did you tell your father?' she yelled. 'What did you whisper in his ear?' I told her I had said nothing, but she knew that was a lie, for she had seen me. She shook me again, and her face was red with anger. I relented and said, 'I told him where to find the dead man.' 'What kind of nonsense is that?' she screamed. 'It's the truth,' I said, and began to cry. 'You'd do well to keep your mouth shut if you don't want me to take you away from him,' she said. Then she brought the back of her hand around and smacked me across the face with such force I fell to the floor. When the blow struck me, I saw in my mind the shooting star."

"Mrs. Charbuque," I said, closing my notebook, "I must say—" Here she interrupted me again.

"One more thing, Mr. Piambo," she said, and her voice fluttered nervously. "One more thing."

"Yes," I said.

"My father informed me upon his return that they had found the body at the spot I had described. My mother overheard him say this and was delighted, not by my unusual premonition but with relief that I hadn't divulged her tryst."

"But, Mrs. Charbuque," I said, this time determined not to be put off, "this story you are building, it is rather fantastical, wouldn't you say? I am having a hard time believing that this is all real.

Please don't take this as an accusation, but please, explain to me how I am supposed to take all this."

"What piece of it disturbs you?" she asked.

"I can follow all of it, but the fact that these two identical snowflakes are communicating with you in some psychic way seems, well, if I may be so bold, a good deal of rubbish."

"The story is true, I swear, but as you say, the idea that the Twins conferred supernatural abilities was rubbish. It was the worst, most destructive rubbish, because I believed with all my heart that they did. So did my father. That childhood delusion would shape and eventually poison the rest of my life, Mr. Piambo."

"So you agree with me?" I asked.

"Even God is fallible," she said. Her laughter was prolonged and piercing, and that dim shadow I had been trying to capture on paper now moved wildly, changing shape, calling into question whether there had ever been anything there to draw at all.

THE SIBYL

*I*MAGINE," SHE said, "a friendless child with a mother who does not love her or her father and a father who spends his time reading the will of God in the formations of snowflakes. How could I possibly have been anything else *but* a believer? I needed power and importance, and I desperately wanted to be noticed for more than my ability to spray the specimens as my father held them up on toothpicks. He was my hero, and I wanted to be, like him, a conduit of the divine message."

"So you fantasized the voice of the Twins," I said.

"Not consciously, Mr. Piambo, but yes, I swear to you, I could hear them. Loneliness can make magicians of us, not to mention prophets."

"What of the shooting star, though?" I asked. "What of the corpse of the man from the supply team? You actually did know where he was."

"Undoubtedly coincidence. The picture *was* in the book that had fallen open, but my father had many books with pictures of the heavens. I know from my extensive travels in Europe that there is an entire theory of the psyche being conceived of in Austria now which makes the case that there are no accidents. We are supposedly sentient on many levels, and those desires we do not choose to be aware of manifest themselves through what we think of as mishaps. The other two instances of my seeing the shooting star, when I closed the door and when my mother struck me, might have been more wishful thinking than anything else. As to the corpse, there were very few places on the mountain trail where it would have been as easy to wander from the beaten track in a storm. The path into that meadow forked off the main trail and then died at our picnic spot. Maybe somehow I unconsciously surmised that that was the most likely place for the poor man to have lost his way."

"But you continued with this notion of the Twins as the years progressed?" I asked.

"I became 'the Sibyl,'" she said, "and eventually it twisted my heart."

"The Sibyl?"

Upon voicing my question, the door opened and Watkin announced that my time was up. I remembered that it was Friday, so I wished Mrs. Charbuque a pleasant weekend and took my leave. As Watkin led me to the front door, I said to him, "You have the most uncanny sense of bad timing."

"Thank you, sir. It is my specialty," he said as I passed him and stepped outside.

"I'll be seeing you," I said, and he slammed shut the door.

I was thoroughly exhausted from not having slept at all the previous night. The macabre image of that woman on the street, losing her life through her eyes, had done something to me. It was as if, after witnessing that horror, I had to take in through my eyes all that she was losing through hers, and therefore dared not close them.

As it was, I barely made it to the Sixth Avenue streetcar for the trip downtown. Once aboard and seated, I stared out the window at the multiplicity of faces and figures on the street. People came and went, well dressed and ragged, beautiful and homely, no two alike, all existing together as atoms of the monster known as New York, and yet each unique, each alone with his own, her own, secret self and past, isolated within on distant mountaintops. God may have been fallible, but was there ever a painter who worked with a more varied palette, a writer who struck an irony more perfect than the two-headed racehorse of life and death, a musician who could weave the threads of so many diverse tunes into such an all-encompassing symphony?

God was also a raucous vaudevillian, and I was obviously his foil at the moment. The joke had to do with eyes—Watkin's, the bleeding woman's, my own unable to see Mrs. Charbuque, her confabulatory supernatural sight. Were I to read an account of something similar, even in a novel by a writer of arabesques, I could not help but scoff and close the cover.

The ultimate punch line was that my eyes finally closed somewhere in that morass of contemplation, and I passed my stop by two blocks. I woke suddenly when we halted at Twenty-third Street, and I leaped off just before the car began to move again. My notebook, as light as it was in actuality, seemed as heavy as a rock as I staggered back to my house, half dreaming, thinking only of taking to my bed. Consider my utter disappointment when I saw a visitor sitting on my steps. I tell you, I nearly wept.

As I drew closer, the person waiting stood, having noticed my approach. From his height and wiry frame, the drooping handlebar mustache and wave of raven-black hair, I knew it was John Sills, the police detective who had saved me from a beating the previous night. During his off-hours he dressed rather informally—an old army jacket and the flat lid of a day laborer.

"Johnny," I said, "thank you for intervening on my behalf last night. I have a definite aversion to being clubbed."

I knew him to be a very affable fellow, and now he proved it by breaking into a wide smile and laughing. "Merely fulfilling my duty as a public servant," he said.

"I suppose you are here to explain what the hell was going on with that wretched woman last night," I said.

"No, Piambo, I'm here to remind you that, for the time being, that incident never happened."

"Come now, John," I said. "You can easily buy my silence with an explanation."

He looked over his shoulder and up and down the length of the block. Then he moved closer to me and whispered, "You've got to swear that you will tell no one. I'll lose my job if you do."

"You have my word," I said.

"That woman is the third we've found like that. The coroner thinks she was suffering from some kind of exotic disease brought in on one of the ships from Arabia or the Caribbean, perhaps China. Listen, I'm just a cop, so don't ask for anything scientific, but I understand that the fellows at the Department of Health have discovered a kind of parasite; something they've never come across before. It eats the soft tissue of the eye and leaves the wound unable to heal. It happens very rapidly. At first the victim weeps blood, and then the eyes are gone, becoming two spigots that cannot be turned off."

"And the higher-ups think it better if no one knows about it?" I asked, horrified.

"For now. It's not like a plague that passes rapidly from one person to the next. In fact, there doesn't seem to be any connection among the three victims. As far as we can tell, they're isolated incidents. But if word of this reaches the *Times* or the *World,* all hell will break loose. Mayor Grant wants it kept quiet for now until we can discover the source of the parasite."

"I will keep it close, John. You can trust me," I said. "But if you've come in contact with this woman, what is it that has kept you safe?"

"It appears that once it has fed, the bug becomes dormant. For how long, no one knows, because they have cremated the bodies immediately after studying them."

"Let's hope they can stop it," I said.

"If they can't, we'll all be crying in our beer," he said, and gave a grim smile.

I could tell from this ill-conceived joke that he had finished speaking about the incident. Truly wanting to know, I asked him how his painting was coming along. He had a great deal of natural talent, and over the years, stealing time from his job and his wife and children, he had become a very creditable miniaturist. Some of his works were no bigger than a cigarette case, and many of the images in them were rendered with a brush that held only two very fine hairs. He informed me that he had just finished a series of portraits of criminals and that a few of them would be included in a group show at the Academy of Design.

"It opens next week," he said, and moved forward to shake my hand. "Tell Shenz to come along also."

"I will," I said, and clasped hands with him.

Before leaving, he said in a low voice, "Remember, Piambo, the less we know, the better."

"My memory is a blank canvas," I said.

"Thank you," he said, and walked away up the street.

Once inside my home, I went immediately to the bedroom and shrugged off my coat and clothes, letting them lie in a pile where they fell. I felt as if I could have fallen asleep standing up, but there was one more thing I had to do. There was the matter of the notebook, and an assessment of the sketches I had made at Mrs. Charbuque's. I took the tablet to bed with me, and when I was comfortable, with my head propped up on the pillows, I set about reviewing what I had done.

I flipped the pages, past sketches of a neighborhood cat, Samantha in a kimono, one of a telephone pole on East Broadway, outside the Children's Aid Society, Reed's goldfish, a portrait of a young writer sitting at a corner table at Billy Mould's Delicatessen. Then I came to the first of the sketches done in Mrs. Charbuque's drawing room. Staring for a moment, I then turned the sketchbook to see if I had not had it positioned differently while drawing. What I saw before me was an amorphous blob made up of scratchy lines. Hard as I tried, I couldn't make out the figure of a woman at all. To tell the truth, I couldn't even make out the figure of a person.

Irritated, I turned to the next. Again I beheld the mere shadow of a cloud. The next, another charcoal puddle. None of them exhibited any recognizable trace. I lay there wondering what it was I thought I had witnessed projected on that screen. At one point, I remembered thinking I had actually captured the outline of a facial profile, but what was transmitted to the sketchbook now made me wonder if I was not, weakened by my sleepless condition, doing a bit of projecting myself. While Mrs. Charbuque was relating to me her tale of allowing fancy to infect reality, I had been going her one better and putting it into practice. An indistinct movement of shadow had become a woman.

I cursed and threw the sketchbook across the room. It slammed against the top corner of the dresser, twirled in the air, bounced off the arm of a chair, and landed, no lie, directly in a trash can I kept in the corner. As Mrs. Charbuque had said, there was no such thing as an accident. My eyes closed, and I fell into a dream of snow.

DREAM WOMAN

SATURDAY BROUGHT with it the urge to paint. I rose early, well refreshed, and went out for breakfast to Crenshaw's on Seventh Avenue. After a greasy repast of steak and eggs, two cups of coffee, three cigarettes, and the perusal of a story in the *Times* concerning a land grab ensuing in Cherokee Creek, Oklahoma, where people were shooting one another over parcels of dirt, I returned home to my ethereal pursuit of the ineffable Mrs. Charbuque.

I had a canvas stretched and prepared in my studio, waiting for me to attack it with color. What with all my recent dithering about—the unveiling of Mrs. Reed's portrait, sessions before the screen, Samantha's play, and my visit to Shenz—I had not lifted a brush in over a week. That demon inside me, the one that can only be placated through the application of pigment to canvas, was chafing at the bit. I prepared my palette and, dipping my brush into ochre, moved forward to claim my own parcel of territory. Then the specter of absence that was Mrs. Charbuque rose up in my mind in all her negative glory, the folds of her nonexistent dress spreading outward, the voluminous emptiness of her hair burgeoning. The exquisite lack of her crowded out all else, extinguishing the insistence of the paint demon and stultifying my intention to create. The brush seized an inch from the canvas, and my hand slowly carried it back to my side. I placed the palette and brush on the table and sat down in utter defeat.

For the longest time I simply stared at that expectant rectangle on the easel before me. As usually happened when I turned my attention toward trying to envision her, she finally cohered out of the miasma of nothingness, and I saw a woman, but as with Proteus in the *Odyssey*, whose form shifts endlessly from that of one creature to another, this was a woman of many women. I took deep breaths and concentrated, trying to halt the rapid metamorphosis of face into face, blond to brunet to ginger. The process was frustrating, like trying to determine when precisely to step onto a swiftly spinning carousel.

One thing that struck me for the first time that morning was that every incarnation that passed before my eyes was an instance of classic beauty. But was Mrs. Charbuque beautiful? To tell the truth, it had never struck me that she could be anything but. In all the hundreds of images of her I had conceived since first accepting the commission, I had never once envisioned her as plain. "God forbid," I thought. "Say she is outright ugly." Although the women I continued to see in my mind's eye remained handsome, with another, nonpictorial part of my brain I entertained the notion that she might be heavyset, even obese. Perhaps I had been wrong in my assessment of her age, and her years were not equivalent to mine or less, but instead she was a wrinkled crone. What if she were thin as a rail, with no breasts to speak of, bucktoothed, cross-eyed?

That is when I realized that my own sexual desire, my own ridiculous male expectation of the female, would never allow Mrs. Charbuque to be herself. I was doomed to end up painting the portrait of some idealized dream woman, more me than her. My God, I was Reed. I remembered M. Sabott speaking to me one day about the nature of portraiture. "Understand this, Piambo. The first lesson is that every portrait is in some sense a self-portrait, as every self-portrait is a portrait." If my thoughts were in turmoil, my body was completely paralyzed. Had there not been a knocking on my front door to awaken me, my only recourse would eventually have been to drag myself off in search of the bottle.

Samantha stood before me on the front steps, pulling off her gloves finger by finger. Her dark hair was done up in the back in intricate braids, and her face shone in the Saturday-morning sunlight. She was smiling mischievously, and the instant I laid eyes upon her, all traces of the elusive, evolving Mrs. Charbuque were obliterated from my mind.

"What do we have here?" I said.

She laughed aloud, and it was obvious she was up to something. I stepped aside and let her in.

"Are you working, Piambo?" she asked.

"I was pretending to for a moment but found I couldn't deceive myself."

"Having trouble painting the mystery woman?" she asked.

For some reason I hated to acknowledge the fact, as if my admission were one of impotence, but I could not lie to Samantha. I nodded sadly.

"As I thought," she said.

"Did you come to taunt me?" I asked.

"I'll save that for this evening," she said. "I'm here now to help, as always."

"You've heard something about this woman Charbuque?" I asked.

"Heavens, no," she said. "I have a present for you. I have engaged a young actress, an understudy from the production at Palmer's, to sit for you. My idea was to keep you from seeing her. Perhaps you could sit with your back to her and ask her questions. You could practice capturing her likeness through her words."

"Where is she," I asked, "hiding under your skirts?"

She took a halfhearted swipe at me with her gloves. "No, imbecile, she is outside, down the street, waiting for me to arrange the situation."

At first I was skeptical, afraid of failure, but Samantha told me that the entire reason for the project was to see what I could do, not what I couldn't. "Like a dress rehearsal," she said. I acquiesced and went to my studio to arrange the easel and a chair for myself. It was then I realized that painting was out of the question and that it would be more useful to simply sketch. I needed to work quickly so as not to think too much. Contemplation had been nothing but a hindrance to me. I went to my bedroom and retrieved my sketchbook from the trash pail. A few minutes later, after dragging my drawing board around to face the back wall, I heard the front door open and close. Two sets of footsteps approached down the hallway from the parlor.

"Piambo," I heard Samantha say, "this is Emma Hernan."

"Hello," I called, having to remind myself not to turn around.

"Hello, Mr. Piambo," said the voice of a young woman.

"Are you ready to have your portrait done?" I asked.

"Yes," said Emma.

"Please do not be upset if I miss the mark."

"She understands the situation," said Samantha.

"It will be somewhat awkward, but if you two will simply engage in a protracted conversation and allow me to eavesdrop, I will try to capture several quick images of both of you," I said.

"Do you mean gossip, Mr. Piambo?" asked Emma.

"We shouldn't have a problem with that," said Samantha, and the two laughed.

They settled themselves on the couch and began to discuss the previous evening's performance, in which one of the principal actresses had not shown up due to illness and Emma had had to fill in. Even if Samantha had not told me that Emma was young, I would immediately have identified her age by the clarity of her voice and the enthusiasm she exhibited in talking about the craft of acting. I listened intently for a time, moving my hand and the charcoal inches above the page, unable to commit a line. Closing my eyes, I pictured Samantha speaking, and slowly brought into view her respondent. At first there was merely a shadowy form sitting next to her, but then the conversation turned to the inadequacy of the poor Derim Lourde, and Emma's figure grew in my mind out of the sound of her laughter. I saw long, wispy blond hair with red highlights and smooth skin, devoid of wrinkles. I made a mark, and that first difficult line gave permission for another.

From the hapless amnesiac ghost, their talk turned to the particulars of a grim story the newspapers of late could not get enough of, namely the trial of Lizzie Borden. There was something vaguely erotic in the way the young woman recited that song all the children were singing about forty whacks. Emma's lips and perfect nose, her small ears, and the curving lids of her wide eyes came to me through that tune.

Then for a time they spoke and although I heard what they were saying I did not register it but was lost to my drawing. I saw them clearly, Emma in a long orange-colored skirt and white pleated blouse. It was a certainty that she wore a ribbon in her hair. One of the things I discovered after the second preliminary sketch was that she had a light dappling of freckles across the bridge of her nose. Her body was thin and athletic with the newly evolving modern look; a contrast to Samantha's fuller figure. I knew that if I were to paint this young woman she would be situated in a lush green garden in full sunlight, sitting on a marble bench. She would be wearing a summer dress, rendered with a number 4 filbert in a translucent quinacridone red, holding a book and staring off as if rapt in a daydream of herself as one of its characters.

I was putting the finishing touches to the sketch, now rendering a quick profile of Samantha's braided hair, when a snippet of the conversation drew me abruptly away from my work.

". . . weeping blood," Emma had just said.

"Bizarre," said Samantha. "That's dreadful."

"Who was weeping blood?" I called out, and nearly turned around.

"A woman in an alleyway. I had been at W. & J. Sloane on Nineteenth Street buying fabric. On the walk home, I passed an alley on Broadway and happened to look in. There was a woman not too far down the way, leaning against the wall. She seemed to be unwell, so I stopped. She noticed me and looked up. I could be mistaken, but it appeared as if she were crying blood. Her tears were red, staining her white jacket. The second she noticed me she turned away as if in embarrassment."

"What became of her?" I asked, and in my agitation now did turn around, seeking an answer.

Emma's eyes widened with my sudden movement, as if I had walked in on her in the middle of dressing, and flustered she said quickly, "I don't know. I left her alone."

I was about to blurt out my own experience on the way home from Shenz's place but remembered my promise to John. Managing a smile, I said only "Interesting."

"Perhaps I should have approached her," said Emma, rapidly shedding my vision of her to confront me with reality. She was short and somewhat stocky—her dark hair in ringlets, no ribbon, not a freckle in sight, and her outfit was a dowdy dark blue affair.

"Who would know what to do in that situation?" said Samantha. "Obviously the woman wanted to be alone in her grief."

"But the blood," said Emma. "I'm sure she was crying blood."

"What heartbreak," said Samantha, shaking her head.

"Indeed," I said.

After I thanked the women, and made plans to meet Samantha after her show, they left to prepare for that evening's performance. I prayed they would not ask to see my sketches and was surprised when they did not. It must have been an arrangement Samantha had made before the session. I doubt there was ever a woman more discreet. Later I tore the drawings from my book and threw them all in the fire. "What heartbreak," I thought, and went to fix myself a drink.

THE ASYLUM

*I*T SEEMED that the remainder of Saturday was to be given over to pointless maundering. I had just settled down in the studio with my drink, prepared for a first-class stare, when again someone knocked at my door. This time it was Shenz, wearing his velvet derby and matching coat, carrying that walking stick of his with an old man's head carved into the handle. He had a hansom cab waiting in the street and seemed very excited.

"Grab your coat, Piambo," he said. "We're going for a visit."

"Why don't you just come in and have a few," I said.

"Nonsense, this is important."

"Whom are we going to see?" I asked, reaching into the closet for my coat. "From the looks of your outfit, I'd guess Whistler is in town."

"Close," said Shenz. "We're going to meet with a lunatic by the name of Francis Borne."

"I've had enough madness for one week," I said.

"No, you haven't. This old fellow once worked for Ossiak as a prognosticator like your Mrs. Charbuque's father."

That was all I needed to hear. I threw my coat on, and we were out the door. As we boarded the hansom, I asked Shenz how he had tracked the man down.

"A little asking about in the right circles," he said. He shut the cab door and then leaned out the window to tell the driver, "Morningside Heights, One Hundred Seventeenth Street and the boulevard."

"That's way up by the Hudson. Where are you taking me?" I asked.

"Bloomingdale's asylum for the insane," he answered.

"Fitting," I said, and the horses began to move.

The day was unseasonably warm; the sky a dab of lead white in a sea of Windsor blue. It was only a little past noon. The streets were crowded with shoppers and the usual bustle of business. In addition to the throng of pedestrians, the streetcars, and the carriages, there were quite a few motorcars maneuvering through the traffic. Together, they conspired to raise a fog of fine brown silt on the major thoroughfares.

I looked across the compartment at Shenz, who sat facing me with his back to the driver, resting both hands on the head of his cane. He was staring intently out the window, as if the melee on the street might reveal some important secret.

"And what certain circles were those that identified this Francis Borne as an ex-employee of Ossiak?" I said, breaking the silence.

"A gentleman I know in the Village who traffics in curatives and elixirs and the like," he said. "The Man from the Equator."

"There's a singular moniker," I said.

"He's a singular fellow," said Shenz.

"Mrs. Charbuque's father plumbed the mysteries of snowflakes. What of Borne? Astrologer? Dream reader? Divination by analysis of the corns on one's feet? What was his specialty?"

"I don't know the official name for it," said Shenz. "Some kind of turdologist."

"What are you saying?" I asked.

"He predicts the future by way of the past, so to speak," he said, and smiled.

"Excrement?" I asked.

Shenz nodded, and we both howled with laughter.

"I thought that was the devil's end," I said, wiping tears from my eyes.

"You should read more of the Transcendentalists," said Shenz, shaking his head. "The Oversoul is everywhere. Besides, we're not going for a seminar. All we need do is find out if he ever saw your patron in the time he was with Ossiak. Even if she was only a child, he might be able to clue us to her hair color and some distinguishing features."

"Good God, man," I said, and lit a cigarette. We rode the rest of the journey without speaking but occasionally bursting into fits of laughter.

As we pulled off the road onto the grounds of the asylum, I caught sight of the main building, an impressive structure of brick and stone, partially hidden by old maples and oaks. As we drew closer, other buildings scattered here and there about the property came into view. It was a lovely setting, unindicative of the mental anguish and dysfunction it sheltered—much like many individuals one meets in the course of a day.

Shenz gave the driver the fare for our journey and asked him to wait for us. We were only allowed an hour's interview with Borne. My companion had set up the meeting by way of telephone, telling the attendant that we were old neighbors of Mr. Borne's curious to see how he was getting on. We were met on the steps of the main building by a Mr. Calander, the fellow with whom Shenz had spoken earlier. He seemed affable enough, suspiciously cheerful, with a penchant for rapid speech.

"Things are somewhat in turmoil," Calander told us. "We are moving to a new location next year out in White Plains, and my people are doing an inventory just now. Since your friend Borne is not in the main building and is quite a docile patient, it should be no problem for you to see him for a brief time."

"Wonderful," said Shenz. "And which structure does Francis reside in?"

"Come, I'll show you," said Calander.

As we walked across the grounds, the verbose attendant regaled us with the recent history of the asylum. He explained that although its location had been perfect when it was first built, as it was far removed from the rest of the city, now that the developers were encroaching, relocation was called for, since no one wanted to live in close proximity to the insane.

"It's too late," Shenz said in response.

Calander stopped speaking briefly and gave my friend a quizzical look before proceeding at breakneck speed. "Also, the land here with its beautiful view of the Hudson is choice real estate. I don't think it would be saying too much to suggest that there are numerous powerful entities who would like to own the rights to it," he said. "We admit nearly four hundred and fifty new patients a year. A veritable heaven compared to Wards Island, though." There was more, and the man spoke so frantically fast, eventually just mouthing facts and figures interspersed with a quote or two from *Hamlet,* that I began to suspect him of being a patient himself.

We passed a chapel topped by a stone bell tower, then crossed more lawn to a large house the attendant told us was named Macy Villa. "Here are housed those whose problems are not so pronounced but who suffer from certain fractured or illusory views of the world," said Calander. We entered, and I saw that the place was peaceful and well kept. We ascended a set of steps to the second floor and then walked down a long hallway. As we went, Calander lightly touched each closed door, naming the residents of the apartments: "Mr. Scheffler, Mr. Cody, Mr. Varone . . ." Finally he landed upon the door of Mr. Borne.

"A moment, gentlemen," he said, and entered the room. A few

minutes later Calander came out and told us, "Francis has been ex-pecting you."

I glanced at Shenz, who had told me Borne had no idea we were coming. He raised his eyebrows and shrugged as if to say, "Well, the man *is* a prognosticator."

As we entered, Calander told us, "Only an hour, please, gentle-men," and then he left. In the middle of a neatly ordered one-room apartment, light spilling in through two high barred windows with plants on the sills, there sat a very old man, fully dressed in a tuxedo whose style had gone out of fashion two decades earlier. He wore rather large spectacles with thick lenses that magnified the size of his eyes. His body was painfully thin, like a cornstalk in a suit of clothes, and his face appeared to be made of loose, well-broken wallet leather. Upon seeing us, he bowed his head and smiled in our direction. "I was wondering when you two would arrive," he said.

"You knew we were coming, then," said Shenz.

"I saw it," he said.

We moved close to him and sat down, myself on the divan and my companion on a bench that had obviously been drawn near to Borne for that very reason.

"Where did you see it?" asked Shenz.

"Two days ago, in the results of Monday's lamb stew."

I winced, but Shenz kept a straight face. "Sounds like quite a repast," he said.

"I can't imagine a more prophetic product," said Borne, "unless the thing were to grow lips and speak to me."

"The Man from the Equator sends his greetings," said Shenz.

"Ah, Goren," said Borne. "How is he?"

"Getting on in years, but a wonderful advertisement for his mer-chandise," said Shenz. "Still stirring his cauldron for the ailing."

"A knowledgeable man," said Borne.

I introduced myself, as did Shenz, and the old man lifted a skele-tal hand and gave a meager handshake to each of us.

"We were wondering if you could tell us something about your time working for Malcolm Ossiak," I said.

"Those were the days," Borne said, and looked past us as if caught up in a memory of long ago. That memory must have been something, for he sat staring for whole minutes before finally speaking. "I had my own laboratory and over a hundred specimens at a time from which to discern the course of future events. Row upon row of glass jars, representing the movers and shakers of the time. I had a cobralike piece of President Lincoln in my possession that was a veritable Rosetta stone of political portent. As long as Ossiak's money was behind me I had credibility, but the minute he met with financial ruin I was labeled insane, and someone sent the Department of Health after me. People fear the truth of the chamber pot. They have no idea how old and venerable a tradition divination through evacuants is . . ."

A SOLILOQUY IN BROWN

ORNE WENT on for a good half hour relating every kernel of the history of that odious science he was so obsessed with. From prehistoric coprolites to the Dalai Lama's powdered good-luck droppings, he spoke sometimes like a Harvard professor, sometimes like a revivalist preacher, laying bare his excremental vision. When finally I feared we would run out of time with him, I rudely interrupted in the middle of a disquisition on Swift's volume *The Human Ordure,* saying, "Do you remember, when you were with Ossiak, a man who made predictions based on the formations of snowflakes?"

My question was like a wrench thrown into the gears of a talking machine; his verbal diligence grinding to a definitive halt. He retreated again to his silent reverie, staring at the wall.

"Snowflakes," said Shenz as a means of pulling him back to the present.

"Ossiak called us two his bookends: heaven and earth," said Borne. "He gave us more credence than the others. We both, at one and the same time, predicted his financial ruin. Grasp the profundity of this, if you will, gentlemen. In one of Ossiak's own golden movements, I discovered two specimens of precisely the same weight and size, both shaped like goose eggs, exact twins in every feature and giving off the aroma of wild violets. This should be an impossibility, but there it was, right under my nose. And Londell, the yin to my yang, reader of the excrement of the skies, found something equally devastating, though I was never informed as to the details of what that was."

"Londell?" asked Shenz.

"Benjamin Londell," said Borne. "A very fine fellow. Some of those whom Ossiak employed in this capacity were charlatans, but I can tell you Londell was serious. He worked very conscientiously and subjected his family to great hardship in order to see the future."

"What hardship would that be?" I asked.

"They had to traipse up a mountain every year and stay in the most ungodly surroundings for six months or so to get the precise crystals he was after. At least in my discipline specimens were always readily at hand."

"He had children?" asked Shenz.

"A daughter," said Borne. "That, I believe, was all."

"Do you remember the girl?" I asked.

"A sweet child," he said.

"What did she look like?" asked Shenz.

The patient shook his head. "It's difficult to remember, for soon after I began paying any attention to her at all she went incognito."

"She disappeared?" I asked.

"No," said Borne, "she had a sort of act she performed when they would come to the city to confer with Ossiak. She hid behind a screen and made predictions or something along those lines. Once she took to the screen, I don't believe I ever saw her again. This was only a few years before Ossiak's empire fell apart. As a matter of fact, the year she became the Sibyl was the same year both her father and I made our startling discoveries. By then, although we sensed only the first inklings of it, things had already begun to crumble."

"The Sibyl," I said, hoping for more information.

To this, Borne simply nodded and said, "Yes, that was what she was called."

"Her hair color?" asked Shenz.

"Either chestnut or blond, perhaps strawberry," said the old man. He slowly lifted his hand to play with one of the buttons on his threadbare jacket. "It's all locked away now in the warehouse."

Borne looked sad, as if dredging up the past was a painful task. Sympathizing with him, I said, "It only remains in your memory, eh?"

He turned and peered at me through those thick glasses. "No," he said, "the warehouse. Ossiak, before committing suicide, began gathering what little of his wealth was left and bought warehouses in which to store the stuff. He didn't want his creditors getting everything. At that point he had gone somewhat insane himself and dreamed of eventually rising from the ashes to rebuild his empire. All my instruments, specimens, notes, what have you, were confiscated and locked away. Londell, the poor man, had a stroke and died when they took his precious snowflake equipment and research from him. Those were grim days."

"I suppose these things have since been dispersed," said Shenz.

"No," said Borne. "They are still there. I know where they are. I followed the men who took them. I know exactly where they are."

"Yes?" I said.

"Do you know the chemists on Fulton, the ones with the big building? The Fairchild Brothers, I believe. Fulton and Gold? I can't imagine they've gone out of business. Around the corner, heading east toward the water, there sits an old one-story warehouse made of brick. On the front is an O painted in white. It must be quite faded by now. All of it is there; the detritus of the entire saga."

Calander, exhibiting a more irritating punctuality than even

Watkin, appeared at that precise moment. I had a hundred more questions for Mr. Borne, but it wasn't to be. The old man shook our hands again, and we were ushered out of his room. Before the door was closed, Borne shouted to us, "Remember, gentlemen, to move forward you must first look behind."

"Borne doesn't seem like such a bad sort," I told Shenz on the ride back downtown. Night had begun to blossom by then, and the temperature was dropping.

"Reed lives a more illusory existence than that poor fellow," said Shenz. "At least Borne understands what he is made of, but his predilection for the mysteries of shit is altogether repugnant to society at large. Can you imagine his neighbors' horror when they realized he was collecting it? We live in an age in which everyone pretends to be an angel. Think of all the painters who have taken that winged theme as their subject."

"On the other hand," I said, "he wasn't simply analyzing it with an eye toward diagnosing one's health; he was predicting the future with it. That seems somewhat deranged. Not a bad old man at all, though."

"Useful too," said Shenz.

"He at least corroborated much of Mrs. Charbuque's story and gave us her maiden name, Londell," I said.

"A name we can trace," said Shenz.

"It also reminds me that at some point I must get around to asking her about her husband. Who, then, is Mr. Charbuque?"

"Of course," said Shenz, "but one thing we need to give some time to is that warehouse Borne told us about. The one on Fulton with the O painted on it. We need to get in there and have a look around."

"It doesn't seem as if anyone would have the key at this point, though. Didn't it sound as if Ossiak stocked the place and then died? I'll wager no one knows who owns it, and they just assume someone does. There it sits, like an ancient tomb, guarding its treasures."

"I thought I was the Romantic," said Shenz. "I have an acquaintance who can get us in there."

"The Man from the Equator?" I asked, smiling.

"No, a man from West Thirty-second Street."

"One of the Kitchen's dignitaries?" I asked.

"An artisan in his own right," said Shenz. "This man knows locks the way Borne knows what he had for dinner last week. He has crafted a ring of skeleton keys that is legendary in the underworld, on a par with the Holy Grail, and wields a hat pin with more finesse than Vermeer did a brush."

"Why should he help us?" I asked.

Shenz laughed. He took out his cigarette case and drew forth one of his opiate specials. After lighting it, he blew a stream of smoke out the window and said, "Cash."

"You propose we break into that warehouse?"

"Think of what we might find there, Piambo," he said. "Besides, I'm curious to see Malcolm Ossiak's golden eggs, not to mention that nugget of Abraham Lincoln's. Now *that's* historic."

"I had better call Bloomingdale's asylum and reserve you a room. I'm not about to break into a warehouse. Come now, you're more adamant about this commission of mine than I am. Get a hold on yourself."

He sat back in his seat, as if my words had wounded him. Turning his gaze out the window, he watched the passing lights of Broadway. When his cigarette was three quarters finished, he tossed the rest into the street and closed his eyes. In minutes, he was asleep. As I sat studying his features in the intermittent light from the boulevard, I felt remorse for having rebuked him.

Shenz was somewhat older than I, his age in the middle ground between those of Sabott and myself. It was becoming increasingly obvious to me that the opium was beginning to erode his health. His skin tone had become more sallow in recent months, and he had lost a good deal of weight. When he was younger he had been quite muscular and had always exuded a great sense of energy. His exuberance now, though, had a frantic edge to it, more like the nervous excess resulting from the consumption of too much coffee. Also, his work had begun to decline in its precision and freshness, and the commissions he now drew were less than choice—the Hatstells' children were a good example.

I wondered if I was looking at a portrait of myself in another few years. I also wondered if perhaps Shenz, when looking at me, was seeing a portrait of himself a few years younger when he still had an opportunity to marshal his powers and, as my father had entreated me, "create something beautiful." It came to me that perhaps that was the reason for his resolute insistence that I succeed in my bid to portray Mrs. Charbuque precisely.

When the cab stopped at Shenz's address, I woke him. He came to with a start and then smiled, his eyelids opening to mere slits. "I had a dream, Piambo," he said.

"Was it of that model of Hunt's again, the girl sitting on that wag's lap in *The Awakening Conscience*?" I asked.

"No," he said, and slowly shook his head. "I was trapped in a glass jar, and Borne was peering in at me. I tapped the glass with my walking stick, desiring to be let out. He paid no attention, though. I saw he was at work making a label. On it he wrote in large black letters LUNCH."

I saw my friend to his door. Before he passed over the threshold, I said to him, "Listen, Shenz, I do truly appreciate your help. I'll consider going to the warehouse. But first let me see what else I can learn from Mrs. Charbuque."

He fixed me with a look of grave weariness. "I never told you this," he said, "but before Sabott died, I had a conversation with him one day when he turned up at the Player's Club. No one would acknowledge his presence, and they were watching him closely, prepared to eject him if he should get out of hand, but I went over and sat with him out of due respect. Luckily he was having a rare lucid moment. He bought me a drink and spoke brilliantly about the painting by Waterhouse of the Sirens depicted as birds of prey with women's heads, surrounding Ulysses, who is bound to the mast of his ship. Before he left, he mentioned you, and said to me, 'Shenz, keep an eye on that boy for me. I haven't had the chance to tell him everything.' Then he left. Two weeks later he was dead."

SUNDAY MORNING

I WOKE VERY early Sunday morning to a suffused gray light and the patter of a driving rain against the window. Although it was cold out beyond the blankets and the counterpane, Samantha lay next to me, enveloping me in her warmth. There, on our intimate island of calm, I felt temporarily safe from the concerns that presently plagued me. Swarming just beyond the confines of the bed, I knew, was that flock of female images waiting to descend and peck at my consciousness, tear apart my reason. I thought I would remain where I was, lashed to the mast, so to speak, for a little while longer.

I turned away from the world and watched Samantha breathe, wondering what dreams she moved through behind the screen of sleep. Her long dark hair swept over and around the pillow, wild in its configurations. There were curious minute angles at the corners of her closed lips—either a smile or a sign of consternation. Her eyelids fluttered slightly, and I could read her pulse by concentrating on her neck. Evident now also were the creases around her eyes and mouth, betraying her age. The blankets lay at a slant across her body exposing her right breast, and seeing her at that moment made me think what a perfect subject she would be for a portrait. I had to wonder whether in all the portraits I had done of her, most when we were younger, I had ever really captured her essence, or if what I had painted was, expanding upon Sabott's dictum, only something of myself.

I lay there swinging rapidly back and forth between specific memories of my days with Samantha and moments of clouded uncertainty when her sleeping figure mocked my belief that I knew anything about her at all. In an attempt to circumvent the troublesome half of this equation, I concentrated on the kindness she had shown the previous day by bringing Emma to my studio. I smiled when considering how poor a job I had done in rendering the girl's looks, and then, suddenly, miraculously, I had a thought that was not centered upon myself.

I dressed and left the house in such haste that I did not remember an umbrella, and by the time I reached Broadway, I was soaked to the skin. As happens during such torrential rains, the thoroughfares had been turned to mud. When I had to leave the safety of the sidewalk and cross the street, I sank in to my ankles. I nearly lost a shoe to the suction but, in all, fared better than a deeply mired automobile I saw another block down, uselessly spinning its wheels and sending up a geyser of brown muck. The horses showed up their mechanical competitors, but even they moved at only a plodding pace.

Upon reaching the address of W. & J. Sloane, I ducked in under the stone overhang of a doorway to find a moment's relief from the downpour. The wind felt brutally cold, and I was surprised the precipitation had not turned to snow. The gloves I wore had no lining, and my hands were freezing. I took off my hat and tipped it to let the water roll off the brim. Then, standing still, I surveyed the Sunday-morning desolation of the street, trying to remember if Samantha's friend Emma had mentioned whether she headed south or north from the fabric merchant's on her way home. I had already passed a number of alleys on Broadway, but I thought I would head downtown a few more blocks and then inspect each one on my way back home.

Only then did I consider that it might have been a good idea to check the newspaper to see if there had been any women who had gone missing in the last few days. It was possible that the woman whom Emma had seen crying blood was one of the poor victims that Sills and his men had already discovered. Since Emma had not given an exact date in mentioning the incident, but, as far as I could remember, had just said "the other day," I was unsure about how long ago her brief glimpse of the weeping woman had taken place.

Next door to Sloane's, heading downtown, was a church whose doors stood open but which seemed as empty as the stores. I passed apartment buildings and shops, but the structures here were built with walls butting up against each other, leaving no room for alleyways. The same held true for the next few southerly blocks, so I turned around and began working my way back toward my home.

I was every bit the undaunted investigator while walking along Broadway, but when I came to the first alleyway and looked into its grimy darkness, my courage quailed. It struck me that the very last thing I wanted was to discover a body with the eyes leaking blood. As I mentioned before, the eyes hold a sacred position in my personal psychology. Being that the crux of my profession and my art is the manipulation of light on canvas, to say that sight is essential is an understatement. The mere thought of a sty makes me queasy, and now, as I inched into the dripping shadows to find what I might, my hands shook and sweat mixed with the rain on my face.

This alley was a miniature throwback to old New York when people would toss their refuse into the streets for the pigs to root through. A few yards into the canyon of brick, I was walking on all manner of offal and discarded newsprint. There were some staved-in barrels, a few empty crates, but I reached the end, a tall wooden fence, and breathed a sigh to have discovered no corpses. I went mincingly down two more of these grim passageways and, in the last, discovered only a starving old mongrel hiding in an overturned barrel. The creature barely stirred when I went scuttling past it through the debris.

Emerging once again onto the sidewalk from the last of the three alleys, I felt an overwhelming sense of relief as well as a twinge of righteousness for having taken the trouble to brave the weather and make my search. As I turned to head toward Twenty-first Street and home, my gaze happened to scan the other side of the avenue, and I noticed an entrance to yet another alley. "Is it possible that Emma crossed the avenue on her way home?" I wondered. I shook my head and took a few steps before turning and looking back at the opening. I cursed roundly and stepped down into the muck of Broadway.

The wall of one of the buildings that defined this particular alley belonged to a tobacconist's shop, so there were quite a few casks stacked high, giving off the rich scent of their recent contents, and a good deal of rotted whole leaf, both tied in bunches and loose on the ground. The aroma made me desire a cigarette, and I stopped halfway to the end of the alley to light one. This bolstered me a bit, and I continued. I neared the end and was about to turn back when I saw a shoe; a woman's laced ankle boot. Then there was movement, as if the ground were shifting. I finally heard squeals above the sound of wind and rain echoing down the passage. I peered closer and made out no fewer than a hundred rats like a slick, living blanket of shadow covering something. The cigarette dropped out of my mouth as I groaned. At this sharp sound the filthy creatures scattered to reveal her. The blood had coagulated, and the face held two huge, erupted scabs instead of eyes. It was difficult to tell that the dress had once been white, so drenched it was in the brick color of dried gore. It was all I could do not to retch. I turned, fighting an overwhelming paralysis, and forced myself to move forward one step at a time.

When I reached the street end of the alley and finally stepped out onto the sidewalk, a passerby nearly walked into me. I was slow in my movements, and the other individual brought himself up short at the last instant.

"Please excuse me," the gentleman said, and then stepped around me.

I said nothing, but did take in his countenance. Only later, after I had walked to Crenshaw's in a daze and used their telephone to call police headquarters, did I realize that the man I had nearly collided with was of all people Albert Pinkham Ryder. I was beginning to sense that condition Mrs. Charbuque had alluded to when speaking of the first time she believed the Twins had whispered to her—as if she were being singled out by God.

Samantha was still asleep when I arrived home. I did not wake her but changed out of my wet clothing and went directly to my studio. Taking up my palette and brush, I set to filling the canvas I had prepared the previous morning. I worked furiously and had only a vague idea that I was painting a woman. I let the paint and the sensation of its application dictate the attributes of the figure, taking my cues from the colors I chose with no lengthy deliberation—the picture itself directed my creation of it.

Sometime in the late afternoon I felt Samantha's arms close around me from behind. Only then did I become fully aware of what I had rendered: a portrait, definitely of a woman I did not know, seated, with long light hair, dressed in a robe of phthalocianine green sporting a paisley design in cadmium yellow. Her smile was as mischievous and mysterious as that of Leonardo's Giaconda, but her eyes were fountains of red, red everywhere, in a million droplets, more copious than the downpour outside.

"Tell me, Piambo," Samantha whispered to me. "Speak to me."

My own eyes filled with tears as I related to her what had occurred on the way home from Shenz's place, my promise to John Sills, my discovery that morning. I lifted the palette knife as I spoke, and scraped the canvas clean.

THE WOLF

NEAR THE end of winter, one night when I was with my father out in the frozen laboratory, he questioned me about how I had known where to find the corpse. In all things save the self-delusion generated by the pursuit of his profession, he was an honest man, and I could not lie to him. All he need do was squint his right eye and smile with the left side of his mouth, and the truth would out. I confessed that the identical snowflakes had bestowed some strange power upon me, an ability to know things I should not be able to. With so much time now passed, I can't recall the words I used to describe the phenomenon to him, but I was an intelligent child and made myself understood. I knew he would not laugh derisively as any sane parent would, but I was fearful he might be angry with me for calling attention to the Twins. What he actually did was nod gravely and touch me lightly on the forehead.

"He called it the second sight and said that, although I was always to keep the existence of the Twins a secret, I should develop this ability in order to help others and myself. Then he told me, 'Ossiak will not be able to support my work before too long, and it will be

necessary that you begin preparing to make your way in the world.'
I nodded, although I had no idea what he was alluding to.

"He told me to fetch the lamps that sat at the perimeter of the
laboratory. 'Bring them and put them on the viewing stage, Lu,'
he said. As I ran to fulfill his request, he started up the ladder to
his seat on the optical magnifier. I returned with the two lamps
and placed them one on each side. 'Now lie down, faceup, so that
I can focus upon your eyes,' he said. 'I want to get a look inside
you.'

"I did as I was told. The stage was frigid. Once my head was
beneath the huge lens, he called, 'When I bring down the barrel,
try as best you can to hold your breath for as long as possible.
Otherwise it will fog the lens.' I heard the machine begin to descend, one gear tooth at a time, and for a moment feared that my
father would absentmindedly crush my face, forgetting that today's
specimen was my head and not a flat board full of snowflakes. He
halted it only an inch or two from my face, or that is how I remember it. 'Stop breathing,' he called, and I took a deep breath.
'Open your eyes as wide as they will allow,' he said. I did this too.

"In my attempt to ignore the discomfort of not breathing, I
listened to the wind outside. Suddenly I saw something move in
the lens above me, an image that eventually settled into a hori-
zontal line, like a pair of giant lips displaying a monumental lack
of emotion—a magnification of my mother's usual expression. A
moment later those lips finally parted, revealing themselves as
eyelids, and I beheld an eye of immense proportions. I felt its
gaze penetrating me, scratching my very soul, and knew that it
could see all my secrets. There was no doubting now that I
would forever be scrutinized from above by an omniscient judge.
I desperately wanted to scream with the fear of being so completely exposed but would not allow even a murmur to leave my
mouth.

"I tell you, my face was probably blue by the time I noticed the
lens above me beginning to ascend. 'Take air,' yelled my father as

I heard his feet hitting the rungs of the ladder. I did, and I felt his hand on mine, pulling me up away from the machine. He knelt on the frozen floor and hugged me to him. 'I saw it,' he said. 'I saw everything.' I began to cry, and he patted my back. I tried to clasp my arms around his neck, but he pulled me gently from him and held me by the shoulders so as to look directly at me. 'Within you,' he said, 'I saw the universe. A million stars, and at their center a star composed of stars that shone with a clear brilliance—the imprint of the Almighty.'

"Believing himself to be a scientist, of course he had to double-check his findings. So he asked me to try to concentrate upon the voice of the Twins and remember whatever it was they next showed me. All I could do was nod. I was stunned by the idea that now not only was God watching me, especially me, but He was also inside me in the form of a swirling universe of stars. I did little more for the rest of the day than sit on the broken-down couch at the back of his study and stare out the window. Later on, when my mother called us to dinner, I felt the locket's heat against my breast, felt its chain tingle around my neck, and heard the faint stirrings of identical voices, one in each ear. Those words became a picture in my mind. I saw, moving through the trees on the shore of the lake, a large dark wolf, saliva dripping from his tongue, his eyes bright yellow.

" 'A wolf!' I yelled aloud, and at that moment realized I was looking out the window through the twilight and had actually seen some darker shadow passing into the forest at the edge of our homestead. Father spun around in his chair and said, 'Where?' 'The Twins,' I told him, 'they showed it to me. It's coming.' Right then my mother came to the door of the study and told us dinner was getting cold. As soon as she left to return to the kitchen, my father nodded, letting me know he understood, and then put his finger to his lips.

"After that incident in his study, I saw the wolf repeatedly in my thoughts and, if truth be told, still see it lurking from time to time at the edges of my consciousness. I was afraid to go out into the forest to play, as was my custom. Sticking close to the house, I had my games, but with one ear I was always listening for its approach. Two days passed and the wolf had not materialized, but my father kept his rifle loaded as a precaution against an emergency. I thought the plan was not to mention it to my mother, but I suppose my father feared for her safety, and at dinner the second night he told her to be wary of wolves. 'It's the season,' he said. 'It's the season.' My mother gave a mocking laugh and replied, 'What season? We haven't seen a wolf up here for four years,' but still, from that point on, she exhibited a certain nervous agitation.

"On the third night following the day of my so-called prediction, our small family was in the sitting room, reading by the lamplight. I still remember that through the winter of that year I was reading a collection of fairy tales my father had purchased for me in New York City the previous summer. When it was nearly my bedtime, I heard a noise outside the house; something moving through the crusted snow. I stood up from where I lay on the floor, and as I rose, so did my father from his chair. He went to his study and brought out his rifle. 'Put that away,' said my mother. 'Someone is going to get hurt.' He ignored her as he slipped his feet into his unlaced boots. She literally leaped out of her chair and placed herself between him and the door. I was as startled by her action and the emotion behind it as I was afraid of what might be outside. He gently moved her aside and pulled back the dead bolt.

"Tense minutes passed while he was outside. I kept expecting to hear a growl or a gunshot, but neither came. When he finally returned to the house, he was very quiet, much as when he was in his study pondering the mysteries of the snow crystals. 'Did you see the wolf?' I asked when he returned from putting the rifle away and again took his seat. 'Footprints,' he said. 'It's a big one.' I was then sent to bed. The next day I searched all around the house for the prints of the predator. It hadn't snowed, and the wind had not been high through the night, so they should still have been there. All I managed to find were boot prints.

"THE FOLLOWING day I was sitting in my father's study on the couch, and he turned to me and said, 'Lu, go see if your mother has any twine. I have to tie these old notes up in order to store them.' I went on my errand, first searching in the kitchen and then the bedroom. She did not seem to be in the house at all. I put on my boots and coat and went outside to see if she was fetching water or using the outhouse. It was a clear day and somewhat warmer than usual, the first sign that year that spring might actually arrive. I did not find my mother in any of the usual places, so I went to the tin shed that held the optical magnifier. She was not there. Out behind that building, I found the clothesline half hung with the day's laundry, the other half still heaped in the wicker basket. When I drew closer, I saw the trail of my mother's footsteps leading away into the forest. The wolf burst into my thoughts then, and I ran screaming back to the house.

"My father again took his rifle. He told me to stay in the house and bolt the door behind him when he left. I watched from the window in his office as he trudged across the snow beneath the blue sky toward the tree line. The waiting was interminable, and in that time I wanted to rip the locket off my neck and throw it as far from me as possible. It was the first time I realized that the secret of the Twins was much more a curse than a blessing. If only I had followed my impulse. I don't know how much actual time passed, ten minutes, a half hour, hours. Finally the anxiety became too much for me, and I ran to the door in the sitting room and unbolted it. I stepped outside, and that is when I heard, from a great distance, like the whisper of the Twins, my mother's scream followed by the report of the rifle. I took two steps in the direction of the woods, and the rifle sounded a second time.

"I met my father a few yards from the tree line. He moved slowly as if in the clutches of a great weariness. 'Where is

Mother?' I asked. He seemed in a daze, and his complexion was blanched a terrifying white. He shook his head and said, 'The wolf took her and I shot the wolf.' I knew this meant she was dead, and I began to cry. My father cried too as we held each other. I can mark his physical and mental decline from that moment. The fact that it matched the decline and eventual destruction of Malcolm Ossiak's empire is an interesting side issue. Twin tragedies."

"Your mother's body, was it ever recovered?" I asked, and briefly looked down to see that I had sketched not a woman but a wolf.

"No, Mr. Piambo, nor was the corpse of the wolf. I will tell you, though, that in the spring, when we were packing our things to descend the mountain and return to the city, I discovered in a box kept in the corner of the laboratory a broad-brimmed hat and a fur coat made from the pelt of an animal."

I was anxious to ask Mrs. Charbuque a rather obvious question, but she interrupted me as I mouthed the first word.

"By the way, Mr. Piambo," she said, "what were you doing out in that terrible rain on Sunday?"

Her query caught me off guard for a moment, and when I recovered I asked, "How do you know I was out in the rain?"

"Why, I saw you standing on Broadway. My carriage passed, and I only glimpsed you for a moment. It looked as if you were with that other artist, the one who does the seascapes, Ryder."

"You have seen me?" I asked.

"Certainly. Last week you sat at a table at Delmonico's drinking wine with your lady friend, Miss Rying. I was at the table next to yours." She laughed then, briefly, as if as an afterthought.

Her admission stunned me, and while emotions of betrayal and anger collided, I tried to think back to that night. When I looked around within my memory of the restaurant, I saw gowns and suits, cigar smoke, fine china, silver, and crystal, but everyone, even the waiters, was faceless. Then the door opened, and Watkin entered the room. I quietly gathered my things with trembling hands and left.

A GIFT FROM A CHILD

ON THE streetcar heading downtown, I finally took charge of my emotions and wondered if I had a right to feel so thoroughly abused by Mrs. Charbuque. She was playing me like a pennywhistle, and whatever visage I eventually concocted of her would have to manifest in some way a streak of sadism, but did it matter to our proposition whether she was engaged in spying on me? Was the sum of money she offered license enough for her to know every bit of my life? It struck me then that the aspect of the situation that distressed me more than any other was the fact that her presence was loose in the world, as if a bejeweled lamp once belonging to an ancient sultan had been rubbed and a mischievous djinn were now free. As long as I had known where she was, in that quiet room, situated behind that screen, the enigma was contained, and as frustrating as it might be, I could approach it on my own terms. She had been of equivalent status with, say, a character in a book, a figure out of mythology, and I was merely to be her illustrator. But now she roamed the world, and this notion ensured a certain physicality while at the same time negating a definitive location. She could have been anyone, the woman sitting next to me, the young girl passing outside on the street. I could not even discount disguise, so for that matter she could have been the streetcar conductor. Having gone to see Samantha on the stage innumerable times, I had witnessed convincing portrayals of women by men and vice versa. With the possibility of her being anyone, she was, potentially, everyone. My scalp prickled as I felt the fine tendrils of paranoia growing within and around me. I felt it on the back of my neck, in my stomach, with every beat of my heart, until I was trapped in a net of gazes, a thick web of stares. I was, undoubtedly, being watched.

I scanned the faces of my fellow passengers, searching for telltale signs in each that he or she might be my patron. Long before my stop, I forsook the streetcar for the sidewalk, where I could escape the claustrophobic feeling that made it difficult for me to breathe. In the open air, I was somewhat less a specimen on display, and there was at least the illusion of freedom in personal locomotion. A woman, a complete stranger, leaving a dry-goods store, flashed me a brief smile and nodded. Why? I frowned disapprovingly at her, and she quickly turned away. Wherever I looked I found a pair of eyes trained upon mine, and the weight of these gazes eventually made me stop in my tracks. The throng moved around me like a stream around a large rock, and I turned in circles trying to see all those who were seeing me. To calm myself, I closed my eyes, and there, behind the screen of my lids, I had a sense that the entirety of the teeming metropolis had me in its sights.

When I eventually felt steady enough to again open my eyes, I found standing before me a young boy of six or seven, wearing a cap and a threadbare coat. His round cheeks were red with the cold, and his smile showed the absence of at least three teeth. At first I thought he was begging, for he held his hand up toward me. Only when I was digging into my pocket for some change did I realize he was handing me a card.

"I been paid," he said, and shoved the square of paper into my hand.

"What are you doing?" I asked. "What is this?"

Before I could finish my second question, he was gone, running off into the swirl of passersby. I turned to watch him, but in seconds he was lost amid the multitude. It quickly became evident to me that I was now literally making a spectacle of myself, blocking traffic on the sidewalk. I moved quickly forward. Only when I reached the solitude and safety of a bench in Madison Square Park did I inspect the gift from the child. Turning the white rectangle over, I noticed words rendered in ink, a message in desperate script. After I stared at it for a solid minute, the words registered their meaning.

WHY ARE YOU SEEING MY WIFE?

CHARBUQUE

I quickly shot a glance over each shoulder and then scanned the park before me. When I again turned my attention to the message, I tried to see it in a new light, but still the words exuded a sense of menace, a definite threat. Rising, I slipped the card into my coat pocket and headed for the sidewalk. I hailed the first cab I saw, and went directly to my home. Once inside, I locked the door and checked each of the rooms.

Sitting in the studio, I pondered that day's events. It was becoming increasingly clear that Mrs. Charbuque was, in her subtle way, trying to undo me. How artfully she had dropped the news of her knowing my every move. "Is she paying for a portrait or for a subject to amuse herself with?" I wondered.

Out of thin air, her husband had materialized to insinuate a new thread into the tapestry. I wouldn't have been half surprised to find that she herself had written out the card and had Watkin find an urchin to deliver it. She obviously wanted me to ask her about her husband. Perhaps the whole exercise was as I had suspected earlier: a chance for her to tell her life, our meetings akin to attending confession. The twisted nature of the entire charade was mind-boggling.

I determined then and there that I would not play the fool for Mrs. Charbuque. I would eventually ask about her husband, but not when *she* required it. She was not playing fair, and I no longer felt the need to do so myself. What I needed was some systematic plan of attack, an approach to discovering her countenance in a more definitive manner than simply conjuring it through her questionable autobiography. Also, I would begin to subtly drop a hint or two during our daily dialogues that I might know more about her than she suspected. For now, some of these morsels could come from the information imparted by Borne; others I would simply manufacture. What I wanted above all else was to shake her confidence as she had shaken mine.

The tension of the afternoon settled upon me, but I tried to throw off my predicament, and set to work at the drawing board. On a large sheet of paper that covered the entire face of the board, I began illustrations for each of the characters and settings that inhabited her story so far, keeping each sketch small. I wanted to crowd them all onto one surface so that I could take them in at once. The house on the mountain, the optical magnifier, the face of her mother, her father, the tracker who was obviously tracking more than corpses. I also drew the wolf and the locket on a chain, the book of fairy tales opened to an illustration of Aladdin's lamp, and entering the picture frame from the side was a single manly hand offering a card with a message written upon it. Filling the empty spaces between objects, I drew six-pointed snow crystals—no two alike. God could be fallible, but not Piambo.

I worked rapidly, with a reserve of energy that had not made itself evident until I began. When I finally rose and backed away from the board, I stared at my depiction of all Mrs. Charbuque had told me. Like one of those antique paintings of the life of a saint, each saintly act depicted at one and the same time on the same plane as if time had been halted and history could be viewed as a single event, my drawings had captured everything from the broken-down couch in the study to the murder amid a stand of lonesome pines of Mrs. Londell and her lover by the warped crystalogogist.

Unconsciously I had arranged the elements of the story in a great circle on the page. In viewing it, I smiled with satisfaction at the unplanned but perfect balance of the piece. Only after I had patted myself on the back, so to speak, did it become clear to me that at the drawing's very center, around which everything else seemed to turn, there was a smaller circle of unsullied white. Of course, this emptiness was where the portrait of the child, Luciere Londell, belonged. It stared back at me.

I was too weary to engage in one of my usual bouts of self-pity. The fact that I had accomplished anything at all toward the commission, had at least made some marks on paper, was enough for the time being. I set down the charcoal pencil and retired to my bedroom.

I removed my shoes and was about to undress when I heard a noise emanating from outside the house, as if someone was walking on the stones just beyond my bedroom window. The fear I had felt earlier in the day returned immediately, and I stood stock-still, listening so hard I could feel my ears move. For an instant I actually considered getting down on my hands and knees and hiding beside the bed, but then from somewhere in the creeping paranoia, a stronger emotion of anger surfaced.

"Ridiculous," I said aloud, and stormed over to the window. With real determination I drew back the curtain to reveal the portal filled with night. It hadn't registered with me that I had spent so long at the board. The darkness made me quail a bit from my intended mission, but I bolstered my courage, unlatched the pane, and swung it open.

A blast of cold night air swept around me and lifted the curtains. "Who's there?" I demanded.

"Shhhh," I heard in return. "Piambo, it's me."

I immediately recognized the voice of Shenz.

"Shenz, what in good God are you doing out there?" I asked.

"Shhhh," he said. "Quietly, Piambo. Whisper only. We are here because we did not want anyone to see us at your front door."

"Who is with you?" I asked, softening my voice.

By then my eyes had adjusted, and I saw Shenz step toward the window. In the light coming from the bedroom I could make out his face directly beneath me. From out of the shadows another figure slowly sidled up next to him—a large woman in a great black overcoat, wearing a flowered kerchief around her head. I squinted to see more clearly and noticed that this might have been the ugliest woman I had ever seen. Her face had thick crude features and, upon closer inspection, a few day's growth of beard and mustache.

"Hello," she said in a deep voice.

I said nothing but moved back a bit.

"Piambo, this is our passage into Ossiak's warehouse," said Shenz, pointing to her.

"I thought you said the locksmith was a gentleman," I said.

Shenz quietly laughed, and his companion smiled. "He is in disguise," said my friend. "Say hello to Mr. Wolfe."

THE REMINDER

*I*T WAS a cold, moonless night with a light mist in the air that made haloes around the street lamps. We walked a good way downtown, Shenz and I on either side of Mr. Wolfe, before we came upon a hansom cab waiting for us at the curb on Seventeenth Street. We entered the carriage, and without a word the driver spurred the horses forward at a great pace. Inside the compartment, we found two oil lanterns and two crowbars.

Up to that point in our journey, no one had spoken. My nerves would not allow me to contain myself any longer, though, and I whispered, "Do you have your ring of keys, Mr. Wolfe?"

Shenz, who sat next to me, shoved me in the ribs with his elbow. I turned, and he shook his head, silently admonishing me for having spoken.

"There is no ring of keys," said Wolfe. "I'm the ring of keys." He held up his open hand, knuckle side out, before my face. It was a rather squat, round mitt, the fingers like sausages, but from their tips grew exceedingly long nails that had been precisely trimmed to the thinnest width. At their very ends, those of the pinky and ring bearer were cut in a serrated pattern, the thumb bore a three-

inch hat pin, and the remaining index and middle sported eruptions of nail that evidently would fit a lock's baffles.

He made a fist, leaving the thumb protruding. "I call this one the
Reminder," he said, adjusting his kerchief with his other hand. I
looked quickly to see if that one also had keys for nails, but from what
I could see, they appeared trimmed short in the normal manner.

"Once I shoved this darling all the way up a man's nostril and
tickled his brain. He didn't laugh, but I did. From then on, he
bothered me no more. Last I heard he was refusing all sustenance,
wasting away to a skeleton, counting the stars." Wolfe pulled his
hand back in a flash and licked the tip of the Reminder. "I think
I can still taste the memory of his first kiss," he said, and broke into
a bellowing laugh.

"Get ahold of yourself, Wolfe," said Shenz.

"Beg your pardon, sir," Wolfe said, and slumped back in his seat
like a reprimanded child.

After leaving the carriage, with crowbars and lanterns, and
walking two more blocks south to Fulton, we finally came to the
warehouse with the white circle on it. As Borne had predicted,
the sign was faded but still fairly legible. The building was made
of brick, one tall story with two grimy windows in the front. On
the hasp of the huge oaken door was a very rusty padlock.

Wolfe had barely seemed to touch the ancient device before he
was holding it in his hand. "Sometimes these old ones take a little longer," he said, pushing open the door. The hinges wailed like
banshees, and we waited and watched up and down the block for
a good five minutes before entering. They complained miserably
again as I shut us into the dark expanse. Shenz lit a match and ignited the two lanterns. He adjusted their wicks to lessen the glow
and then handed one to me. With that odd light shining up to il-
luminate his face, my colleague appeared truly satanic. We could
not see very far into the shadows even with the lanterns, but I
squinted and began to make out that we were surrounded by rows
of shelves constructed of iron scaffolding and planks.

"Let's see what we can find," said Shenz.

With great trepidation, I set off down an aisle. Wolfe followed closely, and I wasn't sure which was more daunting, the dark or having him behind me carrying a crowbar. I stopped at one of the many crates and whispered, "Give this one a go." He wedged the end of the bar into the frame of the crate and gave one quick shove. The box cracked open, and a large object, obviously made of glass, fell to the cement floor and shattered.

Wolfe and I exchanged looks, mine I'm sure exhibiting more concern than his. I squatted down in order to bring the glow of the lantern around the fallen object. As I descended, a putrid stench rose from the scattered contents, which only then could I see had been partially liquid. Soon enough the culprit came clearly into view.

I fled that aisle, knowing it was the repository of Borne's legacy, and began searching down another. All the time I could hear Shenz breaking into and rifling through distant boxes.

"What are you looking for?" asked Wolfe as I motioned for him to attack another crate.

"I'm not sure," I said.

"Amateurs," said Wolfe, handing the crowbar over to me. He turned and wandered off into the dark.

I opened three more crates on my own, each one containing thousands of the same little slips of paper. Written on them was either the word *yes* or the word *no*. I could only wonder at what banal manifestation of paranormal science I was gazing and marvel at the dizzying depths of foolishness that had directed the course of Ossiak's incredible fortune. The entire journey to the warehouse was quickly beginning to seem pointless to me when Shenz called me to him in an excited voice, more a hiss than a whisper.

I navigated the dark maze of shelves, holding my lantern out before me until I saw the corresponding glow from my friend's.

"Here we are," he said as I approached him. He held his lantern up next to a crate that had the name Londell written across its planks in grease pencil. There were two other such crates to the left of this one.

"Shall I?" I said to Shenz.

"Get on with it," he said.

I placed the crowbar and pushed forward with all my might. Two of the planks squeaked violently and then popped free onto the floor. A surge of white crystals spilled through the opening, glittering in the lantern light and forming a small dune at our feet. I knelt down and grabbed some of the odd snow in my hand. It was completely dry.

"These are the prepared specimens from the father's research," I told Shenz, lifting a fistful and securing it in my coat pocket.

"Like fairy dust," he said. "The old crank was certainly busy."

I rose and pried off the other planks of the crate to gain fuller access. After handing Shenz the crowbar, I reached one arm in and swept more of the fossilized crystals onto the floor. Eventually I felt solid objects protruding through the white. The first thing I pulled out was a book. Shenz set down the crowbar and took the volume from me. He brushed it clean against his coat in order to read the title.

"Fabulous Tales from Around the World," he said, and turned it for me to have a look. There was an illustration embossed on the cover—a scene of a djinn, cohering, headfirst, out of a stream of smoke issuing from a lamp shaped like a boat.

I said nothing but stared in disbelief long enough for Shenz to prompt me to continue. The next item I uncovered was a stack of paper tied up in string. Once out in the light, though, the sheets that made up this small package showed themselves to be green and cut in the shapes of leaves. Each one had a question written on it. "Will Clementine go before the rain?" "Is it right?" "Billy?"

"Where are the damn answers? That's what I'm looking for," said Shenz.

I reached back into the crate to see if I could find something less obscure, and my hand closed around the crown of a circular, broad-brimmed hat.

"I'm underwhelmed," said Shenz at the sight of it, not knowing the story as I did.

"What of this, though?" I said, hauling forth a heavy fur coat that smelled like a horse stall.

"I'll take that," said Wolfe, who suddenly appeared from out of the darkness behind me.

I handed him the coat, and he took his off and put the new one on.

"Like a glove," he said, modeling it for Shenz.

He then brushed past me and lifted the hat where I had let it fall. Removing his kerchief, he placed the broad-brimmed lid upon his head. "Gentlemen," he said, "this is the most pathetic heist I can ever remember participating in. Jars of shit, a children's book, and crates of dandruff. I'm very disappointed."

"That makes three of us," said Shenz.

We opened the other two crates with the name Londell written across them. The second held only snow. Inside the last, at the bottom, beneath all manner of strange optical equipment, I found an old daguerreotype. In faded shades of brown, it showed a picture of Mrs. Charbuque's screen facing an audience of men in suits, some smoking, some drinking.

"Her screen," I said to Shenz, and pointed at the picture.

"Who is she?" asked Wolfe. "The Dog Girl?"

"What are you getting at, Wolfe?" I asked rather defensively.

"Look here," he said, and used the Reminder as a pointer. "What do you make of that?"

Shenz and I both squinted to see what he meant. Then I saw it. At the extreme right side of the screen, at midlevel, the hand of someone hiding behind it was clutching its frame as if to reposition that panel. Something of the forearm was also visible, but no part of that appendage appeared to belong to a human being. The hand was like a paw, and it and the rest of the arm that could be seen were covered with thick dark hair.

"That's not an ape?" asked Wolfe.

"It's the Sibyl," I said.

For at least an hour we searched for more crates marked Londell but were successful only in discovering another vein of Borne's specimens in the dark cavern. Shenz was crestfallen that the outing had not been more fruitful, and told me so as Wolfe restored the padlock to the oaken door.

"Nonsense," I said. "I found it completely worthwhile. Everything we found has corroborated Mrs. Charbuque's stories."

"That arm, though," he said, pointing to the picture whose border jutted from within the pages of the book of tales I now held in my hand.

I was not prepared to think about that hirsute development at the moment and simply nodded as a sign that I too found it puzzling.

"Morning approaches, men. Let us depart," said Wolfe, and we moved swiftly off toward where the cab had left us earlier.

On the ride uptown, Wolfe told us that he was on his way to spend time with the wife of a fellow who left for work every morning at five o'clock sharp. "As usual," he said, "there will be no sign of forced entry." Considering the fact that he now wore the tracker's coat and hat, I should have warned him about how illicit amorous affairs could end in fairy-tale tragedy, but I had no idea where to begin to explain. I was sunk so deep in the morass of Mrs. Charbuque's effluvia, I could hardly make sense of it all myself.

The thief was the first to be let off, the cab pulling up in front of an address in the West Village. Before Wolfe left the compartment, Shenz paid him. Wolfe then shook both our hands and said, "The two of you are distinct failures as criminals but good fellows nonetheless. I wish you all the turds and snowflakes you require. Good day."

A VISITOR

"THROWBACK" WAS the word that Shenz left me with as the cab, he now its sole passenger, departed for the West Side. An image of a large organ grinder's monkey in a white lace gown slouched through my thoughts, methodically tearing down every scrim of scenery previously conjured by the words of Mrs. Charbuque. I balanced our photographic discovery atop the already tenuous house of cards that was the whole mad affair, and could tell without letting go that the structure would not bear this new freight. My frustration was intense. Could Isaac Newton have discovered gravity with an orangutan swinging through his calculations? Could Shakespeare have written the sonnets beset by an expectation that at any moment a chimp might barge through his window, spill the inkpot, attack his wife's shin, and make off with his best pipe?

Weary to the point of collapse from our midnight caper, I was snared in that odd condition of being too exhausted for sleep. Sitting on the divan in my parlor, I thumbed through the volume of Luciere Londell's fairy tales until I came to where I had stowed the cursed daguerreotype. There was the glimpse of that anomalous arm in sepia tones, gradations of sienna and umber and off-white. Wolfe was right, it was unmistakably hairy. "The painter undone by the camera, how fitting," I said aloud. I shook my head and tossed the picture onto the floor. There was always the slim possibility that what presented itself was merely a devious play of shadows, and I leaned upon that insubstantial prospect with the full weight of my desire.

The book was another story—a lovely edition, published in London in 1860 by Millson & Fahn and illustrated by Charles Altamont Doyle. There were a baker's dozen of stories in the table of contents, some of which I recognized and some I'd never heard of. In keeping with the weird train of coincidence my involvement with Mrs. Charbuque had set in motion, I came across an illustration of a wolf in a snowbound forest. The ferocious beast was tracking a sweet young girl who carried a picnic basket. A few pages later on I discovered a story entitled "The Monkey Queen." Its attendant illustration showed the tale's subject decked out in a yellow dress and tiara, sitting on a throne, while beneath her were gathered her human subjects. It was my belief that if I were to continue looking, I would find among those pages a piece called "The Foolish Painter," and its corresponding picture would be a portrait of myself. I set about looking for it, but somewhere between the middle of the book and the end, I finally fell asleep.

Upon waking what seemed like only minutes later, I groaned, for staring at me through the parlor window was twilight and the fact that I had missed my meeting with Mrs. Charbuque. Cursing roundly, I tried to lift myself off the divan but found that my body had seized in the odd position in which I had sat throughout the day. My neck was especially stiff, and it was all I could do to work through the pain to straighten it. I sat dazed, staring around the room and then up at the clock on the mantel. It was five-thirty, which reminded me that I had promised Samantha I would drop by Palmer's to catch a rehearsal of her new show. The fat ghost had rapidly sifted through the floorboards, borne down by the newspapers' less than flattering reviews, and now the troupe was about to launch a production of something called *The Brief Engagement*, in which Samantha had a role as an heiress to a huge fortune.

I hoisted myself up off the divan and tottered away into the bedroom to wash and change my clothes. Images of the previous night's warehouse break-in darted through my memory as I repeatedly admonished myself for having missed an opportunity to sit before the screen. While shaving, though, I managed to put things in perspective by telling myself that I needed a respite from the recent events. Things were teetering on the brink of insanity, and it was imperative I take a step back. As I wiped the remaining lather from my face, I made a promise to myself in the mirror not to attempt any further illegal activities in the name of discovering my patron's visage.

Feeling somewhat refreshed, I dressed and put on my coat and hat. As I passed through the parlor to the front door, I chanced to look down at the floor and noticed that the daguerreotype was gone. I quickly searched my thoughts and distinctly remembered it gliding down to land in the middle of the room upon the braided rug. I checked the divan and saw the book of tales lying atop the cushion where it had fallen out of my grasp during sleep. My first thought was that the old photograph had somehow been pushed under the couch when I had gotten up a little while earlier. I bent down and looked into the partial shadows beneath that seat and then under all the other furniture. My efforts netted me an old number 10 sable brush and a nickel, but no picture.

A chill ran through me as I stood in the middle of the room. Was it possible that someone had entered my house while I slept and taken it? I strode to the door and checked the lock. I always secured the door upon arriving home, yet now I found it not so, offering free admittance to anyone with the nerve to simply turn the knob. Had I been that tired? Attempting to consider what might have happened, I pictured myself sleeping on the divan and watched with my mind's eye as one by one different suspects entered and lifted the daguerreotype. The first thief I fabricated was Watkin, poking his bald head in and wrinkling his nose to sniff if the coast was clear. Following him came the queen of the monkeys, picking nits from her scalp and treading on the train of her yellow dress. After these two culprits came a smudge of a figure, a faceless, sexless, amorphous being. Instead of corporeal fingers lifting the picture, a slight gust of wind rose and carried it out the door along with the shadowy phantom.

I was both weak with fear and overwrought with indignation, for I, Piambo, had been robbed. In the next moment, though, I considered the fact that I had come upon the picture by unlawful means myself. My hypocrisy struck me as somewhat amusing, even in the face of the unsettling mystery. In my own home I was now subject to the prying gaze of Mrs. Charbuque. Who was studying whom? In this game of ring-around-a-rosy we were playing, I pursued her as she pursued me as I pursued her . . . It was precisely that phenomenon of the mirrors at the local barber shop, where the one on the back wall reflected the one on the front wall, and I, sitting in the middle, could see myself reflected ad infinitum as Horace the barber snipped away at the edges of my life. Mind-boggling, to say the least, but somehow I knew in my gut that we had been observed entering Ossiak's warehouse.

Miraculously, I arrived at the theater on time. Samantha was rushing about, preparing to begin the rehearsal, but she stopped to kiss me. The director, who was an old friend of hers and quite a devotee of her thespian abilities, asked me if I would mind watching from one of the special boxes that jutted out above either side of the stage, to see if the movement and placement of the players was "balanced."

"I'll do my best," I told him. He ushered me off the stage and to a door opening on a stairway leading up. My ascent was blind, for the house lights, save those illuminating the action of the drama up front, were dark. On arrival at the landing, I groped my way forward, pushing aside a velvet curtain to enter a small box holding four seats. Creeping slowly to the brass rail, ever nervous of great heights, I peered over the edge. I could see through the wide expanse of shadow beneath that I was the sole audience member. The view of the stage was remarkable, and I now knew why these seats were so expensive. I sat down and waited for the play to begin.

It was a great pleasure of mine to witness these rehearsals before actually seeing the show. For some, I imagine, it would ruin the experience of the drama, but I found the creative process as enchanting as its ultimate product. M. Sabott had taught me how to read a painting, to see beneath the illusion of form and notice the brush strokes, the various pigments, and how they had been applied. Each picture then became a manual on how to achieve a certain effect, how to employ a particular technique. At times I could see so deeply into the confluence of color, texture, and canvas that I caught a glimpse of the artist staring back. It struck me at the moment the actors took the stage that this method of dismantling and reconstructing was what I needed to perform on the emerging drama that was my present commission.

A man in a straw boater and seersucker suit strolled across the stage, and when he opened his mouth to speak the first lines of the play, I felt a hand run through my hair. I jumped slightly in my seat but as quickly realized it must be Samantha, having come up to sit with me until her first scene. Then the fingers fiercely wrenched my hair to the point of pain, and at the same moment I saw her on the stage beneath me. Before I could open my mouth to cry out, I felt a cold sharp blade at my neck, either a knife or a straight razor, and heard a deep male voice whisper, "Quietly now, or I will have to cut your head off."

I was stunned into utter submission.

"Do you know me?" asked the voice.

My lips quivered, my throat was dry, but I managed to say, "Watkin?"

"Nonsense," said my assailant.

"Mr. Wolfe," I said.

"You'll wish it was Mr. Wolfe."

"Charbuque?" I whispered.

"What are your intentions?" he asked.

My mind was spinning, and sweat was already running down my face. "What do you mean?" I said.

His grip tightened, pulling my head farther back, though not far enough for me to see my attacker. "Why are you seeing my wife?"

"She has commissioned me to paint her portrait," I said.

I heard a quiet rasping sound come from his mouth, which was at most an inch from my ear. At first I thought he was choking, but then realized the horrible noise was laughter. "You're lost," he said.

"Yes."

"I'll be watching you," he said.

I said nothing.

"For now, I can't kill you, but the game may soon change," he said, and released me.

I spun around to try to catch sight of him but saw only the velvet curtains swaying as they closed, and heard his soft footfalls as he raced down the stairs. My hands were shaking terribly as I reached up to rub my throat where the blade had touched me.

"Mr. Piambo," someone called from the stage below.

I turned back and looked down. The characters were frozen in various positions. "Please, Mr. Piambo, we need silence," said the director, smiling up at me.

"My apologies," I stuttered, trying to use my fingers as a comb.

The play then resumed, and the plot thickened, but I spent the rest of the evening looking furtively over my shoulder.

THE MONKEY QUEEN

"I MISSED YOU yesterday, Piambo," she said as I sat in the chair.

"Please forgive me," I told her. "I was extremely tired."

"It is your prerogative," she said. "You shouldn't stay out so late, though, especially in this season. You'll catch your death."

"Sound advice," I said, although I wanted to say much more.

"I know you want to know all about my time as the Sibyl, so I have been trying to recall for you as much of the origins of it as I can. I have a great deal to tell you."

I remained silent for a long time.

"Hello, Piambo?" she said.

"Yes, Mrs. Charbuque, I'm here. Before you continue with your life, *I* have a question for *you*," I said.

"Very well."

"This is a little odd. Hypothetical, so to speak. But if you could be any animal in the world, what would you be?" I asked.

Now it was her turn to be silent. Finally she said, "I've never thought of that. A wonderful question, to be sure. Like a game . . ."

"Any animal," I repeated.

"I suppose this is somewhat of a cliché, but probably a bird. Specifically, *not* a bird in a cage. I believe I would enjoy a bird's freedom of flight. Perhaps a tern, living by the ocean."

"What about a dog?" I asked.

"Are you trying to insult me?" she said, and laughed.

"No, certainly not," I said, laughing along with her.

"Too pedestrian. Too slavish," she said.

I paused for a moment and then asked, "A monkey?"

"Good heavens, Piambo, I think you are teasing me."

"I'm serious," I said. "What about a monkey?"

"Well, Mr. Darwin thinks I already am one," she said.

"I suppose, according to him, we all are."

"Some more than others."

"What do you mean by that?" I asked.

"What do you think I mean?" said Mrs. Charbuque.

"Some, perhaps, have more primitive attributes. A jutting jaw, a low brow, more . . . hair."

"Actually, I was speaking metaphorically," she said. "There are those who seem merely to mimic others, those who are more foolish, getting into mischief all the time."

"And your husband?" I asked, trying to catch her off guard.

Without missing a beat, she said, "Certainly not a monkey. A jackal, maybe. A hooded cobra, certainly. That is, if he were still alive."

"You are telling me he is deceased?"

"Some years ago. Of his bones are coral made," she said.

"A shipwreck?" I asked.

"You are astute, Piambo."

"Can you tell me more?" I asked.

"For you to understand the complexity of our relationship, I must go back to the Sibyl. Nothing in my later life will make sense without your knowledge of it."

"The Sibyl it is, Mrs. Charbuque. As you wish," I said, with the understanding that I was the most pathetic of strategists. I sat back, holding the charcoal pencil at the ready, determined to capture an image on paper that day. There was the sound of movement behind the screen—the scraping of her chair against the floor as she repositioned it, the rippling of her dress like a distant flag blowing in a breeze. Then I heard something make contact with the cherrywood frame at the right side of the screen. I looked quickly to catch a glimpse, for she was pulling it toward her an inch or two, as if what she was about to say made her feel more vulnerable than before.

The hand that gripped the wooden border, I tell you, was not human. I saw it from the lower quarter of the forearm to the tips of the fingers, and the sight of that thick black hair covering every inch to the second knuckle would have had Mr. Darwin reconfiguring his theory in a mad sweat. As for me, I simply gaped, wide-eyed, at that monkey paw with its dark cuticles and rough digits performing this human task. My glimpse of it lasted no more than a second or two, but it brought immediately to my mind the image of the Monkey Queen.

I might have sat there stunned all day, but another wonder followed hard upon the heels of the first—a half-dozen large green leaves flew over the top of the screen and fluttered down to land at my feet. To have had nothing but a voice for all those days and now to have something so substantial threw me into a state of confusion. I leaned over and lifted one of the leaves and found they were made of green paper. As she began to speak, I realized that they were the same as those we had discovered at the warehouse tied in a bundle in the crate of dry snow marked Londell.

"With my mother no longer casting her doubting glances, frowning those grimaces of disdain, there was no impediment for my father and me. We rushed headlong into belief. The Twins were our new religion. Firmly convinced that they conferred the power of second sight upon me, we looked everywhere for proof of prophecy and found it. The most insignificant happenstance was fraught with multiple layers of meaning, and all the connections formed a spider's web of paranoia we were ecstatic to be snared in. I know how ridiculous this all must sound, but when you are a child, and the one adult you are in close contact with, a parent you love, tells you again and again that every dream you have, every imagining, every word you pronounce is a valuable prophecy, this then becomes your truth.

"I'm not sure how it works, but I swear to you that there is something about this process of thought that once embarked upon propagates happy accident, quirky twists of fate, and eventually leaves one believing that she is at the very center of creation. Perhaps the truth was that my father and I were searching so diligently for these coincidences that in actuality we were willfully projecting them at every turn. Be that as it may, I became a magnet for felicitous circumstance."

"You need not convince me, Mrs. Charbuque," I interjected. "I am a recent student of the phenomenon."

"Every morning he would ask me what my dreams of the night had been. On one occasion I told him, 'I dreamed of a horse swimming in the ocean,' and I had. The day went on as usual, and then after lunch, he called me into his study to join him at the window. 'Look there, Lu,' he said, and pointed toward the sky. I looked but saw nothing. 'At what?' I asked. 'Look, girl,' he said. I looked harder, expecting to see a hawk or a buzzard, but there was nothing. 'I'm sorry, Father. What am I looking at?' 'Dear God, girl, do you not see that large cloud? It is in the perfect shape of a horse. Don't you see its streaming mane, its galloping hooves, the blasts of steam coming from its nostrils?' 'I see a ship,' I said. 'No, no, please look more closely.' Then I stared hard for a full five minutes, and all of a sudden the airy white frigate revealed itself to be a running horse. I clapped my hands. 'I see it, I see it,' I said. He put his hand on my shoulder and leaned down to kiss me. 'Your dream, you see,' said my father. 'A horse swims in the vast blue ocean.'

"At other times, he would stop what he was doing and turn to me and say, 'Get a piece of paper and a pencil and jot down a number between one and a hundred.' Of course, I did as I was told. In the evening, while we read in the sitting room, he would say, 'I will now think of a number,' and close his eyes. Sometimes he would lift his reading glasses and pinch the bridge of his nose. 'Very well, I have it,' he would say. This was my signal to go and fetch the piece of paper with the number I had scrawled earlier. 'Go ahead, read it to me,' he would say. I would read, say, the number thirty-five. 'Incredible,' he would exclaim, and then shake his head in wonder.

"In the final weeks before spring of the year my mother was taken by the wolf, my father devised the stage act that would eventually become my life and subsequently my cage. Even in my youthful excitement owing to all the attention he was lavishing upon me, I was overwhelmed by the fact that this previously unassuming man, a scientist who had been content to quietly study snowflakes his entire life, should exhibit such an intuitive facility for, not to mention interest in, the art of showmanship. Maybe he had his own premonition about how important the act would be to my survival and knew that before too long he would no longer be able to help me.

"His plan was that the audience members would ask questions of me, and I would then concentrate upon the Twins and offer up whatever images I was shown through their voices. 'Tell them nothing but what you actually see,' he said, for when he introduced me, he would let them know that I would merely give clues to the future and it was the individual's job to understand the message or to keep a watchful eye open for its realization in the near future."

"In other words," I said, "there was no chance of your being *wrong*. The onus for the prophecy would be on the inquirer."

"Precisely," she said. "And that was the beauty of it. They loved it because they were given the opportunity to participate in the prophecy. No matter what question was asked and what images I divulged, there was always a way to reconcile the two, given time and a modicum of imagination.

"When we finally returned to the city, it was my father's plan that we should test out my act at one of Ossiak's dinner parties. What was missing, though, in his estimation, was a certain air of mystery. After again taking up our summer residence on Fourth Avenue, we had a few days before the night of the gala. One afternoon after Ossiak had sent over my father's yearly salary, we were out shopping for a dress for me, and we walked into a store that sold all manner of exotic objects from around the world. There were ostrich eggs, African masks, Eskimo harpoons. It was in that shop that he found this screen imported from Japan. No sooner did he see it and its design of falling leaves than he conceived the idea of the Sibyl. Are you familiar with this character of ancient lore, Piambo?"

"Only by name," I said.

"There were a number of sibyls in ancient Greece and Rome. A sibyl was a woman who foretold the future. The most famous was the Cumaean Sibyl, who lived in a cave, unseen by the populace. If someone desired to know the future, he would go to the mouth of the cave and speak his question. The sibyl would then write her answer on leaves and place them at the mouth of the cave. In our version of the legend, we reversed the procedure. The participants wrote their questions on paper leaves, and I answered from my hiding place."

"Interesting," I said. "So the screen has a meaning."

"Everything has a meaning, Piambo," she said. "That day in the shop, we also bought another object of mystery to use in the act, something from Zanzibar."

"What was that?" I asked.

She did not answer, but I heard her chair move again behind the screen. Brusquely enough to make me jump, the monkey hand appeared at the top of the middle frame, its fingers curling around the cherrywood. I pushed my own chair back at the sight of it.

The ugly paw did not rest there long but continued to rise up all the way to the elbow. Then abruptly, it fell forward over the screen and landed on the floor in front of me. I jumped out of my chair and gave a short scream. I blinked four times, my heart racing, before I realized that the appendage was the work of a taxidermist. At the shoulder end was a wooden pole with which to hold it.

Mrs. Charbuque was in a fit of hysterics. She laughed so hard she choked slightly and gasped for air. "What about a monkey?" I heard her barely get out before exploding into another paroxysm of mirth.

I stood frozen for the longest time, trying to comprehend this woman. Then I stamped my foot angrily like a spoiled child. Folding over my sketchbook, I prepared to leave, but when I put my pencil in my coat pocket, I felt there the dry snow from the warehouse. I grabbed a mere pinch between my thumb and first two fingers, walked up to the screen, and threw it high over the top so that it would shower slowly down upon her. This done, I turned away. Just as I was closing the door behind me, Mrs. Charbuque suddenly went silent. When I was halfway down the hall, she screamed my name, and I smiled.

HAPPY ACCIDENT

I TELL YOU, I think she is mad," I said to Shenz. We sat at a streetside table in a café on the corner of Park Avenue and Sixty-fourth Street. The sun was beginning its late-afternoon descent, and although there was little wind, the air was quite cold. The waiter had looked at us oddly when we said we would like to be served out-of-doors, but we needed privacy from the other customers who crowded the place.

"Piambo, you are a regular Auguste Dupin. Insane, you say? Heavens, how did you chance upon such a remarkable notion?" he asked.

"Everyone is abusing me today," I said, lifting my coffee cup.

"We have a woman who hides behind a screen and asks to have her portrait painted—a woman, no less, who is in possession of a mummified monkey arm. I don't think it takes an assiduous application of ratiocination to determine that her reason has gone fishing."

"True enough," I said.

"But," said Shenz, closing his eyes as if to concentrate, "this sibyl thing is interesting in more ways than one."

"How do you mean?" I asked.

"The Cumaean Sibyl lived a very long time. It seems that when she was young, she made herself very attractive to the sun god, Apollo. Overwhelmed by her beauty, he offered her anything in exchange for spending a single night with him. Her plan all along had been to gain a kind of immortality, so her wish was to have as many years as the grains of sand she could hold in her hand. The sun god acquiesced, but once the sibyl had her prize, she spurned his advances. In turn Apollo, not to be trifled with by a mortal, did not grant her as many years of youth, so as the years swept by she aged and shriveled but remained alive."

"There's an inconvenience," I said.

"Quite," said Shenz. "She withered to nothing but a small lump of dried-out flesh, but the pulse of life still beat within her. Her remaining form was placed in a hollow gourd and hung from the branch of a tree. Children would come to her tree and ask her what she wished, and she would whisper that she wished only to die. In one story, she petitions Charon, the oarsman who rows the recently deceased across the river Styx from the shores of life to the land of the dead. Charon, though, could not take those who were either still alive or not properly buried. These poor souls remained on the banks of the river forever, flitting aimlessly about, unable to pass to the underworld. At this point in the story there is a part I forget, but as it turns out, the only time a person who is not truly dead or not properly buried can cross the flood to the underworld is when he is granted a golden bough by the sibyl. Charon honors this bough like a ticket on the el and takes them over."

"Shenz, I don't know who traffics in more of it, you or Borne. What does this have to do with anything?" I asked.

He laughed. "It has to do with *you*. You have gone to Mrs. Charbuque for the golden bough so that you can make the passage to a new land."

"I was thinking more along the lines of cash," I said. "Let's not rush the Styx crossing."

"In mythology, Death is not always death. Very often it is symbolic of a great change. You seek freedom from this life of portraiture you are now trapped in."

"At times you amaze me," I said with true admiration.

Shenz waved off my compliment and said, "I checked the papers, and there was no news of our break-in. It seems we have pulled off the perfect crime."

"Yes," I said, "but there is a new wrinkle." I proceeded to apprise him of the involvement of Charbuque, his message to me and my fearful meeting with him at Palmer's the previous night.

Shenz sat forward, a look of excitement in his eyes. "We must find out who he is, where he is. He could very well be the key to discovering what his wife looks like."

"No doubt," I told him, "but I'm afraid that will be impossible."

"Impossible, but why?" asked my friend.

"Mrs. Charbuque told me only this afternoon that he is dead. A shipwreck, I believe."

"A razor-wielding spirit?" said Shenz. "Interesting. Listen, find out what ship it was that he was on. I'll look into it."

I nodded. "If he doesn't kill me first."

"You might want to start carrying a weapon," he said. "This is getting dangerous. A pistol wouldn't be a bad idea."

"No, Shenz, a pistol would be a very bad idea," I said. "Thank you, but I'll keep my toes."

"Where are you with the painting?" he asked.

"Absolutely nowhere."

"You are in your second week. You've a mere two and a half weeks left," he said. "I'd better arrange a visit to the Man from the Equator."

"What will he do for me?" I asked.

"Focus your vision, perhaps."

"Perhaps," I said, and finished my coffee.

"You said you are meeting Samantha?" asked Shenz.

"She has been spying on Mrs. Charbuque's house for me today,"

I told him. "I'm to meet her at five on the steps of Saint James Church up at Madison and Seventy-first."

"There's a woman ready for canonization," said Shenz.

"By the way, how are the Hatstells?" I asked, circumventing one of my colleague's lectures on why I should marry Samantha.

"Walking, breathing endorsements for the childless life. I'll be finished with them in another week or so. I've probably spent my entire commission already on cakes and candy. The little one calls me Uncle Satan, the older one, Grandfather Time. My opium consumption has doubled."

We each had another cup of coffee, and before we parted I reminded Shenz of the yearly show Sills had mentioned at the Academy of Design the following evening. We agreed to meet there.

Night had fallen by the time I reached the steps of Saint James Episcopal Church. The sidewalks had emptied somewhat, since it was the dinner hour, and the traffic in the streets had thinned. A wind had come up since I had left the café, and with it the temperature had dropped yet a few more degrees.

The church itself seemed deserted, and I sat down on the bottom marble step and lit a cigarette. One of my favorite pastimes when roaming the city at night was to stare at the lighted windows lining the streets and wonder what dramas, comedies or tragedies, were playing just beyond those bright rectangles. At times, given the architecture of a certain building, its neighborhood, a hint of something within visible from the street, I could even imagine the characters and their lives. My God, I could see their faces and what they were wearing. Here a nude, there a man in shirtsleeves bouncing a child on his knee, a fellow drinking his pail of beer, a gray-haired grandmother in a rocking chair saying her rosary. If these people, completely unknown to me, could show me their faces and forms, if I could readily see the nuanced figures of the characters I merely read about in novels, then why did Mrs. Charbuque remain such a tantalizing blank?

I was interrupted in my reverie by the approach of a woman.

She was of the same height and figure as Samantha, and I was about to rise and greet her, but at the last moment I saw a lock of blond hair showing from beneath her hat. She nodded to me and said, "Good evening," and I touched my fingers to my hat brim. "Hello," I said, and she passed down the street. As her figure disappeared into the dark, I thought to myself that it could very well have been Mrs. Charbuque spying on me, and concentrated on remembering her face.

A few gentlemen passed by and another woman, too short. Then I saw a familiar figure approaching from the north. I had only to think for a second before realizing how I knew this person. A big, burly woman in a large dark overcoat, she wore a kerchief tied around her head, and as she drew closer, I made out the thick crude features of her face. When she drew even with me where I sat on the step, I said, "Wolfe, is that you?"

"Piambo," she said, "who is Wolfe?"

I stood then and peered more closely. Finally the voice registered at the precise moment I realized her face was devoid of Wolfe's facial hair. "Samantha?" I said.

"How do you like my look?" she said. "Duenna of the night."

I was giddy with what Mrs. Charbuque had earlier that day called *happy accident*. Leaning forward, I kissed the wrinkled face and came away with greasepaint on my lips.

AN APOLOGY

IN THE hansom cab on the ride downtown to my house, Samantha used the kerchief to wipe the makeup from her face. Seeing this paint removed gave me a great appreciation of the artistic flair with which it was applied, for mere strokes of the darker shades gave convincing indications of thickness and weight to the flesh, prominence to the bone structure, and a frightening depth to the eyes. One minute she could have been Wolfe's sister, and the next she was her own beautiful self, her eyes sparkling with a kind of childish joy at the theatrics of having played a spy.

She then removed the overcoat to reveal a set of small couch pillows secured with twine, one to each shoulder. Around her middle, fastened with a belt, was a larger bed pillow. Once she was free of all her prosthetics, and the ugly old woman lay in a heap on the seat beside her, she reached back, gathered her hair together, and flipped it into a simple knot.

"A command performance," I said, and we laughed.

"That was fun, but I wouldn't want to be that poor woman every day. The coat and pillows kept me warm, but round about four o'clock I really started to feel the extra weight. I'm exhausted, and my feet are killing me," she said.

"When did you get there?" I asked.

"A little after noon," she said. "I saw you arrive and leave the house. You didn't stay long."

"Mrs. Charbuque and I had a bit of a falling-out. I'll tell you about it later, but first, did you see anything?"

"As far as I witnessed, no one came or went until you arrived. I slowly made my way up and down the block, trying not to seem too conspicuous. Occasionally I sat down on the steps across the street. Aimless Old Wretch was the character I portrayed."

"And after I departed?" I asked.

"You passed directly by me on your way down the street and appeared to be having a heated argument with yourself under your breath," she said. "But a half hour after that, a bald fellow with a walking stick left the house, and I followed him."

"Did you see that he was blind? He's remarkable, wouldn't you say? Mr. Watkin is his name."

"Piambo," she said, and started laughing. It was that same type of mocking jollity I had heard from Mrs. Charbuque earlier.

"I am hilarious today," I said, somewhat piqued.

"Forgive me. I hate to disillusion you, but if your Mr. Watkin is blind, I'm Evelyn Nesbit."

"What are you saying?" I asked.

"Please, Piambo, that old fellow is the worst actor I've ever seen. By comparison he makes Derim Lourde seem worthy of playing Hamlet."

"But did you see his eyes? Deathly white, devoid of any color whatsoever."

"Yes, yes, a stage trick. Thin lenses made of glass, cast in a milky white with pinprick holes in them to allow the actor a limited range of vision. I first saw them used five years ago in a production of *The Golem*. They are a favorite of directors of plays whose theme is supernatural. Fitted up under the lid, they are uncomfortable but effective in giving that otherworldly look."

I was about to speak but found I had nothing to say.

"The man's conception of being blind is merely barging here and there giving things a slight tap with his cane. Did you think he had memorized the entire city and accounted for where each pedestrian would be at any given moment, not to mention autos and streetcars and horses when crossing from one side to the other? Occasionally he will remember he is supposed to be blind and cock his head suddenly this way or that as if attempting to listen to the dark world around him. A pathetic, melodramatic performance, for sure."

"My God," I said. "I was so convinced. It was those eyes. I'm paralyzed when something is amiss with the eyes."

"Don't feel bad," said Samantha. "Everyone on the street believed his performance as well, giving him a wide berth."

"Where did he go?" I asked.

"I passed close enough to touch him and then turned and followed him at a distance. He went into a small corner market and bought a rather expensive little container of nutmeg. Then he went down the street to a florist. Here is where I made my own mistake, though. I'm sure he noticed me when he left the market, and when I followed him to the florist, he turned, and I saw him look directly out at me through the window. I got nervous then and scurried back to Mrs. Charbuque's. It had been in my mind all along that he might have been a decoy and that perhaps she would slip out while I was following him. I stayed in the vicinity of the house until a little before five, but he did not return."

"You're a wonder," I said. "I can't thank you enough. But no more of this. I have a feeling Watkin can be dangerous, and I now suspect, with what you have discovered, that it was him at the theater last night. Why, though, I have no idea."

When we arrived at my house, I had Samantha stand on the steps while I searched for a possible intruder. The darkness I passed through on the way to the light switch in the parlor was ominous, and then what a relief to be able to see. The modern age had its advantages, to be sure. I slid along the wall on the way to the bedroom and then leaped around the corner to surprise any would-be assailant. The room was empty, as was the closet.

By the time I reached the huge shadowed expanse of the studio, my heart was pounding. Nothing is worse than feeling like prey in your own home. I switched on the light and gasped slightly. There was no stranger there to confront me, but there was something strange. Sitting on the table that held my painting equipment was an enormous vase of flowers. The sudden vivid colors were what drew a reaction from me. A large faux Chinese vase held an array of blossoms—red carnations, yellow roses, acanthus, ivy, and lavender. It was an odd assortment—either hastily chosen or fraught with meaning, I could not tell. Leaning against the container was a small violet-colored envelope. As I approached, I was swamped by the lovely aroma of the arrangement.

I lifted the envelope and held it tentatively for a moment, recalling the feel of the straight razor against my throat. Then I tore up the flap to find a card, whose front was blank. Opening it released a few flakes of dried snow, which fell slowly to the floor. On the inner fold was written:

Dearest Piambo,
Please forgive my foolish joke. I will be waiting for you tomorrow.

Love,
Luciere

Of course, my attention was drawn directly to the word "Love," for this seemed to me to be the most bizarre development of the entire ridiculous pageant that had been my dealings with Mrs. Charbuque. I sensed a genuine contrition and deep emotion from the few words that made up the message, and was contemplating this in relation to everything else when I heard something behind me. I spun around to find Samantha standing there holding her coat and pillows and soiled kerchief. I don't know why, but I blushed as if she had caught me at something dishonest or illicit.

As I have said, it was difficult for me to hide anything from Samantha. She gave me a cynical smile and said, "A secret admirer?"

I wanted to slip the card into my pocket unnoticed, but it was too late for that. Instead I tried to convince her that my embarrassment was really befuddlement at this odd turn of affairs.

"A message of apology from Mrs. Charbuque," I said, and threw the open card on the table. "First she abuses me, and then she sends me flowers. Does she take me for a fool? I tell you, I'm beginning to despise this woman."

"No doubt," Samantha said, and then turned and left the room.

Later we made love, but through it all, I felt as if someone was watching me. I half expected Watkin to pop his head out from beneath the bed and critique my performance with the words "Strictly nutmeg and mold, Mr. Piambo." The entire session was perfunctory and somewhat unsatisfactory for both of us. We lay side by side afterward, and I told Samantha about the monkey arm. She did not share my now trumped-up outrage, reacting rather blankly to the whole story.

When she fell asleep, I crept out of bed and returned to the studio. There I reread the card several times and sat staring at the flowers while smoking a cigarette. I imagined the room with the high ceilings, the two windows, and the screen, darkened as it would be at that late hour, but this time I was behind the sacred boundary, looking at Mrs. Charbuque sitting naked, bathed in a slanting beam of moonlight. She turned and saw me and, in that soft lunar glow, held out her arms toward me. I clearly saw her face, and she was beautiful.

I blinked and looked back at the flowers, but when I concentrated again on the image in my imagination, it was the same. Now she was motioning for me to come to her. I got up and ran across the room to fetch charcoal and paper. Returning to my seat, I closed my eyes just as she stood to embrace me. Then the pencil touched the paper, and I drew without thinking.

NOTHING IS SAFE

WHEN I awoke the next morning Samantha was gone. I vaguely remembered her having told me that she had an audition at the Garden Theatre for a part that would follow her present one in *A Brief Engagement*. Neither of us was a particularly early riser, and we maintained an unspoken pact not to wake the other unless there was a verifiable need.

I closed my eyes, deciding to sleep for a little while longer. No sooner were my lids shut, though, than I remembered the reason for my late hours. I saw in my mind the sketch I had made while sitting before the vase of flowers on the paint table, and immediately rolled out of bed. As I got into my robe and slippers, I clearly remembered the drawing, and my excitement over it was rekindled. The promise of seeing it again sent me rushing through the house to the studio.

I had finally executed an actual picture of Mrs. Charbuque, and if I do say so myself, it was a wonderful job. Granted, it was still merely a sketch, but I had rendered enough detail in the face and form of the body so that the sight of it triggered in my mind again that clear vision of her standing naked in the moonlight behind the screen. Yes, even the specific features of the eyes and hair had revealed themselves clearly to me. This then would be my touchstone. One glance at it, and my subject would be standing before my mind's eye, willing to pose for as long as I required. I felt a warm glow emanate from my solar plexus, a certain giddiness invade my bloodstream, and I truly believed that I had captured precisely what she looked like. Mrs. Charbuque would have her painting, and I would succeed at the impossible.

Staring at the sketch, holding that vision of her in my mind, I also felt a trace of sexual longing for this woman I had created. "Could anything be more narcissistic?" I wondered, but I could not deny my feelings. To do so, I feared, would transport me back to the other side of the screen. At that moment, I looked around for the violet card from my patron. It lay on the table between the sketch and the vase of flowers. As I reached for it, I noticed that its envelope lay next to it and that now there was writing upon that as well.

Dear Piambo,
I will meet you this evening at the Academy of Design.

Love,
Samantha

She had copied Mrs. Charbuque's handwriting and the format of her note precisely. Obviously this was meant as a joke, but there are jokes and there are jokes. The placement of the envelope directly next to the card troubled me somewhat. I had been obsessing over the project of late, there was no doubt of that, but it was work and a monumental turning point in my career. More than likely it was evident to Samantha that my attention was always keenly focused on it, although in conversation during our private moments I might pretend otherwise. Surely she was not jealous, or was she? Samantha, in full daylight, could at times be more mysterious than Mrs. Charbuque in hiding. Perhaps she had meant to remind me of this very fact, placing her note next to the other to claim a kind of equality. I shook my head, not willing to be distracted from the task at hand. I instead turned my attention back to the sketch and the unique pleasure of strategizing how I would convert it into a full-fledged portrait.

I spent the remainder of the morning and early afternoon preparing a canvas and jotting down notes concerning color, placement of the figure, props if any, and so on, so that upon my return that evening I could begin. One decision I made that excited me was the determination to show Mrs. Charbuque as I had conceived of her—naked, a solitary figure adrift in a sea of deep shadow. She would be the light source of the painting.

I remembered Sabott telling me how the old Dutch masters had manufactured their own pigments because they knew that certain substances, ground to certain textures, would refract the light at specific angles. They were aware that configurations of these angles of refraction would focus light in precise areas of the composition and make it glow, seemingly of its own accord. I wished I had paid more attention to Sabott's lectures on pigment and light. When I was younger, I thought using anything other than readymade paint was hopelessly primitive, the drudgery of mortar and pestle nothing more than a pointless inhibitor of my artistic muse. That was before I came to realize that a good sable brush was worth ten yards of emotive genius and that painting was a two-headed beast—part craft and part inspiration. What I would have given to have listened more closely, for it was the magical effect of light I now hoped to achieve.

At one o'clock I made my preparations for the journey uptown. Formal attire was necessary, as I would go directly to the opening at the academy from the day's meeting. I was full of energy and goodwill, now that the project was so clearly defined. I put on my coat and hat, picked up my sketchbook, and made for the front door. As I turned the knob I was reminded that someone had entered my house without my knowledge twice in the past two days. Nothing was safe, I realized.

Returning to the studio, I carefully rolled up the sketch. Then I made a tour of the rooms, searching for a place to stow it where an intruder would never think to look. I finally settled on stuffing it into the arm of a dinner jacket that hung at the back of my bedroom closet. This was not completely satisfactory, but on the other hand no one but Samantha and I knew of the drawing's existence.

It was a beautiful day, warmer than those of late, and I took the opportunity to let my ideas percolate, choosing to walk a bit before boarding an uptown streetcar. There is nothing like that steady rhythmic motion, the fresh air, and open space to fan the creative spark into a genuine blaze. The sidewalks were crowded, and I made a game of trying to walk as many blocks as I could without coming to a full stop, dodging passersby here and there, looking ahead to anticipate tight gaps between pedestrians, and slipping through at the last second. All the while I was contemplating whether or not to depict Mrs. Charbuque from the waist or from the knees. Considering the question, I found that either prospect thrilled me.

At the corner of Park Avenue and Twenty-sixth Street, the game was up. A crowd of nearly two dozen people had gathered there, waiting for three automobiles and twice as many carriages to pass before they could cross uptown. I joined the group and patiently waited for the vehicles to move on. When the street was finally clear and the horde began to cross, my attention was drawn to the left by the blare of an auto horn. A mere second later, from the right, I could swear I heard a female voice whisper, "Piambo, I love you."

I turned my head quickly, but no one was there. Either my ears had played a trick on me, or the speaker had moved on ahead with the surging crowd. I hurried across to catch up. The group seemed to be composed completely of women: hats and hairdos, parasols and handbags. Before I could reach them and see their faces, they had gained the opposite sidewalk and scattered, some entering shops and the rest going east or west or continuing north. The incident unnerved me for two reasons. The first was that I was very possibly deluding myself, which, given recent events, would not be so unlikely. The second was that the voice I heard, although its message was very much the opposite, carried the same quiet tone and inflection as that of Mrs. Reed's wish for me.

I boarded a streetcar at Twenty-ninth Street and arrived at Mrs. Charbuque's house with a good ten minutes to spare before the appointment. Watkin answered the door in his usual slightly irritated, perfunctory manner, but with what Samantha had told me, I saw him in a completely new light. I now had the courage to stare into those white eyes and found in them an unnatural quality of reflection. Upon close inspection, I could see they were not real. Beyond that, though, they were so pathetically fake that I nearly laughed out loud at my naïveté. In order to elicit a performance, I asked him if he had seen the lead story in the morning newspapers. "Surely you are jesting, Mr. Piambo," he said, and his gestures quickly corroborated everything Samantha had said about his erratic manner. Either his movements were those of a normally sighted person, or they involved a melodramatic positioning of the head, like a bird listening to the call of its mate.

Watkin escorted me to the antechamber and then went to check on the readiness of Mrs. Charbuque. In those short minutes I conceived of a plan to disturb Mr. Watkin. Opening my sketchbook, I turned it horizontally on my lap. I took out my pencil and wrote in large dark letters WATKIN IS AN ASS! Admittedly juvenile, but I wanted something that might get a rise out of him.

When he returned, I was waiting for him, standing with the book open in front of me. He stopped short at the entrance to the small room, and I saw a blush suffuse his forehead and cheeks. "This way," he said curtly, but he did not append the phrase "Mr. Piambo" to it as he usually did. I followed him, trying to consider the purpose of Watkin's threadbare disguise. As we passed through the formal dining room, he pointed to his left and said, "We've acquired a new piece." He did not stop to give me time to study it, but I turned my head quickly enough to see, framed and hung upon the wall, the daguerreotype from the warehouse. While ushering me into the room with the screen, his visage sported a wide, ugly grin.

THE RED HERRING

*S*HALL I mark your presence here today as an acceptance of my apology, Piambo?" she asked.

"Yes," I said.

"I'm sorry to have startled you with the monkey arm, but my sense of humor has grown strange from my self-imposed isolation. I expect my words and schemes to be taken in a certain way, but I am often disappointed with the results. After all these years, I remain unable to calculate how the presence of the screen will alter my intentions."

"I understand," I said. As I listened to her words, I conjured the image of the sketch in my mind. The more she spoke, the more the minute details began to fill themselves in—the curve of her ear, the insignificant creases at the corners of her mouth, the length of her neck.

"We used the monkey arm in the act as what my father called a *red herring,* something to both confuse the audience and delight their sense of wonder. I don't know if you noticed, but the thumb has a spring inserted in it so that it closes tightly against the palm. This feature had been added before we purchased it. What its original use was God only knows, but for our purposes it acted as an eccentric clasp to secure the paper leaves people wrote their questions on. By thrusting out the fake arm to accept the leaves from my father, I could remain completely hidden."

"Reaction to it must have been interesting," I said.

"Very. It led people to believe that I was some kind of monstrous anomaly cursed with the attributes of an ape yet blessed with divine knowledge," she said.

"My mentor, M. Sabott, used to say, 'The public loves a neat package of contradictions,'" I said, entertaining the notion that perhaps the arm had been a red herring for me as well and that she really was some bizarre creature. Having come too far to allow myself to be plunged back into the pit of doubt, I banished the thought as quickly as it had arisen, and focused again on my memory of the sketch.

"That first time, at Ossiak's dinner party, was exciting for me. I was just eleven years old, and actually quite timid, but the screen gave me an uncharacteristic courage. I still remember the first question asked of me. My father read it aloud to the audience. 'Will it happen?' he said, and I held out the monkey arm. With an elegant flourish, he clamped the green leaf under its thumb. Upon retrieving it, I read it again to myself and then closed my eyes to concentrate on listening for the voices of the Twins. As I have told you, I was a fervent believer, so there was no apprehension. They came to me immediately, their whispers turning to images in my mind.

" 'It is raining,' I said loudly in order to project my voice beyond the barrier. 'The path is muddy. There is a cat and a crowd. I see an open window through which everything passes. It will happen at the end of the day, and there will be peace.' When I was finished, a few moments of absolute silence reigned in the dining hall, and then the voice of a young man called out, 'Thank you.'

"That evening I responded to the questions jotted on a dozen leaves and subsequently read aloud. When my father announced

that the session was over, there came a thunderous applause. I left
the room in the same manner as I had entered: the lights were
briefly extinguished, and I fled through a nearby door, my father
preventing anyone from following me. We had arranged to have a
carriage waiting for me outside the building, and like some fairy-
tale princess racing against the approach of midnight, I rushed to
it and was on my way before I could be spotted. Back at our
apartment, I waited alone for him to return, hoping that I had
done well. Eventually I fell asleep on our parlor couch, for he did
not return until daybreak. As he explained to me, when the fes-
tivities were over, Ossiak met with him, and they discussed the results of that year's snowfall.

"He was both troubled and delighted. The act of the Sibyl had
been a great success, but his news of financial ruin did not sit well
with his employer. Still, Ossiak was not so ignorant as to blame the
bearer of bad tidings. He entreated my father to put the question
of the fate of his fortune to the Sibyl.

"Our performance was an interesting entertainment, and I
doubt that many of those present thought of it as anything more,
that is until three days later, when the daily paper brought some
shocking news. The first person whose question I had answered
was a young man who, owing to his economic station in life (I believe he was a waiter or laborer at some hotel or tavern), would
not normally attend one of Ossiak's affairs. He was present that
night because he had recently come to the aid of one of Ossiak's
nieces on the street when she was accosted by a ruffian. To repay
this young man's gallantry, Ossiak sent him an invitation to the
gala.

"As it turned out, the young man had a vision of his own. Over
a period of years, he had saved a sum of five thousand dollars. The
Tuesday following Ossiak's affair, he took a day off from work and
went to Hanover Racetrack. There, at the betting window, he put
all his money to win on a horse by the name of Calico. Calico was
a well-respected Thoroughbred, but that day it rained, which

turned the track to mud, and Calico lost the race. Later that afternoon, the young man committed suicide by slitting his wrists with a straight razor, thereby finding peace from his overweening desire for success. Instead, it was I who found success. All those who had been in attendance the evening of my first performance now believed I was imbued with special powers."

"A sad story," I managed to say, while my memory of the sketch of Mrs. Charbuque was replaced by the harrowing image of Ryder's *The Race Track*.

"Do you see the irony in it, Piambo? My prediction was pure fabrication, but at the time, I believed quite ardently in its veracity. The crowd allowed themselves to be deluded in the name of entertainment, and the young man, wanting so desperately to be a winner, took my words as an assurance that he would be. Add to this the trumpery of the ape's arm, my father's sudden new guise as a huckster of marvels, and Ossiak ignoring the warnings that his economic empire was fragile. This maelstrom of illusion coincided to produce not one but several tragedies."

"Besides the suicide, which probably could not have been avoided, what other misfortunes came of it?" I asked.

"Well, most important to me, an innocent young girl was transformed into a monster. From the time my father told me of the young man's demise, I felt the weight of the responsibility I carried. He was so jolly over it, it made him red in the face, and when I broached the question of whether my response had in some way spurred the poor man to place the bet, he responded, 'Nonsense, dear. A fellow like that, in his situation, could hear a thousand messages of warning, and still they would all sound to his addled ears like the same affirmation to proceed unto glory.'

"No one knew for certain that I was the Sibyl, although I'm sure many suspected it from the tenor of my voice and from their knowledge my father had a daughter. We had numerous visitors following the performance and its subsequent revelation. Friends of my father's, Ossiak's other employees, would drop by the apartment looking for a chance to ask the Sibyl a question. My father told them that the Sibyl had left town for a week or two and would most likely give another performance somewhere in the city the following month. These visitors would eye me suspiciously, and I would turn away. I felt that to return their gazes would engage the voices of the Twins, and I would be forced to speak their fates in cryptic phrases.

"Eyes became very frightening to me. I felt their gaze almost physically, as if they projected beams that searched every inch of my body and soul for signs of their bearer's future. Each sighted orb was like that giant eye that had stared down at me through the optical magnifier.

"With the help of Ossiak's influence, Father found another venue for the act at one of the better hotels. I no longer recall which one, but it was an upscale establishment catering to society's elite. We had our second performance there and this time charged for it. Once more situated behind the screen, I felt safe for the first time in weeks. I again served as a conduit for the whisperings of the Twins, and we took in a small fortune.

"What I did not learn until later was that Ossiak himself was in the audience, and one of the leaves I received bore a question from him. My father read it: 'Does the future hold more?' and my answer involved images of a splintering throne, a rotten apple, a half-empty glass. I heard from the other side of the boundary a solitary groan rise from the audience and did not realize it at the time, but I, an eleven-year-old girl, had tossed the pebble that initiated the avalanche of his financial ruin.

"For the next month we performed at the hotel once a week. In the interim between shows I began spending more and more of my time behind the screen. When people visited the apartment I would run and hide. My father never worried about or admonished me for my growing shyness, for having dedicated so much of his life to his crystalogistics, he thought it only proper that I should become dedicated to my profession.

"Then one day the police came to the house. I hid behind the screen as they questioned my father about the fate of my mother. When he told them that a wolf had carried her off, they laughed at him, and I heard one of them say, 'Come, come, Londell, do you take us for fools?' There were things said that I did not want to hear, so I shut them out, refusing to listen. Although I worked hard not to acknowledge what was said, the one thing I do recall is the sound of my father opening the chest within which he kept the proceeds from the shows. Soon after, the police left. It was immediately following this incident that we began doing five shows a week. That is when my fear of the world outside the protection of the screen grew into a mania. When I was caught in plain sight, I would tremble and cry hysterically, but when I was safely hidden behind the falling leaves, I felt I was God."

CONSULTING THE TWINS

A SINGLE green leaf fell, sawing back and forth in the air past the static depiction of its autumnal kin. "I will demonstrate for you," said Mrs. Charbuque. "Do you have your pencil?"

"Yes," I said, still trying to digest her statement that she had felt herself to be God.

"Write out a question," she said.

I leaned over in my seat and lifted the paper leaf from the floor. It took only a second to think of what to ask. You do not have to be psychic to guess what it was. "I have done so," I said.

"Place it carefully beneath the thumb," she said, and I saw that insane monkey arm inch its way slowly up from the top of the screen. The sight of it now made me smile, and I heard Mrs. Charbuque giggle quietly like a girl in church.

I stood and secured the leaf in the hairy hand. Then it lowered with the same comic slowness as it had risen.

" 'Do I see it clearly?' " Mrs. Charbuque read aloud. "A moment now, Piambo. I am consulting the Twins."

Knowing the entire thing was a farce didn't matter. I still felt a kind of mild excitement tingling in my chest as I waited for her pronouncement.

"I see fire," she said, ". . . and snow. There is a shiny coffin, a smile, and an angel on the beach at sunset. That is all." A few moments passed, and then she laughed. "How was that?"

"Curious imagery," I said, "but I'm afraid I'm no wiser than I was before asking."

"In all the time I actively portrayed the Sibyl, I don't think I ever actually answered anyone's question," she said.

"Your record remains unbroken," I told her. "How long did you perform as the Sibyl? You've already said that you continued with the act after your father passed away."

"I not only continued, Piambo, I became famous and, as you can see by the trappings of my life, wealthy," she said. "Yes, for someone who for all intents and purposes did not exist, I did quite well."

"Tell me about how that happened," I said as I sketched the twin arches of her eyebrows.

"My father and I were to go to the mountains twice more, and in the summers following each season of snow, we performed in the city. A goodly piece of everything we made on the act was handed over to the police to keep my father from being prosecuted for the murder of my mother. This weighed on him, not out of guilt but because he was loath to share our wealth. As much as he enjoyed playing the assistant to my Sibyl, he was still first and foremost a crystalogogist. Once we were back in the mountains, he buried himself in his work. The tale told by the snowflakes became grimmer with each reading, but barring his obvious concern for the future, he was always pleased to trudge out to the tin laboratory and climb the ladder to the optical magnifier.

"Then, at the end of the second summer, Ossiak called father and all the other diviners on his payroll to a meeting at his estate on Long Island. I did not attend, but when my father returned, he was pale as death. He told me that Ossiak had never made an appearance, but one of his underlings had told all those present that they were being let go and that their records and equipment would be confiscated. That was it. With his work gone, my father had no will to continue. I told him we would make our way by performing the act, and he sighed and nodded, but I could never get him to agree to set new dates at the hotel. Eventually he took to staying indoors and sleeping much of the day away.

"One afternoon, while sitting in his chair in the parlor, he asked me to take up my guise as the Sibyl and foretell his future. I told him I didn't want to, but he insisted. He made me go into the bedroom and bring out the screen. Once it was set up, I slipped behind it and sat on my chair. 'Sibyl, what does the future hold?' he called out in a weak voice. I was quite upset, but I tried to calm myself and concentrate on listening for the Twins. Nothing came to me. He waited patiently for my answer. I got no sign from the benefactors in my locket and felt they had abandoned me. Of course, I knew that Father was in a bad state, so I consciously fabricated pleasant imagery. 'I see sunshine,' I said, 'an ocean of sunshine and great good fortune,' and other such satisfying bits of nonsense. When I was done, I listened for his response. I thought he might applaud or perhaps even say 'Eureka,' but there was absolute silence. When I finally came around the screen, I found him dead in his chair. His eyes stared with such frightening intensity, and . . ."

Mrs. Charbuque's voice trailed off into silence. I had stopped sketching halfway through her story, and only a day after wanting to strangle her, I felt the greatest sympathy.

"You were thirteen," I said.

"Yes."

"Did you have any other family to take care of you?" I asked.

"Believe it or not, Piambo, I took care of myself. You cannot fathom the struggle I went through to make the arrangements necessary for my father's funeral. Each individual I met with was an appointment in hell, but I wanted to be left alone eventually, so that no one could see me. If I were to seek out relatives or depend on the relief agencies for assistance, I would never be free from their glances, their looks."

"That took courage," I said.

The door opened, and Watkin entered.

"Good grief," I said, my annoyance obvious.

"Your time is now up," he said.

I gathered my things and put on my coat.

"Tomorrow, Piambo," said Mrs. Charbuque, and I read a wealth of emotion in her salutation.

"Tomorrow," I said, trying to imbue mine with as much.

Watkin wore the same grimace as he had earlier when showing me into the room. As I walked toward him, I stopped short, suddenly remembering a question that nagged at me, and called back, "Mrs. Charbuque, you said your husband was lost in a shipwreck. I am curious to know the name of the vessel."

"You will have to wait until tomorrow for that," said Watkin.

"Now, Peter, it's quite all right," she said from behind her screen. "If I'm not mistaken, it was the *Janus*."

"Thank you. Good day," I said.

Out on the steps, I turned to Watkin and said, "Have a tedious evening, Peter."

He, of course, slammed the door in my face.

I had a good two hours before the event I was to attend that evening. Even though the National Academy of Design was on East Twenty-third Street, not far at all from my house on Gramercy, rather than going home I chose to arrive early and spend some time wandering the halls of my old haunt. The sun was setting as I approached the building, and the sight of the warm glow emanating from its tall arched windows induced a wave of nostalgia. I stood for a moment outside the low wrought-iron fence and took in the building's architecture of gray and white marble and bluestone, before proceeding up the left side of the double stairway to the entrance.

Classes were still in session, and I took great pleasure in roaming down the halls, peering in at the earnest students, mostly young but some old, laboring in the fields of art. Many of the instructors were professional artists, and I knew almost all of them. Of the people who had passed through those halls, one could compile a roll of America's most famous artists—Cole, Durand, Ingram, Cummings, Agate; the list was long. On that particular evening, though, I moved stealthily, not wanting to be discovered by any old friends. From the moment I entered and smelled the familiar aroma of the place, I had a specific destination in mind.

On the main floor, in the far corner of the east wing, was a small gallery in which the academy displayed works from its private collection. Certain paintings hung therein that were perpetually on display: a Thomas Cole landscape, an Eakins portrait, and the one I had come to visit. With my busy career, I could usually make time only once every year or two to commune with this piece. Every time I entered the gallery I experienced a moment of trepidation in which I would entertain the fear that perhaps the work had fallen out of favor and been removed to storage. On that evening, I was not disappointed.

The gallery was empty but for me, and I walked quietly to a bench and sat down in front of Sabott's masterpiece, *The Madonna of the Manticores*, the same work my father had taken me to see so many long years before.

Because of what Mrs. Charbuque had just told me about the loss of her father, my thoughts were on the loss of my own. I am speaking not of my birth parent but of Sabott. It was just down the hallway from the very spot where I sat that I had first encountered him. He had been teaching a course in painting for the academy that season. I had been a student for a few years, and at an early age, not so many years older than Mrs. Charbuque when she had become the Sibyl, I had already developed a distinctive painting style.

Luckily, the classes at the academy were free. Although my

father had left us fairly well off when he died, my mother had to budget this money carefully because no more would come in until I was able to make a living. I was forced to dress poorly and could not always afford the necessary supplies, but I had some innate talent, and the teachers usually helped me out with extra expenses when they could.

Then Sabott came to teach. I did everything I could to be accepted for his course, even though it was reserved for more accomplished students, who were usually older than I. Mr. Morse, the man who subsequently invented the Morse code, was the president of the academy at the time, and he happened to be a great supporter of mine, having known my father. He pulled the necessary strings to get me into Sabott's painting class.

Sabott was a strict teacher, and many of the students did not like him. I, on the other hand, was completely devoted to him because of my father's admiration for his work. Throughout the weeks of the class, he said only the same two words to me again and again. He would come to look at one of my paintings, point to something in the composition, and shake his head. Then he would lift the palette knife and hand it to me. "Scrape it," he would say, which meant I was to clean the canvas and begin again. This I did without a word of protest. During the final week of the class, I worked on a portrait from a live model, a woman dressed in only a pink robe. Every day I expected him to tell me to clean the canvas, but he didn't. It was the finest piece of work I had ever done. On the last day, as I was adding some highlights to the robe—finishing touches—he discovered a problem with her hair. "Scrape it," he said. I almost cried, but I did as he instructed.

The class ended, and I had not even one completed canvas to show for it. Sabott left, as he was not going to teach the following season. Exactly one month later he arrived on the doorstep of our house in Brooklyn. That day, he asked my mother's permission to take me on as his apprentice. From then on, he clothed me, fed me, educated me, took me with him on his travels, and worked me like a dog, demanding that I become the finest painter I could be.

I discovered that his stern demeanor was an act he put on in the classroom, for he was always a wise and kind gentleman. Most important, he taught me how to see where the arts and literature and science coincided with everyday life. Even his technical lessons involved larger issues of human philosophy.

Sitting there, staring up at that great work of the imagination, I felt his absence deeply, and through this sense of loss found what struck me as an intense kinship with Mrs. Charbuque.

THE GALLERY

SHENZ WAS dizzy with opium, three sheets to the wind, as they say, his eyes more glassy than the fake orbs of Mr. Watkin. We stood with John Sills in front of his entry in the show, a set of miniature portraits of criminals. The fete buzzed and whirled around us, wealthy patrons hobnobbing with artists—some students, some academicians, some reigning masters in their fields.

"Amazingly well done," I said to John.

The police detective bowed slightly and thanked me.

"This damsel looks familiar," said Shenz, pointing to the last picture in the row, his entire body tottering as if thrown off balance by the discovery.

I drew close to the painting, bent down, and squinted. The portrait was of a homely woman wearing a kerchief. I also recognized the subject.

"Was it an affair of the heart, Shenz?" asked Sills, laughing.

Shenz did not register the joke but merely said, "No doubt."

We chatted some more, and then Sills announced that he needed to see a gallery owner who was interested in representing his work. Before he moved away, he took me by the elbow and leaned in close. "I have to speak to you before you leave tonight," he said in a whisper.

I nodded, and then he vanished into the crowd.

I turned to Shenz, who was still studying the portrait of Wolfe, and said, "You look positively lacquered tonight."

"Yes," he said. "There's a good reason."

"What's that?" I asked.

"Because I am," he said, his eyes focusing for the first time since he had entered the gallery.

"You'll lose commissions," I said. I hated to be prudish, but Shenz's career had taken a precarious turn of late, and I felt he was doing himself a grave disservice.

"The ship," he said, changing the subject. "Did you inquire the name of the ship?"

"The *Janus*," I said.

"A figurehead at both prow and stern, I suppose," he said. "Did you find out what port it hailed from? What was its destination?"

"All I could get was the name," I told him.

At that moment I looked up and saw, of all people, Mrs. Reed, making her way slowly toward us along the row of paintings. I nodded in her direction, and Shenz turned to look.

"She may have a derringer in that purse, Piambo," he said. "Disperse!" He laughed quietly and staggered away toward the champagne.

I lit out in the opposite direction, keeping my eyes peeled for her husband, who I knew could not be far off. For an hour, I made the rounds, meeting and greeting colleagues and professors, catching up on old times and talking art for art's sake. It was always a pleasure to hear of the various philosophies and techniques that others were employing in their work. At one point I came upon a former student of mine, standing before what I surmised to be his painting. He was young and wore his hair long in the manner of Whistler.

"Edward," I said, greeting him.

Upon seeing me, he put his hand out and said, "Mr. Piambo, how have you been?"

We shook hands, and I stepped back, making a great show of taking in his work. His painting was of a historical nature, vibrantly colored, in a clear, realistic style that had been popular back when I first started in the field. The subject was Salome and the beheading of Saint John the Baptist. The executioner's scimitar had just lopped off the saint's bearded head, which now lay at the feet of the femme fatale. Sabott's influence was in strong evidence, and it pleased me to see this young man keeping my mentor's artistic memory alive.

"Wonderful brushwork and color," I told him.

"Thank you," he said, bowing his head in embarrassment.

"But," I said, "if I may offer a comment . . ."

He nodded.

"There is no blood. This fellow here has just had his head severed from his body, and there is not a drop of blood in sight." It was true. The end of the saint's neck still attached to the torso looked for all the world like a healthy ham steak.

Edward's eyes widened, and he brought his hand to his forehead. "My God," he said, "I will have to put it back on the easel tomorrow."

"Nothing to worry about, it's a fine piece," I said. "When you fix it, leave word with the academy to get in touch with me. I am interested in purchasing it."

Seeing his smile was worth three times whatever I would end up paying for the painting. "This is quite incredible," he said. "Just this evening I was also commissioned to do a portrait for a gentleman. My first."

I wanted desperately to tell him to forget the portrait. "Portraiture is a trap that will relieve you of all your heart's inspiration," I was about to say. Instead, though, I patted his shoulder and congratulated him before moving off.

Samantha arrived soon after, looking particularly lovely dressed in a blue watered silk gown, her hair done up in intricate braids. We had a glass of champagne together, but I was soon separated from her by a long line of her admirers. It amused me that no matter how revered some of the artists present in the gallery were, they could not compete with the interest generated by a popular actress. Samantha was, as always, gracious, speaking candidly with each of her well-wishers. At one point, while I was still standing at the fringe of her crowd, she looked up and smiled at me, as if to apologize. I nodded and smiled, knowing I would have her to myself later.

I turned away and was surprised to see Albert Pinkham Ryder. Although he had belonged to the academy for a time, he had always had trouble showing his work. The other members were quite wary of his style and did not know what to make of it. Eventually this had caused him to join a group of others, who had also met with the academy's intractable stuffiness, and form the Society of American Artists. They held their own juried shows, and of late their rival organization had grown in popularity.

He stood alone, dressed in a silk jacket, clutching an old-fashioned top hat, staring across the gallery at a sketch of an angel by Saint-Gaudens. I was delighted to see my hero, his presence giving me the same thrill experienced by the students upon meeting me or the other professionals. As I moved toward him, I conjured up a fitting introductory line.

"Excuse me, Mr. Ryder," I said. "I wanted to apologize for having nearly run you down on Broadway this past Sunday."

He turned and looked at me, focusing his weak eyes. For a moment he just stood there as if recently woken from a dream. Then he smiled. "Piambo," he said. "Yes, it happened so abruptly, I did not realize it was you until I was halfway down the block."

I was elated that he remembered me. "Are you enjoying the show?" I asked. "There are quite a few luminaries represented this year in the catalog."

"It's not the luminaries I come to see," he said. "I prefer the work of the novices. In their pieces I find sparks of passion that have not yet been doused by the academy."

"I understand," I said.

"Which brings me to wonder why you have nothing hanging in this show. Call it coincidence, but the other day after I nearly collided with you I was in a gallery uptown, and they were selling one of your earlier works, a painting of Tiresias. You had captured him at the exact moment when he was being transformed into a woman, and the figure showed attributes of both sexes. The sky was torn apart by lightning, and the whole composition, though obviously influenced by Sabott in the subject matter, was raw and wild."

"I'd nearly forgotten it," I said, thinking back to the days when I had painted it. I had a brief memory flash of Sabott nodding before that canvas and saying, "This is the way."

"Very inspirational," said Ryder. "It made me consider going back to the myths. I was thinking of the story of Siegfried, something I've toyed with before. I tell you, if I were flush with cash at this juncture, I would have purchased that painting myself."

Now it was my turn to bow my head in embarrassment. I felt a surge of energy in me that I had not experienced since my early days, when every technique and notion I learned was the discovery of a new continent of the imagination.

Before I could reply, John Sills was insinuating himself between Ryder and me. "Excuse me, gentlemen. Please forgive the interruption, but Piambo, I must speak with you."

Ryder nodded, smiled, and turned away. I was in a daze as John put his hand on my shoulder and led me out of the gallery.

THE BEHEADING OF
SAINT JOHN

OUTSIDE THE gallery a group of artists stood gathered in conversation, smoking cigars. They nodded to us and said hello as we passed. We walked to the corner of the hallway and turned left. Sills was about to speak, but a couple came into view. It was a man and a young woman, obviously, like ourselves, seeking privacy. To my surprise I saw that it was Reed. The young lady, though, was most definitely not Mrs. Reed. I nodded, but my erstwhile patron looked through me as they passed, pretending I was not there. We continued on to the smaller gallery at the back of the building where I had sat in reverie earlier that evening.

Once we were alone in the room, Sills asked me what I thought of the opening.

"Wonderful," I replied. "And I was pleased to see what progress you have made in your own work."

"I nearly didn't make it here tonight," he said. "There was a fire at a warehouse on Fulton Street this afternoon. The building burned to the ground, and it was assuredly arson. It's not my district, but they were short of men and wanted another detective to fill in. I had to pull some strings to get out of the assignment."

I wanted to ask him if the burned building was one with a faint white circle painted on it but could guess what his answer would be. "Is this little meeting about the incident we discussed outside my house last week?" I asked.

He nodded. "I shouldn't be telling you, of course, but being sworn to secrecy about this matter doesn't sit right with me," he said. "I think they're wrong to keep the public in the dark. Since I've already told you what I know, I thought I would keep you apprised and also relieve some of my frustration."

"There have been more victims," I said.

"Yes," he said, and his admission came with a look of weariness and shame, as if he were personally responsible for the safety of the entire populace of the city. "Two more since you and I spoke. An anonymous caller tipped us off to the whereabouts of a corpse last Sunday. And another was found in her apartment not too far from your address."

"And the newspapers haven't caught wind of this yet?" I asked.

"Oh, they have, but the mayor has requested that they keep it quiet until more is known. They have agreed, but barely. The editors said that if one more body is discovered, it will be on the front page."

"Does the Department of Health know any more about how the parasite is transmitted and where it came from?" I asked.

He shook his head. "Earlier tonight I heard that they think they might have discovered a common denominator, but nothing more."

I considered telling him that it was I who had found the woman on Sunday, but decided against it. There were enough mysteries circling about in my head to nearly split it open. I did not want to declare ownership of this one as well.

"I'm sure," said John, "that we'll soon be reading about it in the *World*. It's definitely some kind of exotic parasite, but it's odd that up to this point it has only affected women. If I were you I would find a way to warn Samantha to be careful, and especially to stay away from the waterfront."

I couldn't lie. "I've already told her," I said.

I thought he would be angry, but instead he smiled and said, "Good."

As we walked back to the main gallery, I asked Sills if he had made an arrangement with the gallery owner he had sought out earlier. He told me nothing had come of it as yet. The hallways were empty now, and as we approached the exhibition hall, I was struck by the unnatural silence. It was as if the party within had folded up and slipped away.

"Awfully quiet," said John as he pulled back the door to enter the gallery. "Perhaps the judges are about to announce their decisions."

We stepped inside and were met with a scene that could easily have been an illustration from a pulp story. The crowd had backed away to the perimeter of the large room, and in the middle, next to the table that held the champagne, stood Mrs. Reed, a small gun, perhaps a derringer, in her hand. Her arm was trembling as she aimed across a space of twelve yards at her husband, who was backed up against young Edward's *Beheading of Saint John the Baptist*.

I should have been more surprised, but with the manner in which my life had recently been swamped with synchronistic happenstance, I wondered why I hadn't seen it coming. "Did I really have to call for blood on that canvas?" I asked myself.

It probably wasn't that long, but it seemed as if whole plump minutes passed in silence as everyone waited for the shot to sound. Reed was pale, slumped forward slightly, covering his face with one hand and—this would have been amusing if the man's life were not at stake—his groin with the other. "It's really you I love," he said, but his usually ingratiating voice now sounded more like a piece of rusty mill machinery on its last job.

That is when Shenz, as nonchalantly as if he were crossing the street, stepped out of the crowd and stood between Mrs. Reed and her husband. "Madam," he said, "it would be a shame to waste that bullet." He smiled and began slowly walking toward her.

"Get out of the way," she screamed, her face turning bright red.

Shenz continued to advance. "I have a feeling your children will be waiting up for you this evening," he said. "And what's this?" He reached into his jacket pocket and pulled forth a small paper bag. "I have brought some candy for them."

Mrs. Reed groaned, hesitated for another second, and then lowered the gun to her side. Shenz stepped up and put his arm around her. With his free hand, he relieved her of the weapon. She put her face down on his shoulder and wept.

John had already moved into action and was at Shenz's side, confiscating the gun. The crowd broke out in a round of applause for my friend's heroism, while the reporters, who were plentiful, wasted no time in descending upon Reed like a flock of vultures. Many of his business associates were present that evening, and between their eyewitness accounts and what would appear in the papers the following day, he would be altogether finished.

Sills ushered Mrs. Reed out of the gallery, no doubt taking her uptown to police headquarters. As he passed me he said, "Let me know if I get a ribbon." Meanwhile, Samantha had poured Shenz a glass of champagne. There were a few moments in which the crowd, en masse, tried to decide if what had happened was tragic enough to halt the opening or if they felt resilient enough to continue with the merriment. A confused half minute passed, and then there was a collective shrug, a sign that as much as said "Oh, the hell with it," and the patrons and artists moved in from the perimeter of the gallery, the conversation resuming as if someone had flipped an electric switch.

When I saw Shenz dodge his new admirers and make his way out the door, I followed. I did not have to go far to catch up to him. He was sitting on the steps outside, smoking a cigarette in the cold night air. I sat down and lit one of my own.

"Well, she did have a derringer after all, but it wasn't meant for you," he said to me, shaking his head.

"Was that a derringer?" I asked. "You have become as prescient as Mrs. Charbuque."

He smiled. "I think it was the bag of candy that made her reconsider," he said. "I've been carrying that candy around with me for the past two weeks."

"A very foolish stunt," I said.

"I know. It's a sin. I should have let her shoot him. I'll never forgive myself."

"Please," I said, "another Reed would pop up as soon as they buried that one. They turn them out ready-made these days. Besides, you probably saved her from going to prison or worse. Women who shoot men do not fare as well as the reverse."

"True enough," he said.

"What made you do it, though?" I asked.

"Well," he said, and puffed on his cigarette, "I looked around that room and thought to myself, 'Who of everyone present has the least to lose?' I won hands down."

"That drug is warping your mind."

"No," he said, staring across the street into the darkness. "All those fresh-faced youths with their brilliant works. All the established artists with their careers. I am like a snowman sitting in the sun. My talent drips off me and streams away in rivulets, my desire to paint evaporates more with each hour, my heart is cold to the whole endeavor."

"You've got to pull yourself together and work your way back to your old form," I said.

"Easier said than done," he told me.

"You are giving up?"

"Not quite yet. I have to help you flush Mrs. Charbuque from her blind. After that, we shall see."

CLAWS OF OBSESSION

FTER THE opening, Samantha and I walked back to my place. Even though the episode with the Reeds was the spectacle of the evening, and my dialogue with Shenz on the steps had been somewhat upsetting, being the unrelenting egotist that I am, all I could think about were Ryder's words of praise for my preportrait work. How I longed to relate the entire conversation to Samantha, but propriety would not allow it. She would smile and say, "How wonderful," but it was impossible for me not to come off sounding like a self-absorbed novice. Mrs. Charbuque had not cornered the market on lurking behind screens.

Instead, as we strolled along the sidewalk, we spoke about poor Mrs. Reed. Samantha seemed particularly horrified at the woman's situation.

"You would never force me to shoot you, would you, Piambo?" she asked.

"There are moments when I'm surprised you haven't already," I said.

"What does that mean?" she asked, turning to stare at me.

"Good Lord," I said, "I'm not talking about philandering. I simply mean for being such a boor at times."

"Oh, that," she said. "That I can forgive, but if I were to catch you making a fool of me with another woman, I would not be so helpless as Mrs. Reed. I can't tell you how many times I am propositioned, either subtly or outright, in the course of a year. I fend off the advances of other fellows because I have chosen you."

"I'm glad to hear it," I said.

"This is where you are supposed to say that you have also chosen me," she said.

"I thought that was obvious," I told her. "Need I say it?"

"It wouldn't kill you," she said.

"Don't shoot," I said. "Yes, I have chosen you. Are you really that uncertain?"

"Well, you seemed so very pleased by those flowers from your Mrs. Charbuque last night," she said.

"Come, come," I said, "the woman is insane."

"It wasn't so much the flowers," she said. "It was more the look in your face, as if you were hiding something."

"I was astonished that she would do such a thing. I can't believe that after all the women whose portraits I have painted, you are now becoming jealous. For heaven's sake, I painted Mrs. Reed. I didn't hear a word about her from you."

"This commission is not the same," she said. "You are completely preoccupied with it."

"It is rather unusual," I said.

"She has some hold on you, I can tell."

"Nonsense," I said.

"You have not seen her?" she asked.

"I go to her house and communicate with a talking screen," I said.

"Then why, in your conception of her, that sketch you made, is she both stunningly beautiful and naked?"

I stopped walking. Samantha went on and then turned to look

at me. "I don't know," I said. "Perhaps she is like a myth to me, being invisible and so forth. In the classical style, nudity was part of depicting the gods and goddesses of antiquity."

"Goddesses?" she said.

"You know what I mean," I said. "Think of Sabott's paintings."

She cocked her head for a moment, as if reviewing in her memory a catalog of his works. "I can't think of one nude," she said.

"What?" I said, but in quickly reviewing them myself, I realized she was right. I started walking again, since standing still seemed to be making me stupid.

"I tell you, that woman has your mind, Piambo. If you are not careful the rest will follow," she said.

"She has nothing," I said, shaking my head. "Except my money."

Silence reigned for the remainder of the walk to my house and still had not relinquished its rule as we undressed in the bedroom. Finally I could stand it no more and, in an attempt to change the subject, asked, "What did you think of Shenz tonight?"

Samantha sat on the bed, removing her stockings. "His actions were very gallant, but Shenz himself appears old to me suddenly, as if he has aged years in recent months."

I was thankful she had taken my bait and was willing to forget the earlier matter. "The opium has its claws in him, I fear," I said. "It is taking control of him. Insidious."

"There's something you two have in common, losing control to an insubstantial entity," she said.

I turned to her as I removed my jacket. "Please, Samantha," I said. "I swear it is you I love. I have been devoted to you for fifteen years now."

"Twelve," she said.

"Don't doubt me," I said.

She stared at me for some time and then smiled. "I'm sorry, Piambo," she said. "I trust you."

"We've got to trust each other," I said as I hung my jacket in the closet. No sooner were the words out of my mouth than I saw, hanging to the right of the jacket I had just put away, the one that held hidden in its sleeve my sketch of Mrs. Charbuque. Before I could even consider the folly of the act, my hand reached for it. Luckily, I stopped myself short, pulled back my arm, and closed the closet door.

The lights were turned off, the nutmeg candle, whose scent I had come to loathe, was lit, and we lay there beneath the covers. My mind was filled with the image of the sketch, and it alternated with my own complete vision of Mrs. Charbuque in the moonlight behind her screen. I did not want to disturb these thoughts and prayed that Samantha would quickly fall asleep.

My prayers, alas, went unanswered, as Samantha turned to me and I launched into it with a pervasive sense of doom. My implement of desire was as useless to me that night as it turned out Mrs. Reed's derringer was to her. I did not need the Twins to foretell that there was a lot riding on this misadventure. The pressure was intense, and out of it was born true American ingenuity.

It was not long afterward that Samantha's breathing regulated to the slow, steady rhythm of sleep. I lay still and waited for a few minutes, and when I was certain she was truly out, I waited yet another few minutes. Then, with stealth and grace combined, I slowly pulled back the covers on my side of the bed. Exerting great control over the musculature of my body, which, believe me, was not easy, I more levitated than sat up. I remained there on the edge of the bed for a moment or two, waiting to see if I had roused Samantha. When I could finally hear her steady breathing over the beating of my heart, I continued, carefully getting to my feet.

I literally tiptoed around the bed and across the room, like one of Mr. Wolfe's compatriots slinking through a darkened warehouse. I knew the hinges on the closet door were going to be murder and they were, but I opened it quickly so as to not draw out their whine. I turned and looked back at the bed. She lay facing me, but her eyes were closed. Reaching down the row of hanging garments, I found the smoking jacket and dug down into the arm. The sketch was there. That was a major relief, as I'd half expected it to be missing. With one quick pull I retrieved the tube of paper from its hiding place. Common sense prevailed, and I left the closet door ajar, not wanting to risk worrying the hinges again, and turned to leave the bedroom.

Before I stepped out into the hallway, I realized I should extinguish the candle. Leaning over the dresser, I gave a quiet puff and then stood in utter darkness.

I nearly jumped when I heard her speak. "She has you, Piambo," Samantha said.

I hoped against all odds that she was dreaming, that she had spoken in her sleep, but I wasn't going to stay to find out. Without so much as looking back once, I went directly to my studio. There, I turned on the lights and built a blaze in the fireplace. Then I sat down and unrolled the sketch. I perused every inch of it carefully until it reignited the original vision in my mind, and that part of me that had but an hour or so earlier proved despondent in the physical fray now stirred to attention.

HANDS

B Y THE time I finally pulled myself away from the sketch, the fireplace had gone cold and daylight was trickling in through the skylight above. I returned the sketch to its hiding place and crept back to bed. Later, when Samantha rose, I pretended to be asleep. She left, but I remember that she kissed my cheek before going. Then I did fall asleep and dreamed of my conception of Mrs. Charbuque in a hundred sordid scenes, rendered in paint and hung on the walls of the main gallery of the Academy of Design.

When I woke later in the day, her image followed me out of sleep, and I saw her projected, like one of Edison's moving pictures, upon the day—a miasmatic phantom looking over my shoulder in the shaving mirror, drifting through my parlor, hovering above the crowds on Madison Avenue. I speak neither metaphorically nor literally here, but somewhere between the two. Samantha had never been so right. Mrs. Charbuque had my mind the way the Sun has the Earth and the Earth, the Moon. For my part, haunted as I was, I was certain that my vision of her was correct, and on my journey uptown that afternoon I verily beamed with self-satisfaction.

I even had a kind word for Watkin, complimenting him on his violet suit. It seemed to fluster him more than when I was rude. On our usual jaunt through the house, he actually missed a corner and lightly hit his shoulder on a doorjamb. And then I was in the room, before the screen. I took out my sketchbook, brought the charcoal pencil to bear, and she spoke.

"It is the last day of the second week, Piambo," she said.

"I'm aware of it," I told her. "I've begun your portrait."

"Am I coming together nicely?" she asked.

"I should say. At present I am fleshing out the details of your hands. Hands are important to a portrait; in their intrinsic physical character and their placement within the picture, they are second only to the face. A person holds the story of her life in her hands."

"You know I can't describe my hands to you," she said.

"Of course not. Please just continue with your story from where we left off," I said.

"I will tell you about that time, but allow me to focus on one particular incident as well. It has everything to do with hands."

"Perfect," I said as I drew the half-moon in a thumbnail.

"After paying for my father's funeral and settling all his debts, I had a substantial amount of money left over. Enough, in fact, to allow me to subsist in a moderate fashion for two full years. In that time, my days were like those of Thoreau at Walden Pond or Defoe's shipwrecked Crusoe before him. I remained isolated, seeking out no acquaintances, forming no bond with any other person. Sitting behind my screen, I read libraries of books in those years. As isolated as I was, the world flowed into me and reinforced my belief that I was its hub. The Twins were my only companions, and they whispered to me daily, showing me their prophetic imagery, solidifying our mutual trust.

"My nights, on the other hand, were quite different. When evening began to fall, I would put on a kerchief, pull a wide-brimmed hat down low to hide my looks, and sneak out of the

building to buy my groceries before the markets all closed. I
avoided people's glances as well as I could, but I went forth with
the knowledge that no one knew me. Anonymity is its own form
of invisibility. After securing the few things I needed for my meals
and perusing the bookstalls that remained open, I liked to walk the
streets for a few hours. Very often I would see enacted scenes and
incidents that had been predicted by the Twins. I returned home
to the safety of the screen before it grew so late that the streets became dangerous.

"I was completely content with this life, but after two years had
passed, Father's money began to run low, and I was forced to consider working. I knew all along that I would again return to my
role as the Sibyl. There was something about the performances
that validated my sense of omniscience. I put an ad in the newspaper and interviewed applicants for the job of manager. The act
needed a second, someone who could deal with the audience so I
could remain an enigma. I also required someone to book the
shows, a task that required face-to-face contact with the owners of
the different venues.

"Remember, Piambo, I was no more than fifteen or so at the
time, yet I understood clearly what was required, and proceeded to
arrange the situation. I interviewed quite a few people in my
apartment. Of course, I remained behind the screen while I spoke
to them. It had not been so many years since the Sibyl was the talk
of the town, and many of these applicants knew full well that
procuring the position could eventually make them wealthy.

"The man I chose for the job was a gentleman who had worked
for some years for P. T. Barnum and before that had a history in
vaudeville. His name was Carwin Chute, and he had all the attributes I was looking for—a sense of the melodramatic, a keen
mind for organization, a willingness to perform his duties without
ever actually seeing his employer. It was his idea to insert pure
white theatrical prosthetics in his eyes and pretend to be blind. I
had told him of my aversion to being seen and to the sight of eyes

in general, so he thought that if I chanced to see him, the illusion that he was sightless would be a comfort to me. Also, in relation to the act, he had said, 'Think how appropriate, Luciere. A man who cannot see, bringing to the public a seer who cannot be viewed.' I knew my father would have loved the juxtaposition. It was, like the monkey arm, another red herring."

"Chute, then, is Watkin," I said.

"Of course," said Mrs. Charbuque. "I have paid him very well through the years, but no matter how he has benefited monetarily, I owe him much more for his dedication to service. The man has proved a godsend. I will tell you honestly that what motivates him, and his personality, are as mysterious to me as I must be to him. He has never laid eyes on me, yet he remains ever devoted."

"I will have to reassess my estimation of Watkin," I said.

"He booked us for the highest amount being paid in hotels, theaters, meeting halls, and at private parties given by the wealthy. Once again the Sibyl was voicing her visions to the populace and receiving praise and adulation. By the end of the first year, I was wealthy. And beyond mere money, I was able to influence the powerful, to coax from them whatever favors I needed. From that, Piambo, comes a wealth that exceeds any to be made by laboring for an hourly wage, no matter how grand.

"After two years of working the city, Watkin—as I had begun to call him, for by then Chute had completely dissolved and re-formed as the blind person you now know—came to me and suggested that in order not to saturate the public's desire for the Sibyl, we should take our performance on the road. I thought it was a wise move. We traveled anonymously by train, each of us at different times so that he would not know me. He would go ahead and set up a room for me in a particular city or town, and I would arrive later, either under cover of night or in some disguise. Remaining hidden from view was a chore, but my desire to do so was so great that I managed the ingenuity necessary to make it happen. St. Louis, Chicago, San Francisco—the Sibyl took all these cities by storm, and in the small towns of the prairie and the South, I believe I came to be revered in a manner bordering upon the religious. We never stayed too long in any given place, just long enough to satisfy the citizens' appetite for the future, and then we moved on.

"It was somewhere in the Midwest—Missouri, Oklahoma, they all seemed the same to me; the people all asked the same questions, reacted in the same manner to my pronouncements—that I discovered I had become a woman. I had recently turned seventeen, and when I caught sight of myself in a mirror one day, a practice I tried to avoid, for the sight of my own eyes disturbed me as much as anyone else's, it was evident that my body had changed drastically from that of the lonely little girl who had spent her winters in the Catskill Mountains. The reality of it struck me all at once, more deeply than even the actuality of menstruation had two years earlier. Please excuse the candor of my language, Piambo."

"I am not easily offended," I said, but the charcoal left the paper with her declaration.

"The Twins began to show me imagery of a very graphic nature, so to speak. My reading had included romances as well as smutty dime novels, and all of this had been digested by my mind without my conscious acknowledgment. Now it all seemed to fall into place. I wanted to remain behind the barrier of the screen, but at the same time my body longed to explore the physicality of the world at large. Do you understand?"

"Sexuality?" I ventured, and felt a certain heat rising beneath my collar and elsewhere.

"I'm so pleased I can speak openly to you," she said. "At night, in my bed, after the shows, I would fantasize about the male voices from the audience that would offer a word or two of thanks after one of my predictions. From those few meager words, whole men sprang to life in my imagination. They were every bit as vivid as the images sent me by the voices of the Twins. Their hands, Piambo, became mine. Their fingers groped in the dark like those of the blind, and what thrilling discoveries were made."

I heard Mrs. Charbuque move in her chair behind the screen. Then came the rustling of material, and if I was not mistaken, the rhythm of her breathing changed from its usual measured pace to an almost inaudible panting.

SHOUTS AND MURMURS

LONG SECONDS passed in silence. There was then a soft sigh, and Mrs. Charbuque began speaking again in a dreamy voice, the emphasis of certain words falling in the wrong places, unforeseen pauses, more panting.

Good Lord, I thought, should I leave? But she continued with her story despite all this breathy interference.

"One night in one of those wretched towns, I was giving the first performance of our engagement, which was to last for a week. I thrust out the monkey arm and retrieved a green leaf on which was written the question 'Will she return?' I forget what my response was, but when I had given it, the gentleman who had obviously written the question said, 'Thank you so much, Madam Sibyl, you have forestalled my heart from breaking.' I was struck by the earnest tone of this man's voice, his ability to speak candidly about a private matter before a packed audience. I continued with the show but remembered his words later and built a grand scenario that evening concerning lost love and a passionate reunion. I can still see . . ." Her voice trailed off into heavy exhalations.

"Please go on," I said, leaning forward in my chair.

"The next night the same man asked the same question of me again. I conjured for him a reply that had more to do with my imagined scenario than with the imagery whispered to me by the Twins. He, in turn, said something equally enchanting, as on the first night, and this fired even more my interest in him. What came of it was that I decided I had to see him. I could easily have asked Watkin for a description but felt my infatuation with this stranger was somehow illicit, and so instead devised another way.

"Excuse me for a moment," she said, and I heard her chair begin to squeal slightly as if she were rocking back and forth in it. "For the third night's show I dressed in black and carried a black shawl. I also took a hat pin with me onstage. Before the event got under way, while the audience was taking their seats, the lights were usually very low . . ."

There came a noise something like wet kisses in rapid succession followed by a gasp. If there had been others in the room, I would have been the first to appear scandalized, but knowing we were alone made all the difference.

"That is when I reached forward from my chair and made a pinhole in the screen. This hole would never be detected by someone sitting only a few feet away, but if I leaned forward and put my eye to it, I could view a wide field, taking in a goodly portion of the seats . . . and . . ."

Frustrating seconds passed filled with brief murmurs of delight. When she spoke again, her voice had a slight edge of urgency. I looked over my shoulder and wiped the sweat from my brow. I shooed a disturbing image of the monkey arm from my thoughts.

"I was unusually nervous about the performance, hoping all the time that the fellow with the question 'Will she return?' would return. His was the very last leaf passed to me. I pronounced the imagery of his future just as the Twins had dictated it to me, and then leaned forward to see who would speak. I saw . . . I . . . I saw a handsome young man in the second row with wavy hair and a trim mustache. I hoped it would be he who would speak. As reality would have it, though, it turned out to be a gentleman five seats away, somewhat older than myself, who stood up. Impeccably dressed in a tweed suit, he had sandy-colored hair and a ruddy complexion and wore small glasses with circular lenses. He spoke, and ohh . . ."

"Oh?" I said.

"Ohhh . . ."

"Yes?"

"I knew what he looked like. As soon as the show was over, I left the theater before the patrons and went outside into the street. There, I ducked down an alley, wrapped the shawl around my head, and waited for him to pass by. He finally came walking past, and giving him plenty of distance, I began to follow him. The walk was brief. He entered a small shop a few blocks away. After he had gone in and locked the door behind him, I passed by it in order to mark the spot clearly. It was, of all places, a tiny museum of some kind. The . . . Museum . . . of Phoenician Antiquities, read the sign . . . above . . ."

An unladylike grunt rose from behind the screen. Then it sounded as if she were beginning to weep until that crying quickly transformed itself back into her story. Her words now came forth with desperately increasing speed and volume. "The next day . . . yes . . . I went there dressed in normal attire. Made believe I was visiting from another nearby town. Staying only a few days. Interested in the contents of the museum. Involved in a conversation. Told me he was . . . yes . . . an amateur archaeologist. He'd been to Carthage on a dig and had . . . oh . . . these treasures. A golden mask . . . a small, armless statue of a young woman with half its face broken off . . . stones with ancient writing . . . a silver lamp with a long spout . . ."

She hit a crescendo, and I got to my feet. I swear, she let loose a groan that sounded to me as if she were expiring on the spot. The panels of the screen rattled. She spoke no more for a time, but her breathing was rapid and pronounced.

"Are you ill, Mrs. Charbuque?" I asked, fanning myself with the sketchbook.

Her answer did not come immediately, but eventually, after catching her breath, she said, "I've rarely felt better." I heard her again shift her position in her chair and then the faint sound of material being maneuvered about. "Now where was I?" Her voice had returned to its normal tone.

"A lamp," I said, returning to the chair.

"Oh, yes. He was a charming fellow, very serious. While he spoke, he used his hands a good deal, especially to indicate a motion, like a boat sailing on the vast ocean, when explaining how the Phoenicians were the masters of the sea in the ancient world. He believed they had circumnavigated the entire globe. I listened with feigned interest to how they warred with Rome and eventually lost the city of Carthage. The Romans destroyed everything, killed all the men, carried off the women, and sowed salt into the earth so crops would not grow there. I was somewhat bored with his lecturing, his rattling off of dates, but I liked to watch his hands in motion. They were like pale leaves falling and rising in an autumn wind.

"I was amazed that I was not more frightened at having left the safety of the screen, that I willingly let his eyes gaze upon me. I was in a kind of trance, as if I were outside of myself watching me play the part of this shrewd young woman. In any event, he made me a cup of tea and told me he did not have many visitors to the museum. 'The people in this town know nothing, nor do they care about the ancients,' he told me. 'They think of me as some kind of fool, but I have more money than any of them. And although I have no official degrees, I am highly thought of in my field. I'll have you know that I was asked to contribute to the research of Francis Borne.'

"That evening he again attended my performance. The next day I again returned to his museum, and he confided to me that his fiancée, whom he hoped to marry upon his triumphant return from northern Africa, had run away to New York City. I comforted him with words, and with this coddling he appeared to take a real interest in me. As I made ready to leave his place that second day, he fleetingly placed his hand upon my shoulder when I said good-bye. He asked if I would be returning, and I told him I would have to see what the future brought. His touch was the first I had felt in years, and it roused my passion.

"After that day on which he touched me, he did not return to my performances. I did go to see him, though, each and every afternoon that I remained in town. On the last day, I told him I would be leaving the following morning. He wanted to know my name, which I had not told him, where I was going, where I lived. I told him nothing, save that I would return that night, late, and say good-bye to him. 'Leave the door unlocked and the lamps unlit,' I said. With that declaration, he reached for me, but I backed away, giggling, and left the museum.

"It was midnight, and I sneaked along the empty streets, staying to the shadows, dressed only in a black dress and my shawl. I had forsaken any undergarments for that assignation. My desire was at the boiling point. The chain of my locket was searing hot, and the Twins were sending out a steady stream of imagery, speaking unspeakable scenes to me that made me slightly dizzy. I arrived at the museum and found the door ajar. I entered into the darkness and crept slowly up the main aisle. Near the back of the place I saw one small candle burning. I went toward it, and as I did, I felt his arms close around me. He had been there, waiting, behind a row of shelves.

"His hands were all over me, as if he had a dozen more than two. I felt them on my breasts, my face, my stomach, between my legs, and when he realized I was wearing nothing beneath the thin dress, he whispered, 'Mother of God.' It was then that he forced his lips upon mine, and the Twins, at that exact moment, ended their hours-long discourse of imagery with one clear picture that formed with the force of an explosion and remained in my mind.

It was of my father. With the presence of that image, the trance was broken. I returned to myself and was repulsed by this groping hundred-handed beast. Frantically I tried to escape his clutches, but he forced himself against me yet more ardently. I felt every inch of him pressing on me, felt his inanity infecting me, and thought I would be suffocated.

"My arms flailed out to the sides, and my left hand grazed against something in one of the displays. I lunged in that direction and grasped a heavy metal object in my hand. With all my fear and my revulsion, I struck him in the side of the head with the object. He quietly grunted, his body went limp, and he slid to the floor. I fled the museum and made my way back to the hotel.

"By the time he probably awoke from the blow the next day, I was on a train, traveling swiftly away from that accursed town. Sitting in my lap was the object I had used as a weapon, for I would not relinquish my grasp on it. The lamp was made of silver or tin or pewter, I could not tell, and was covered with the most amazing filigree—looping knots of design. At the end of its long spout was a stopper, capturing whatever sloshed around inside it. I once had a book of fairy tales as a child, and this lamp was much like the one in an illustration from that volume. The lamp in the story held an evil djinn. I resolved never to remove the stopper.

"Do you know what I learned from this incident, Piambo?" she asked.

At this point I had to clear my throat and wet my lips in order to answer. "What would that be, Mrs. Charbuque?" I said.

"It made me think of my mother. I realized that she had every reason to want more from her life than a lunatic husband who cared less about her than about the insubstantial marvel of snow. She wanted the present, not some illusory future. I saw things for the first time from her perspective. I allowed myself to recognize that she deserved the pleasure she sought with the tracker, and that for this small comfort my father had murdered her. Being a cloistered child, I could never have known that she wanted nothing more than a real life and that my father had enlisted me early on to aid him in keeping her a prisoner. From that moment on the train, fleeing my jackass of an archaeologist, I knew that my act was a fraud and that the voices of the Twins, though they continue to plague me to this day, were a delusion."

"Then why," I asked, "do you remain behind the screen?"

"I seek a kind of freedom a woman cannot find in society. When I don my disguise of anonymity and venture forth into your world, I see in a million instances that I am right. In my world, here, as you witnessed today, I can do anything I want. I can satisfy any whim at any moment, from the most basic to the most complex."

She said nothing more that day. Five minutes later, when Watkin appeared, I wished her a pleasant weekend and left the room. "Be careful now, Mr. Piambo," said the old man before closing the door behind me, and his verbal send-off was eerily devoid of cynicism.

A KNOCK UNANSWERED

FOLLOWING MY meeting with Mrs. Charbuque, it took quite a few minutes out in the cold wind for my temperature to fall within its normal range. That day's installment of her story had required, on my part, the consumption of so many inordinately large drafts of the incredible, I was drunk on the stuff and moved through the crowds on the street like one giddy from excess of spirits. In regard to the, shall we say, heated aural sideshow that had gone on during her recounting, it was impossible to tell if she had been merely fulfilling a whim, as she had said, or if her lustful demonstration had been a bit of cunning subterfuge meant to distract me. Perhaps it was, as her father might have put it, a sizable red herring; nothing, of course, on the order of the one that had so urgently crowded my trousers.

I took the streetcar down to Twenty-seventh Street and made a beeline to Broadway, where I entered Kirk's Saloon. The company of gentlemen, the oak paneling, the famous oil paintings on the walls, the whiskey, all served to subdue me and return my system to its mundane homeostasis. Luckily there was no one there that I knew, so I sat by the main window, looking out onto the avenue, and watched the city perform its daily rituals. I lit a cigarette and tried to rationalize all that I had been told. As I reviewed Mrs. Charbuque's story, small disconcerting contradictions erupted and blew me off course. For instance, the mere idea of Carthaginian remains in a small street-front museum out in the wilds of the Midwest was difficult to believe. But could she have manufactured that detail on the spot?

She had dropped a mention of Francis Borne and her archaeologist's donation to the excremental oracle. That was a turn of the screw that had momentarily spun me once and passed by in a flash as we rushed headlong toward her satisfaction. Watkin was actually a fellow by the name of Carwin Chute, who had readily accepted as his life's work a rather shoddy portrayal of a heinous affliction. The Sibyl, prophesying below the Mason-Dixon line, had gained a kind of religious status. The sudden ascendancy of her mother and the corresponding fall from grace of her father. All of these bread crumbs she had dropped along the path were compressed sagas in which a traveler could lose himself for days.

By my third whiskey, I realized that, unlike the Phoenicians, I would not be circumnavigating Mrs. Charbuque's experiences. With my fourth, I was content to drift aimlessly in the placid Sea of Confusion. It was there, becalmed by my inability to undo the Gordian knot of her confession, that I came to the conclusion that it didn't matter, for clearly shining in my mind was my vision of her, at night, behind the screen. My conception of her had come through the tempest unscathed. I paid my bill and headed home to paint.

After a lengthy nap, I rose around eight o'clock, retrieved the sketch from its hiding place in the closet, and went directly to my studio. I did not sit down and stare at the drawing as I had the previous night, knowing that it would again enchant me. Instead I prepared my palette, chose my brushes, and set to applying a dark base to the canvas. I wanted the foundation of the piece to contain the colors of night—purple, blue, gray, and green—a kind of iridescent, blended indigo, darker than black in its mood and more alive with swirling mystery than the flat absolute. With oils one works from dark to light—a fitting metaphor, I hoped, for my pursuit of Mrs. Charbuque.

Once the ground had dried somewhat, I roughed out the basic form of the nude figure in chromium green, which would eventually be a counterpoint to the flesh tones applied later. Another painter might sketch the subject in charcoal, or in this case, since the ground was so very dark, chalk, but I preferred to work only with the brush. I then set to delineating the structure of the face with titanium white. Using a dry-brush technique that allowed me to create halftones, I indicated the lines, prominences, and hollows that formed her unique expression. Once her fundamental visage had been rendered, I layered white on certain areas to add depth and more completely depict shape. Then I had to let the canvas dry more thoroughly and so ceased work for the night.

It was after three o'clock, and I should have gone off to bed, but my entire system was abuzz with the electricity that attends the act of creation. There is nothing better for one's health than that surge of energy, for it is the unmitigated essence of life. I knew better than to battle against it. Instead I sat before the easel with a cigarette and a drink and contemplated the physical attitude of the pose I had chosen.

It had come to me from out of the blue to portray her from the knees upward, her shins and calves disappearing into the shadows. She was ever so slightly bent at the waist, the right arm thrust out in front of her and the left held so that her hand on that side was at shoulder level. Her breasts did not lie flat against her chest but hung forward at a minor angle. The head was turned a bit to the side, cocked in a manner not quite as pronounced as Watkin's rendition of the blind, listening, chin thrust slightly upward. She would peer from the painting with a sidelong glance and smile, not mischievously, but like a child who has successfully lacquered a snowflake for her father.

Eventually I staggered to bed and slept for a few hours. It was still early, but I was drawn from sleep by my desire to work on the portrait. I would have forsaken breakfast and begun immediately, but the piece still needed more drying time, so I went out to Crenshaw's and ate. There, while I dined on hash and eggs, I read in the paper about the failing economy, Cleveland's stance against "free silver," which led to his resultant ill health in the polls, and about a group called the Anti-Saloon League, who, God save us, wanted a prohibition placed upon alcohol. I could see that, since coming under the influence of Mrs. Charbuque, it was as if I had slipped behind a screen of my own that separated my consciousness from the doings of the world at large. I loitered, drinking too many cups of coffee and chatting with Mrs. Crenshaw. Two hours had passed before I finally paid my bill and returned home.

I probably should have waited a few more hours to begin work, but I was anxious to lose myself again in the timeless trance that envelops me when I am painting. Back in the studio, I reconnoitered my plan of attack. I smiled at the prospect of spending the entire day with Mrs. Charbuque's flesh, for that was, with the exception of hair and eyes and the surrounding night, the totality of the portrait. I do not brag when I say that I was a master at depicting material, its folds and myriad creases, the texture of velvet, the smooth sheen of silk. People often commented to me first about the clothing my subjects wore, only later mentioning the expression on the face or the overall likeness to the original. Now, though, there was something liberating about discarding the clothes and embracing the naked form. I had painted a thousand nudes, but none like this, and the prospect titillated me in a profoundly sensual manner.

Where else to begin but with the eyes? Burnt sienna, of course, to form the outer ring of the iris, but when it came to their actual color, I had to stop for a moment and think about what I had envisioned. At that juncture I heard someone knocking upon my front door. I knew it must be Samantha, but how could I let her in just then? I went to the parlor and peered out from behind the drapes of the window. From my hiding place I could see her on the front steps, dressed in her long winter coat and wearing a woolen hat. Her appearance annoyed me. "She most likely wants me to go somewhere with her," I thought. Then there would be all the necessary explanations once she saw my progress on the portrait. She knocked again, and when I did not answer, her expression turned, with a nearly imperceptible movement of her brow and lips, from her usual one of good cheer to one of subtle sorrow. She obviously knew that I knew she was there. I had never locked her out before. Eventually she turned and slowly walked away down the street. Just before she moved out of my line of sight, she shot a glance over her shoulder, and I saw a look of betrayal in her eyes. I felt it in my heart but made no move for the door.

It made little sense, but I used Samantha's eyes, that woeful glance, to stand in for Mrs. Charbuque's, copying the color, the subdued gleam, and capturing in the aperture of the lids that look of loss. With this small part of the portrait complete, the project took on a reality that drove me forward with increasing confidence. It was as if my painted subject were watching me in the process of creating her. At times when a grain of uncertainty would halt the gear work of my imagination, I would look to those eyes for either approval or a hint toward a new direction.

As I have said, I wanted the flesh to glow, and though I knew that much of this effect would be gained through the various glazes and varnishes I would apply during the process of rendering the figure and after its completion, it was necessary for me to make the skin lighter in tone than usual. Toward this end I mixed the usual portions of cadmium yellow pale and cadmium red but a greater than normal amount of titanium white with just a dab of Windsor blue as a concession to the night and the moon.

Time must have passed, though I never felt its presence at all. When I finally stepped away from the work on Mrs. Charbuque,

I realized that night had fallen and that at some point, though for the life of me I could not recall it, I had switched on the lights and built a fire. As was my custom, I poured a drink and lit a cigarette and sat down before the easel to view my work. There was much to finish, but there was also no mistaking the personality and looks of the figure that stood before me on the canvas. I was pleased to see that the effect of her coming out of the night like a dream was working so far, and could foretell how the varnishes would enhance it. This was the finest portrait, if not the finest painting, I had ever done.

Again I let the excitement dissipate from my bloodstream at its own pace before retiring. Once in bed, I fell directly asleep. My last thought, though, was not of the portrait but of Samantha walking away.

SHENZ OF THE POPPIES

I WAS AWAKENED by the creak of a floorboard and opened my eyes to the dark. Leaning up on my elbow, I listened intently, trying to remember if the noise had been part of a dream. It did not come again, but as my pulse settled I became aware of another, quieter sound emanating from the hallway outside my room. At the same instant that my eyes adjusted somewhat to the murky night, I recognized what it was I heard—the sound of someone breathing. A silhouette of a figure stood in the doorway. I could make out no distinguishing features of my visitor.

"Samantha?" I said.

There was no response, and my heart began to pound.

"Who's there?" I said. I grasped the cover to throw it back.

"Stay where you are," he said.

I recognized the voice from the theater box. "Charbuque," I said. "What do you want?" My hands began to tremble, and the rest of my body went weak with fear.

"I have a pistol aimed at you," he said. "It would be a splendid idea for you to remain where you are."

"Have you come to kill me?" I asked, expecting at any moment to hear the report of the gun.

"Not yet," he said. "Perhaps sometime soon. I'm here to tell you that your painting is all wrong."

"You've seen it?" I asked.

"Rather licentious, Mr. Piambo."

"A classical pose," I said.

"My ass," he said. "In any event, the woman you have depicted is not my wife."

"You've seen her?" I asked.

"I'm her husband, you fool."

I couldn't help myself. "Where have I gone wrong?" I said.

"The question is, Where have you gone right? I've taken the liberty of adding a few strokes of my own to it. And the sketch—you'll find it in ashes in the fireplace. I will give you a hint," he said. At that moment he moved, and I was able to peer through the darkness and make out the vaguest detail of the gun in his hand.

"What can you tell me?" I feared my impertinence might anger him, but I was willing to risk it for just one clue.

"My wife is stunningly beautiful," he said. There was a long pause. "And the most manipulative bitch this side of the Pillars of Hercules."

"Yes?" I said, expecting at least one precise physical characteristic to follow.

I waited for his response until I realized he was gone. As this fact dawned on me, I heard the front door in my parlor open and close. I rolled out of bed and dashed down the hall. As I reached that room, I could hear the diminishing sound of boot soles on the sidewalk outside.

He had left the light on in the studio. I went in and sat before the easel. The painting was completely mutilated, the canvas punctured and sliced. Shreds of canvas hung down showing their white backs. Scraps of it littered the floor. I tried to reflect upon the anger that had fueled his attack, but instead broke down and cried. There is no other way to put it but that I wept like a child. What was worse was that the image I had carried so clearly in my mind for the past few days had also suffered irreparably. When I looked within my memory to find it, I saw the dark room, but instead of Mrs. Charbuque, I discovered that her figure had fragmented into a whirling gyre of snow.

Here was utter defeat. I had but two weeks remaining to as-semble another image and complete the portrait. The task, at that moment, seemed impossible. Charbuque had spared my life but slaughtered my confidence, my hope, my will to continue. I was no better off than when I had begun. In fact, I was a damn sight worse off. My nerves were frayed, Samantha was gravely disap-pointed in me, and I doubted whether I was worthy to reach be-yond my present station and further develop my art. Hours passed, and I sat rigidly still, staring at the tattered remains of my dream.

The sun had been up only briefly, the rays that fell through the skylight having just turned from red to gold, when I heard a knocking at my door. I got to my feet and staggered through the house to the parlor. Upon opening the door, I found Shenz stand-ing on my front steps.

"You look haggard," he said.

"I'm finished," I said.

He broke into a smile. "You've completed the portrait?"

"Come," I said, and led him to the studio. "There it is," I said.

"Were you painting with a razor?" he asked.

I told him all that had happened, about my work and the visit from Charbuque. When I had finished, he shook his head and sat in the chair I had recently vacated. To his credit, I could see that he clearly shared my grief, for he looked as distressed as I felt.

"This romp is over," I said.

He took out one of his cigarettes and lit it. The strange, sweet smell of the opium soon wafted around us.

"Grim," he said, and handed me the cigarette.

I hesitated for a moment and then took it. It was the first taste of the drug I had ever had. We passed it back and forth two or three times, and then he held on to it and smoked it down to a nub.

"How did it look before Charbuque carved it up?" he asked.

I glanced down at him from where I stood. He had removed his hat and rested it on his lap. Something about the way he looked struck me. The sun was shining, golden, upon him, and with his graying beard, thinning hair, and the distinctive lines in his face, he appeared for all the world like some biblical prophet as depicted by Caravaggio.

"You look like a saint just now, sitting there," I said.

"Saint Shenz of the poppies," he said. With this he rose, stepped forward, and pushed the easel backward onto the floor. It landed with a crash, lifting a minor dust cloud. For some reason this struck me as comical, and he and I both laughed.

"Roll your cart over the bones of the dead, Piambo," he said.

"What?" I asked.

"In other words, onward!" he said. "Pull yourself together. Perhaps Charbuque has done you a favor."

"Why would he do that? From the way he has talked during our brief encounters, he thinks he will probably have to kill me sometime in the near future."

"Then you'd better get moving. You have a painting to do. I've come today, at the perfect moment it seems, to take you to see the Man from the Equator. In him, I guarantee you, you will find help."

"We're going somewhere?" I asked.

"How do you feel?" he asked.

"Light," I said. "My head is filled with light, and everything appears somehow clearer than usual."

"You may see and hear some odd things," he told me. "The effects will only last for an hour or two. Then you will want to sleep. So hurry. Get out of your nightshirt, get dressed, and put on your coat and hat."

At the same time that I knew Shenz was cajoling me, I still felt a certain sense of excitement about the prospect of our journey. Why? I couldn't begin to tell you. For all this newfound verve, though, I seemed to be moving twice as slowly as usual.

Out on the street, as we walked over to Broadway to find a hansom cab, the world appeared unusually liquid, the outlines of the buildings blurring and mixing with the sky. At one point I thought I saw Mr. Wolfe, dressed in his female disguise, coming toward us on the sidewalk.

"Shenz, there's Wolfe," I said, and pointed.

"Look again," said Shenz. "That's a police officer."

In actuality, when the figure passed us, I could see we were both wrong. It was a handsome young woman dressed in a blue coat and hat. Shenz and I exchanged glances and laughed.

"Well," said Shenz, "at least I knew it couldn't be Wolfe. Didn't you read in the newspaper the other day that he was shot dead by the husband of that woman he went to meet in the Village after our caper?"

"No," I said. "Poor Wolfe. I rather liked him."

"The husband discovered his wife's high jinks and, shall we say, persuaded her to draw the locksmith into a trap. There is a rumor in the Kitchen that his body was interred sans that remarkable hand of keys and that there are those now seeking a taxidermist to preserve it."

"How poetic, in a way. He will continue to gain entry to secret places even while his spirit cavorts above in heaven."

"Or below," said Shenz as we reached Broadway. He raised his hand to signal to a passing driver, and we had our ride. The address he gave was somewhere in Greenwich Village.

"Shenz," I said as we headed downtown, "I am, as I speak, seeing the city alternately as it usually is and then in ruins, as if it were the remains of an ancient kingdom."

My friend laughed. "You see all manner of bizarre curiosities when under the influence of the poppy. None of it is real, though much of it is interesting. For instance, as we passed Nineteenth Street, I thought I saw a woman standing on the corner, weeping blood."

I was about to slide off my seat and put my head out the window to look back up the avenue, but I caught myself, remembering that I had not divulged my knowledge of this disease to Shenz out of consideration for John Sills. My concern lasted only a moment until I noticed a blue djinn issuing from the exhaust pipe of a motorcar.

THE MAN FROM
THE EQUATOR

W E STOPPED in front of a small shop on Twelfth Street. Above the entrance was a sign on which the letters making up The Man from the Equator had not been painted but instead appeared to have been gouged with a chisel. A wooden figure stood out in front, but it was not an Indian, which is often seen standing guard at the entrance to a tobacconist's shop. This statue was of a very thin man or woman, I couldn't tell which, draped in a robe. The head, with high cheekbones and a pointed chin, faced forward, eyes closed in an expression of ecstasy. Ringlets of hair hung to the shoulders. In each of the hands, held palm up, there sat a miniature replica of the world. I was intrigued by the piece, for it was very deftly carved.

"Nice work," I said to Shenz, nodding at the statue.

"Yes," he said. "I believe it is Eastern in origin."

We entered the shop's dim front room, its floors made from wide, coarse beams. The first thing I noticed was the various scents that filled the air, combining to create a thick, spicy perfume. Inverted bunches of dried flowers and weeds, pale twisted roots, and sprays of brittle fern hung from the low ceiling. There were rows of shelves holding variously shaped bottles. These contained a panoply of different-colored concoctions—some black as tar, some like liquid chocolate, others of beautiful clear blues, greens, and violets. Some of the shelves were stacked with boxes, labeled with odd titles written in grease pencil—Ox Brain Flakes, Powdered Adder Venom, Queen Hebspa's Footstool, Gallstones/Puma. . . . Hanging everywhere on the walls were hand-drawn maps of countries and territories I did not recognize.

"Come," said Shenz, leading the way into the shadows.

I was about to follow when something flew directly over me. I could feel the sweep of wings, and when I ducked and reached up to cover my head, I knocked my hat off. "What in hell?" I yelled.

Shenz laughed. "That's the blasted owl," he said. "I forgot to warn you. The first time I came here the thing nearly frightened me to death. Don't worry, it's harmless."

I lifted my hat off the floor and put it back on my head, meager protection against another low pass. As we moved toward the back of the place, I spotted the bird perched atop a coatrack. Sitting there with its wings drawn in, it looked for all the world as if it were stuffed, a blunt-shaped creature about two feet high with a rounded head and white face. As we passed it, though, it suddenly twisted its head to watch me with large round eyes that reflected the faint light from the front window.

Leaving the main room of the shop, we passed down a long hallway, lined on both sides by floor-to-ceiling shelves of old books. There was a right-hand turn, another hallway of books, and then we stepped into a room drenched in light. With the exception of a low wall running around the perimeter of the space, the rest of its structure was made of large panes of glass. The minute I passed into this new area, I could feel the warmth. Tables ran along each wall and upon them sat rows of potted plants; more plants were suspended from twine above. In the middle of it all, as if awaiting our arrival, stood a tall, wiry man with close-cropped hair. The first things I noticed about him were the smoothness of his skin and the clarity of his eyes. He exuded a sense of vitality.

"Shenz," he said to my friend, and stepped forward to shake his hand.

"Goren," said Shenz, "meet Piambo, the fellow I told you about."

"The painter," said Goren as his hand clasped mine.

"You are the Man from the Equator," I said.

He nodded.

"From where along the equator do you hail?" I asked.

"Brooklyn," he said.

"I grew up there myself. Some of its parts, I would guess, are as exotic as Madagascar," I said.

"And you would be right," he said, smiling. "Come, we can talk in the shop."

The effects of Shenz's cigarette were still upon me but had settled into a feeling of weary comfort. I thought the optical curiosities I had witnessed during the cab ride had abated, but as we left the sunlit plant room, I turned to glance out-of-doors, and just then, framed by a long pane of glass, I saw a configuration of brown leaves falling that was the precise image on Mrs. Charbuque's screen. With my sudden recognition of the design, the leaves froze in midfall for a good two seconds before continuing to the ground. I shook my head and followed Goren and Shenz back into the dim cave of homeopathy.

Goren sat behind a low table in the rear corner of the shop. Two chairs were positioned nearby, indicating that people occasionally stopped in to chat. Shenz and I sat down, and when we were all three settled, the owl flew in and perched atop a large globe that rested upon a columnar stand.

The Man from the Equator began by giving me a brief résumé of his accomplishments. I suppose this was to persuade me that his words had merit. In short, he was a doctor trained at the University of Pennsylvania. He had, from youth, been a loner who liked to wander. Once he had become a physician, he could not settle down but decided to travel the world. He moved off the beaten path, to wild and remote corners of the globe, and in these places witnessed the medical practices of shamans and witch doctors who rendered remarkable cures. When he returned to civilization, he brought back with him the cures he had collected, and set about a course of locating and studying ancient texts in order to cull more. He interspersed all this information with snippets of hermetic and transcendental philosophy that I could not follow and at which it appeared even the owl was rolling its eyes.

"And so," Goren finally concluded, "for some reason our mutual friend, Shenz here, thinks that I can offer you a way of thinking about this commission of yours that will enable you to be ultimately successful."

"Can you?" I asked.

"Let me begin by saying that the entire pursuit strikes me as being wonderfully absurd. I have found in the past that it is often extremely worthwhile to contemplate the seemingly impossible. There is much to be gained by it. One is presented with a brick wall, and the first thing one thinks is, 'How am I going to get around this brick wall?' Instead, you must change your thinking. Meditate upon the existence of the brick wall. Study the brick wall past the point of frustration, until it becomes fascinating. In short, become the brick wall."

"At this point, I am at least as immobile in the face of this problem as a brick wall might be," I said.

"He's always been as thick as a brick wall," Shenz added.

Goren did not smile. "Do you see this image behind me?" he said, pointing to a page ripped from a book and affixed to the wall with a nail. It was a circle, containing equal parts of white and black. They were not divided down the middle but swirled around each other while remaining distinct. In the largest dollop of each lay a small circle filled with the color of its opposite.

"Yin and yang," said Goren. "Do you know what they mean?"

I shook my head.

"Ancient Chinese symbols meant to describe the sun and

moon—the fundamental concepts of the universe—but also having implications for the nature of the human drama. The white and the black are the opposing forces that make up the universe. They are constantly moving, changing, affecting each other. This action is the heart of existence. Light and dark, good and evil, yes and no, male and female, hardness and softness, intelligence and ignorance, you see?"

"Twins of a type," said Shenz, "yet opposites."

"When they are balanced, there is health, there is understanding, there is the potential for creativity. Hence one desires always to reside at the equator. When that balance is disturbed, there is illness and chaos," said Goren.

"My yin and yang are out of balance," I said.

"Now notice this," said Goren, tracing the boundary that contained the yin and yang. "Think of it as an atom, the smallest particle of matter. Each atom contains the full nature of the universe, just as each individual, like a god, contains within his mind the entirety of the universe. Think of the insignificant size of your brain in relation to the immensity of the ocean, yet your mind can encompass the vastness of that entity in a single thought, with room left over for the Parthenon, the entire layout of New York City, the pyramids, and more. To quote Emily Dickinson, 'A brain is wider than the sky.' This concept goes as far back as the earliest recorded human thought. It can be traced from the *Rig Veda* to the *Tao Te Ching* to the teachings of Buddha to Pythagoras to Plato to Averroe to Giordano Bruno to Emerson and my personal friend Walt Whitman."

Here the owl had had enough and rose into the air.

"Do you see what I am telling you?" he said.

"No," I whispered, feeling as if I were back in school and forced to decipher outlandish numbers.

"You, Piambo, contain all the knowledge of the universe, as do both Shenz and I. The portrait of Mrs. Charbuque already exists within you. You must merely discover it. Think about when you have painted a picture for yourself and not a commission. Did you place each brush stroke as if you were laying the bricks for that wall we spoke of earlier? Or was each application of your brush uncovering something that was already in existence in your soul? Wasn't it Michelangelo who spoke of *releasing* the figures from stone? He chose his blocks of marble for the human forms he knew they already contained."

"This, I have experienced," I said. "But how do I uncover Mrs. Charbuque? You don't know her. She is quite an elusive woman."

"The normal course would be five years of exile, isolation, and intensive daily meditation along with a diet of green vegetables, figs, and a liquor made from the pulp of the quince."

"There you go," said Shenz.

"I've got two weeks," I said.

"I am aware of this. So we will need something to catalyze the process. Therefore I have prepared this elixir for you." Goren reached beneath the table, out of sight, and brought forth a large round bottle with a cut glass stopper. It was filled with some sluggish yellow crud. "Ten dollars," he said.

AWAKENING

IN THE cab on the way home, with my eyelids nearly closed, I held fast to my bottle of yellow goo. Goren had told me that this tonic had been used in the realm of Prester John to inspire court-appointed artists to realize the cosmic in their work. He had found the list of ingredients and recipe in a facsimile of a volume said to have been brought back from Asia by Sir John Mandeville and more recently translated by a professor at Oxford. The translated name of the ancient brew was Awakening.

Shenz, who sat across from me, could have used some awakening, for he had nearly passed out. My mind was now unbefuddled enough to realize that my friend had saved me from a dangerous depression resulting from the ruined portrait. For this I was much in his debt. Although his drug was a boon in that it diverted my anguish, I was amazed that he had the vitality to take it daily and yet withstand its ravages. That day's one fling with the poppy was enough to make me wish to avoid it for the rest of my life.

I was on the verge of sleep, and my mind had moved on to a consideration of yin and yang. Picturing them enclosed in Mrs. Charbuque's locket, I saw their black-and-white forms swirling round like two fish chasing each other's tails. Just as my eyes closed completely, Shenz awoke and leaned forward.

"Piambo," he said.

I opened my eyes.

"I didn't tell you, I found some information about that ship, the *Janus*. A couple of old seamen down at the harbor knew of it. About fifteen years ago it left London on a return voyage to New York. It never arrived at its destination, and its true fate was never completely established. In other words, it completely disappeared. The theory is that it went down in a hurricane in the mid-Atlantic. The story was in all the newspapers, and when they mentioned the details to me I seemed vaguely to remember it. One of the old salts told me that from time to time there is a report of it being sighted and then vanishing from view, like a mirage. His partner, though, laughed and said that was all malarkey concocted by bored sailors to frighten women and children and keep one another amused."

"Funny, I don't have any recollection of it," I said.

"The two gentlemen I spoke to were most helpful because they directed me to an official building nearby where a registry of all ships was kept. There, I was allowed to go through the papers concerning the *Janus*. The passenger roster for its last voyage listed no Charbuque."

"Interesting," I said. "Mrs. Charbuque seems to be dealing in a little malarkey herself."

We rode on in silence until we arrived at my house. Before leaving the cab I asked Shenz to remind me what dosage of Goren's elixir I was to take.

"I forget what he said. Take a few snorts every day. If some is good, more is better. But if I were you, I would seriously consider what he told you about Mrs. Charbuque already existing in your mind."

"I thought I had found her," I said.

"Think of that attempt as nothing more than a severed monkey arm. You are getting close, I'm sure of it," he said, and then was off.

I was exceedingly weary, but not wanting to awaken later to the mess in the studio, I spent some time cleaning it. After disposing of the murdered canvas and setting my painting things to rights, I decided to take a dose of my medicine. Half of me considered it a farce, and the other desperately hoped that it would fulfill its promise. When I removed the stopper, a sulfurous aroma wafted from the bottle like an evil djinn. I held my breath and downed a goodly portion of it. After a moment I became conscious of the taste, like a sugary syrup made from rotten eggs, and gagged twice. My eyes watered as the saliva retreated to the corners of my mouth. There was a brief period during which I thought my stomach was going to reject it, and then things settled down.

Going to my bedroom, I removed my shoes and prepared to disrobe when I felt something shift violently in my bowels. I tell you, *Awakening* was not the word for it. *Rude Awakening* might have been more apt. I literally sprinted for the outhouse and proceeded to spend a solid hour there. There is no telling what passed for *cosmic* in the realm of Prester John, but the effects of Goren's elixir seemed, at best, a circuitous route to its discovery.

After my ordeal, I did then go to bed and slept soundly. At some point during the night, I roused very briefly to the dark and again had a sense that someone was with me in the room. My fatigue was so great, though, that I could not muster the appropriate fear and fell immediately back into a dream of walking through a snow-covered wood at daybreak. In Goren's favor, I have to confess that when I woke on Monday morning, I felt completely refreshed and more at ease than I had since beginning the commission. With this said, I still took the bottle of Awakening to the outhouse and dropped the whole thing down into that place where it was in any case ultimately destined to rest.

Later that afternoon I sat before the screen. At this meeting I had a definite mission and did not bother with the sketchbook.

"I saw your friend Samantha Rying on the street yesterday, Piambo," said Mrs. Charbuque. "She looked somewhat forlorn."

I ignored her comment. "Tell me now about your husband," I said.

"Moret Charbuque," she said. "Yes, the love of my life."

"Do I detect a note of sarcasm?" I asked.

"An entire symphony might be more to the point," she said.

"He was untrue?" I asked.

"Yes, but not in any mundane sense. Charbuque was complex if he was anything. We were, for a time, desperately in love. Actually, we remained desperately in love, but our love became something dangerous. If anyone were to see it, they would immediately describe it as hatred, but it wasn't. I'm sure of that."

"From the beginning, please," I said.

"The beginning may be hard to trace, for this type of affair always starts long before the participants become aware of each other, but I will tell you how we met."

"Very well," I said.

"After having crossed the country and returned to New York yet more wealthy and famous, Watkin and I spent quite a number of years performing in the city. During this time I was approached now and then by any number of gentlemen who let it be known that, no matter what my appearance or strange gifts, they would be inclined to enter into matrimony with me. Most of them I dismissed without granting a private audience. When I say private, I merely mean away from the crowd of an audience, mind you, not free of the screen. Occasionally I would get one of my urges, as we have discussed, and I would have Watkin show a fellow to my room, where I would engage him in conversation. To a man, they all failed my review. I was not about to enter into a relationship with a fool, as my mother had done. Of this, I was particularly wary.

"Be that as it may, when enough time had passed that Watkin and I thought the act was again about to reach its limit of interest in the city, we began to cast about for places that might offer new patrons and new revenue. All the time, we were making lavish amounts of money and our venues were growing in size. Since I lived a very contained life, I had only minor expenditures. I put some of my earnings away, and the rest I invested in burgeoning industries. Like Ossiak in his prime, I could not perpetrate a failure if I tried. Eventually Watkin came to me and suggested we head to Europe. 'Madam,' he said, 'your abilities of conquest can only be done justice by a fresh continent.'

"And so we went. Madrid-Rome-Munich-Paris-London was to be our itinerary. We began with those cities that were not English-speaking. It was our plan to end with the easiest, London, because we knew we would be exhausted by that point in the tour. We hired translators, who stood in front of the audience along with Watkin and let my words be known in the local tongue. America has not cornered the market on enjoying being hoodwinked. Although I denied the authenticity of the Twins' whispered prophetic imagery, believing that it was merely my own mind playing tricks on itself, the snowflakes did not fail me even once. The phenomenon continued as it always had with great ease, no matter what the surroundings, no matter how fatigued I was by travel."

"If you had not experienced their illusory messages, would you have continued?" I asked.

"It would have been impossible," she said. "When you have a quiet moment, try to conjure up a list of random images that hint at portending the future. Perhaps you could do it once, or maybe even twice. I doubt it. But to do it again and again, night after night, without repeating yourself, now that would be something. I had enough money. If I were forced to consciously formulate driveling strings of mind-pictures, I would have immediately retired."

"And you were popular in Europe, I take it?"

"The Spanish viewed me mainly as an oracle of romance. The

Italians couldn't have made my job easier, wanting first and foremost to learn about the fate of their relatives in the afterlife. The French saw the entire thing as a brilliant, complex entertainment with metaphorical significance for life itself. I rather think the Germans were frightened of me and therefore were the most adoring. Was I popular? Look around you, Piambo. This house and my estate on Long Island were both built on the gullibility of Europe. Had I the mind to go to China, I would most likely now be an empress presiding over my own province."

I laughed, but she did not. "What of London, though? You did not mention the British," I said.

"London, the city we thought would be our simplest engagement, early on threatened to be colder than the mutton they served. The British are not easily frightened or amused. I thought, from the initial meager audiences, that we would have to fold up and return to the States. Then one night a pronouncement of mine in response to a woman's question could have been construed, I suppose, as hinting at her husband's infidelity. Her husband happened to be a member of Parliament. What the British love is a scandal, and as it turned out, my words prompted the woman to dig into her husband's affairs. Alas, she found not one mistress but three, and in an attempt to ruin him, she went to the *Times* with the story. Had I distributed a million broadsides announcing the show, it couldn't have been better advertised. Another monumental success was on the brink of dawning, and then I fell in love."

HIS LITTLE COCOON

*I*T MAY be true that the sun never sets on the British Empire, but while in London I wondered when it was going to rise. We arrived there in autumn, and the weather was perpetually cold and damp—miserable fogs and drenching rains. Because of having to exit swiftly from the heat of whatever theater we were performing in into the chill night air, I had developed a bad cold by the end of the month. I did my best to ignore its effects, but it remained with me and became serious. Eventually I found I could not draw a decent breath, and my voice could not penetrate the thin boundary of the screen to reach the audience. We had two weeks of shows remaining when I finally told Watkin to reschedule them.

"I was now shipwrecked, so to speak, in my hotel rooms, so absolutely drained I barely had the energy to crawl out of bed to a chair to watch the goings-on in the street below. I tried the usual assortment of home remedies—steam, herbals, compresses—but nothing seemed to alleviate my symptoms. Watkin was frantic, fearing that something might be seriously wrong with me, and insisted that I see a doctor. I told him I was seeing no one and no one was seeing me. But he persisted, and eventually I gave in to his demands—only on my own terms, of course.

"Careful to protect my anonymity, he found an American physician who was visiting London at the time. This young man had recently graduated from medical school and was on the grand tour of Europe and places beyond. He had been at one of my shows a few nights earlier and had chatted with Watkin, merely by way of wishing to speak to someone who had been more recently in the States. My manager assured me that the young fellow was in need of cash and that we could buy his silence if it proved necessary for him to have a direct audience with me. I told Watkin that a direct audience was out of the question but to bring him to me.

"He arrived at my hotel suite on a night when I was at my lowest. I had slept straight through for two days in a row. My spirits were as drained as my body, for with all that inactive time on my hands, now adding up to two weeks of static maundering, I had far too much opportunity to reconsider my life. Memories of my father and mother, my almost fairy-tale existence on the top of the mountain, came back to me both nostalgically and stripped down to reality. What was left was a dark and twisted mess. I wept profusely at never having experienced true love, at my utter loneliness, the curse of the Twins, the murder of my mother, the designs of my father to trap me in this foolish sideshow existence. For all it mattered, I could very well have been a hairy she-ape of a prophet and it wouldn't have made a whit of difference.

" 'Hello, Madam Sibyl,' came a voice from outside my bedroom. I swear, the mere sound of that phrase did something to me. There was a light innocence in the voice accompanied by a real sense of concern. I answered immediately, before I even knew what I was doing, not in my trumped-up stage voice but in my real one. The doctor introduced himself and gave his name, telling me that he was a native of Boston and that his family had originally emigrated there from France. I remember telling him that he had a lovely name. And do you know, Piambo, I was certain I could hear him blush.

"He insisted that I allow him to see me. 'Your secrets are safe with me, Madam Sibyl,' he said. 'I have taken an oath of confidentiality concerning my patients.' We bargained back and forth, and he won. I opened my bedroom door the width of a dime and strode quickly back and forth in front of it three times. When I was finished, he asked me if that was to be the extent of it. 'Of course,' I said, and this drew a peal of laughter from him. He then went on to inquire as to what my exact symptoms were and what my schedule had been like of late.

" 'You are more than likely simply run-down,' he said. 'I believe you have a bad cold and that your body is requiring you to rest both physically and mentally. You are exhausted.' His words made me realize how hard I had been pushing myself and how the strange surroundings had contributed to my weakened nerves. 'You may call me Luciere,' I told him. 'That is my true name. I am a real woman and not an ancient creature.'

" 'Yes, Luciere,' he said, 'I quite suspected that. I want you to stay as warm as you possibly can. Cover up so that you can sweat. Drink hot tea and soup. Tomorrow I will bring you some medicine and check on you.' I thanked him, and he told me how miraculous he thought my performance was. He returned the following day bearing his medicine, which was a kind of hot soup made of cabbage, carrots, and garlic. I had already begun feeling a bit better by then, but I did not let on, because I wanted him to continue to visit. This he did, and on the third day I had Watkin set up the screen for me in the parlor of my hotel suite. I held an audience with him there, thus allowing me to peer through the pinhole and view him. I liked very much what I saw. He was neither large nor small but of perfect stature. He wore his dark hair long, had a mustache, and was dressed casually in a maroon jacket. He wore neither tie nor hat.

"On that day we talked of things other than my health. He told me of his childhood and of his medical studies. I inquired as to his age and found that we shared the same birth year. His favorite pastime was reading, as was mine, and we soon discovered that we had read many of the same works. Our conversation veered into a discussion of Nathaniel Hawthorne's *The Scarlet Letter,* and he concurred with me about how wrongly Hester had been treated by society. All the time we spoke at this meeting, Watkin sat nearby as both an interested party concerning my health and a kind of chaperon.

"On the following day, when Charbuque was due to call, I sent Watkin out on an errand that I knew would last quite a few hours. It was when he realized that Watkin would not be present that Moret began to press me about my relationships, as a means, no doubt, of determining whether I was engaged or married or had a sweetheart. I let it be known that I was altogether unattached, and this pleased him very much. Then he told me he had brought something for me. I reached out the monkey arm, and he slipped beneath the grip of the thumb a small box decorated with colored paper and a pale yellow ribbon. Struck dumb by this gesture, not knowing whether it was too forward or simply an act of kindness, I opened the gift. It turned out to be a cameo; somewhat odd.

"He told me that when he saw it in a shop, he knew it should belong to me. In white relief on a royal blue background was the image of a handsome woman whose hair consisted of writhing snakes emanating from her scalp like a sunburst. 'The Gorgon Medusa,' he said. At first I was shocked, knowing that the Medusa had been a monster in ancient legend. 'And like Perseus,' I said, 'do you plan to cut my head off?' 'Never, Luciere, but I long to be immobilized by your gaze,' he said. 'If you remember the tale, her blood gives birth to the winged horse Pegasus . . . as your voice has given wings to my heart.'

"Utterly trite, I know, Piambo, but when you are a young woman as isolated as I was, such poetry can be the loaves and fishes of your days. This was all it took to win me over. From then on, after only a few days of knowing each other, I was committed to Mr. Charbuque. Watkin never interfered. I think he hoped that the young man would draw me out from behind the screen. He had always told me that I did not need to be a recluse for the act to work and that he thought it unhealthy that I should be forever hidden.

"Our relationship advanced and, if I may speak plainly, as before, reached a point of physical union. It was not that I had decided to reveal myself—that I felt I could not do—but methods for intercourse were devised. Where there is a will, there is a way, you know. I would not allow him to put his hands upon me, but he wore a blindfold, and with me giving directions, I would allow him to approach me from behind. I wrapped myself in a large blanket with a perfectly placed hole cut in it. He called me his little cocoon. We practiced these unusual connections and others yet more exotic with a good deal of frequency.

"The shows that had been canceled owing to my illness were never rescheduled, but I stayed on in London, my time consumed by my new relationship. Two short months following our meeting, we were married in my hotel suite. I sat behind the screen and spoke my vows. Watkin was the witness. It was a joyous day, and we three drank champagne along with the public official who married us. Charbuque had promised me before the ceremony that he would respect my wishes not to be seen and that he thought our lives together, though not run-of-the-mill, could be very happy.

"By the end of the first week together, though, he began demanding that I show myself to him. He told me that when we were together intimately he needed to touch me. Believe me, I considered it. In fact, I wanted it, but my ways were too ingrained by then. There was too much fear, too much, I thought, at stake. My husband's mood then began to grow very dark indeed. He became increasingly belligerent until one afternoon as I sat behind the screen in the parlor arguing this very issue with him for the hundredth time in two days, he dashed the screen aside and lunged for me. The instant he saw me, his eyes seemed to tear right through me. As a reaction to that pain, I lifted the monkey arm, which sat nearby, and batted him across the side of the head. He went down upon the floor, which gave me a chance to retreat to the bedroom and lock the door.

"When he rose from my blow, he spent a long time showering me with the most horrible curses. He called me a *ghost whore,* a *succubus.* He finally left, but not without stealing from me—a large sum of money, my ancient lamp, and some expensive jewelry that I had received from the mayor of Paris for a personal performance I had done for his family and friends. I was distraught and could easily have fallen again into depression, but I too desperately wanted to return to New York. I had Watkin arrange things.

"Charbuque never left me alone. He stalked our every move. At any time of the day or night I could look out my window and see him standing in the street below my window. Daily he sent me letters filled with the most depraved descriptions of sexual violation, mayhem, and murder. One night, while we were awaiting the day of our departure, he attacked Watkin in the lobby of the hotel. The staff managed to subdue him and toss him into the street.

"On the day we were to leave, ever-resourceful Watkin hired some local toughs to, shall we say, detain Moret. Still, he followed as soon as he was able. Luckily we had enough of a lead to elude him, and our ship sailed leaving him behind. He took the very next ship headed for New York, which left port two days after ours. That vessel, the *Janus,* met the storm we had barely missed in our own crossing, and was lost at sea.

"You are sure he was on board?" I asked.

"Positive," she said.

"How can—?" I was interrupted by Watkin's entrance.

"I never performed again," she said, and that was all for the day.

PARTY MASK

"MY LITTLE cocoon," I said under my breath as I walked away from Mrs. Charbuque's house. For some reason her tale of romance gone awry made me think of visiting Samantha to beg her forgiveness for having been so absent recently. At the same time, that blasted deadline, now less than two weeks off, loomed large. I took the coward's path and decided to return to my studio and work for the remainder of the evening. As it turned out, work consisted of polishing off half a bottle of whiskey and two dozen cigarettes as I sat at the drawing board searching my thoughts for a new image of my patron.

I could easily picture her as a snake-haired demon. It was no problem at all for me to see Charbuque, neither large nor small, severing the head of that demon and watching as the spilled blood gave birth to the winged horse, Pegasus. Yes, my mind was a carnival of bizarre scenes, but to summon the face of a real woman, any woman, had become an impossibility. I was so frustrated that I even briefly considered consigning the bottle of Awakening to the pit a grave error. Finally I gave in to exhaustion and went to bed.

The next morning I rose late and went to Crenshaw's for breakfast. While I was drinking coffee and perusing the newspaper, a young fellow carrying a bag with a shoulder strap and wearing a messenger's cap approached me.

"Are you Mr. Piambo?" he asked.

"That's right," I said.

He handed me a lime-colored envelope. As soon as the lad left, Mrs. Crenshaw moved in to see what it was I had received. Using great tact, I ordered another plate of stew so that in filling the order she would have to give me some privacy. I opened it with one tear and took out the card inside. The message read:

> *Piambo: A change of venue this afternoon. The Hotel Logerot at Fifth Avenue and Eighteenth Street. Room 211. There will be a blindfold on the doorknob. Put it on before entering. Say nothing.*
>
> > *Your Creature,*
> > *Mrs. Charbuque*

Before I even had the card and envelope stuffed into my jacket pocket, I began to feel a growing sense of excitement. I surmised that either I was to stand in for Charbuque as a ravisher of cocoons or, equally titillating, she was going to reveal some clue to me concerning her secret visage. "Calm down, Piambo," I told myself. "Proceed with caution." I knew I would eventually rebuke her sexual advances, if that was what she had in mind, but I could not forgo the opportunity of doing so. What interested me in this regard was, if only for a moment, to hold the reins of power in our grotesque relationship. Before Mrs. Crenshaw returned with the stew, I had already paid and left. The day was frigid, but I did not notice the temperature, for I was glowing from within—a dynamo of expectation. I went directly home and washed and shaved.

While I dressed I considered Mrs. Charbuque's use of the word *venue*. It was a word she had used frequently in her descriptions of the places she had performed. Was this, then, to be a performance? Or had they all been performances? It seemed now, with the change in our meeting place, that she was taking her act, as she had put it, on the road. Throughout all my appointments with her there had always appeared some connection, like an allusion, a type of metaphorical link, between what happened in my own life and what happened in her stories.

This line of reasoning led me to believe that perhaps the Hotel Logerot, with its European name, was to stand in as her trip across the Atlantic. If this were the case, then I was, in my role as her gentleman caller, Charbuque, being summoned to a tryst away from the purview of Watkin. The only question that remained was whether I was the Charbuque she was falling in love with or the Charbuque she believed had betrayed her. Not knowing which man I was, I could not be sure which woman she would be.

The Hotel Logerot was a rather new establishment, founded by Richard de Logerot, a bona fide marquis, who moved in the stratosphere of New York society's famous Four Hundred. I arrived at the address a few minutes before our usual two o'clock appointment time. The attendant at the desk asked me what my business was, and I told him I was there to visit room 211. He smiled and told me that I was expected.

I passed up the lift for the stairs. Besides the fact that I was only going to the second floor, I regarded all mechanical contraptions with the same sense of suspicion I had for Reed and his Industrial Revolution. The carpets on the hallways and the stairs were wonderfully thick. The entire place was lavishly appointed with crystal light fixtures and highly polished walnut paneling.

True to her word, there was a blindfold hanging on the doorknob of room 211. It was black and looked much like a party mask sans eyeholes. When I tied its two strings at the back of my head, I made sure they were securely knotted. The last thing I wanted was for it to slip off and negate any chance I had of finishing the commission. Once I was blind, I decided to try the doorknob before knocking. To my surprise, it turned. I opened the door, walked five paces into the room, and stood perfectly still, listening intently for the presence of another. I heard the floor creak quietly and the door closed behind me. It was only then that I realized I could have been playing directly into the hands of Moret Charbuque.

A few tense moments passed during which I waited, not knowing whether I would be knifed in the back or invited to enter into one of Luciere's ingenious games. Then I felt a hand on my shoulder, and its touch was light. She removed my coat and hat. I learned that day that the loss of the faculty of sight does, in fact, increase the acuity of one's other senses. I smelled lilac perfume, heard the excitement in her shallow breathing, felt the heat of her hands just before they touched me. What I wanted more than anything at that moment was to speak just one word in a normal tone of voice as a way of establishing my presence in reality. I knew better than to reach out, I had been warned to say nothing, and I could not see. When those hands removed my jacket, and then my vest, my desire to speak turned into a desire to shout.

There was no mistaking what her intentions were when she began unbuttoning my shirt. The objection I had to her actions was not the only thing on the rise. I knew that to continue any further would be wrong. Moistening my lips, I prepared to speak my aforementioned rebuke, but then my shirt came away and I lost my voice. When I felt her lips lightly graze my stomach, I knew I was in trouble. The tug at my belt spelled certain doom.

She worked quickly then, and in no time at all I was standing completely naked. There was something about the inability to respond to her advances that exponentially increased my desire, and from where she stood I'm sure that was more than evident. I felt her walking around me. After three complete circles, I heard her stop directly in front of me. Before she even touched me, I felt her fingers close around my member, and then they did.

"Piambo," she said.

I quietly gasped at her touch, but at the same instant a thought rose in my mind, slowly as a bubble in maple syrup, making its way inexorably through the thickness of my ecstatic confusion. When it reached the surface and broke, I realized something was wrong. Her voice.

"Samantha," I said, just as the blow to the left side of my head landed, knocking me to the floor. I reached up, not wanting to look but having to. I lifted the blindfold and saw her glaring down at me. My first reaction was to say, "I knew it was you all the time," but . . . Need I say more?

"My new name for you is Reed," she said. That statement hurt nearly as much as the kick to my groin that followed. She strode past me and out the door.

I lay there long minutes before the open door, not caring if I was discovered. There was no avoiding the truth; in mere minutes I had become what I despised. It might have been possible to construct an argument that I had not, in the physical sense, done anything untoward. Another man might even accept the crippled logic of entrapment, but for a woman, intention is everything. There is no charade of pleasing actions, no matter how deftly presented, there are no kind words, no matter how poetic, that a woman will not eventually get to the bottom of. I roundly cursed Mrs. Charbuque, for her commission was costing me more than all her money could buy. Then I got up, closed the door, and dressed.

I sneaked out a back entrance of the Hotel Logerot—a pox on it—and made for the closest saloon. I can't even recall the address of the place, I was so beset with the situation I had allowed myself to fall into. All that remains clear to me was that I took a seat far back in the shadows, where I could talk to myself and weep without anyone noticing me. There I sat for who knows how many hours, steadily drinking and concocting elaborate plans to win Samantha back. Even though I became increasingly inebriated as the afternoon faded into night, I still could not convince myself of the viability of any of the foolish schemes I had worked out with charcoal pencil on linen napkins.

Eventually I passed out, and the waiter brought the manager to evict me. As soon as they had awakened me from my stupor, I assured them that I would leave on my own accord and they would not have to throw me out. "Very well," said the manager. I staggered to my feet, and eyes bleary, head spinning, I tottered toward the door. My recollection is somewhat dim, but I recall actually making it through the door, barging through a group of gentlemen who were just entering, and then tripping and diving headlong into the street.

I pushed myself onto my elbows and looked up to see that the group of men had stayed outside to watch my spill. When my eyes finally cleared, I recognized at least two of them. The portly older gentleman was Renseld, the art dealer. Then there was a tall thin blond youth I did not know. The third was of all people Edward, whose painting of the beheading of Saint John had nearly been the backdrop for Reed's execution. I must have appeared a horrible mess, but still I thought one of them might give me a hand and help me to my feet. Since I did not think I could manage standing, I reached out to them.

"Edward, don't you know that old sot? Wasn't he your teacher or something?" asked the blond fellow.

My onetime student couldn't meet my eyes, and he hesitated ever so briefly before saying quickly, "I've never seen him before in my life." Then they turned and entered the saloon.

I scrabbled to my feet and limped through the cold night toward home, the dirt of Fifth Avenue still in my mouth.

THE MEDUSA

I WEAVED AND stumbled through the night, so nauseated that I had to stop and rest for minutes at a time in shop doorways. Since young Edward's denial, my troubled thoughts of Samantha had given way to fitful memories of M. Sabott. I recalled him telling me once, "Piambo, always keep a clear conscience or your colors will become muddied, your brush strokes erratic." It was far too late for that, though, as I finally fell against the wall of an apartment building somewhere around Broadway and Twentieth Street and vomited. I came ever so close to passing out completely but managed somehow to hold myself together. As I pushed off that wall and began again on my hellish journey, I heard someone behind me say, "That's him."

I looked over my shoulder and saw two large, shadowy figures less than a block away, quickly approaching. When they were aware that I had seen them, they broke into a run. I did my best to flee, but my condition allowed me to go no more than a few feet before I stumbled and sprawled upon the sidewalk. By the time I managed to regain my feet, they were on me.

Each of them took me by an arm, pinning my back against the

nearby window of a shop. They wore their hats low and their collars turned up, so I could not get a good look at them. All I could make out were squinted eyes, rotten teeth, and stubbled jaws. With my bleary vision and frayed nerves, I registered them as twins, each a hideous doppelgänger of the other.

"Charbuque sends his greetings," said the one on my right in a blast of foul, fish-smelling breath. I didn't see the blow coming, but he punched me in the side of the head. Then the other hit me in the stomach. Once the beating started, I retreated to some safe place inside my mind, and there I thought to myself, "They are going to kill me." The next thing I knew, I was on the ground, and they were kicking me. That is when I passed out. I did not come to until I heard the gunshot.

As its echo diminished, I heard my attackers running off. I lay there surprised that I was alive and yet more surprised that, given the night's circumstances, I counted that a good thing. A gloved hand reached out of the dark and touched my shoulder.

"Are you all right, Mr. Piambo?" said a voice.

Terrible aches and pains in my ribs and legs were just then beginning to make themselves known. I could feel that my face was somewhat swollen on the left side. All in all, I did not believe anything was broken or irreparably damaged. The two thugs had beaten much of my drunken stupor right out of me. I managed to get to a sitting position, and then I looked up into the white eyes of Watkin.

"Good of you to save me, Watkin," I said.

He slipped a pistol into his coat pocket and said, "All in a day's work, Mr. Piambo."

"Can I ask what you are doing here?" I said.

"My employer worried when you did not show up for your appointment today. She sent me out to make sure there was nothing wrong. I searched everywhere and was about to give up when a gentleman in a saloon on Fifth Avenue said he had seen someone who fit your description not too long before, drinking like a fish. I followed a logical course toward your home and came upon you being mercilessly pummeled. I drew my pistol, fired it once in the air, and your friends ran off."

"What did Mrs. Charbuque think had befallen me?" I asked as he held out a hand and helped me to my feet.

"She told me she was speaking to you the other day about her husband, and any thought or mention of him makes her generally uneasy. She has made a certain investment in you, and her uneasiness, I believe, spilled over and mixed her past with her present, and she just wanted me to make sure you were well. I hope that explains it."

"Yes," I said. "And to tell the truth, the past *has* spilled over into the present, in the form of Charbuque. Those men said they were his representatives."

If Watkin had not been wearing his white eyes, I know I would have been able to read his fear there, but just by the sudden rigidity of his body and the raising of his shoulders I could tell this was bad news to him. He shook his head.

"This is a dangerous development, Mr. Piambo," he said.

"I thought Charbuque had gone down with the *Janus*," I said.

"If only that were true, but I'm afraid it is wishful thinking on Mrs. Charbuque's part. That ship did sink soon after we returned to New York, and she took the news story and inserted her husband into it for her own peace of mind, but there was nothing to indicate that there is any truth in her belief."

"Is even the smallest bit of any of it true?" I asked.

"In all widespread error there is a particle of truth," said Watkin. "If you were supposed to have died tonight, you would have, allow me to assure you of that. If Charbuque has returned, as the events this evening indicate, that is serious business. The game has changed, my friend, and you are a useful but ultimately disposable pawn."

"And what of yourself, Watkin?" I asked.

"I, sir, am also, as always, expendable," he said, and flashed a grim smile.

"You'd better tell me everything," I said.

"I've already told you too much," he said. Then he whispered, "I'd abandon the commission if I were you." He took something from his coat pocket and put it into my hand, saying, "In order to keep things clear." With this he turned and was off up the street, madly tapping the shop fronts with his stick. "Take care of yourself, Piambo," he called over his shoulder.

Looking down at the object that Watkin had handed me, I discovered it was a small bottle with a plunger top, like the kind used to hold India ink. I hobbled over to the closest street lamp and inspected it. Inside was an amber-colored liquid. I unscrewed the top and smelled it. It would have been as easy to cry as to laugh, but I did the latter, for the aroma was none other than that emitted by Samantha's candle—nutmeg.

I stood for a few minutes breathing deeply the cold wind of the night, wondering if what had just transpired was all that it seemed. The thought of my attackers soon returned to me, and I limped off at as brisk a pace as I could manage, what with all my new aches and pains. Traversing those few blocks to my house was absolutely harrowing. Every passerby, every dog moving in the shadows, made me jump.

I was never so pleased in my life to return home. Once inside, I checked each of the rooms for lurking assassins and, when I found none, went directly to bed. The trials I faced were still many, but there would be no more alcohol, of that I assured myself. I was still beset by troubles to match the plagues visited upon Egypt in the Bible, but that beating had been somehow therapeutic. I went to sleep resolved to lift myself from the slough I had voluntarily leaped into.

Late the next morning I was sitting at Crenshaw's working on my second seltzer water, trying to determine if food was actually going to be an option or not, when someone took a seat at my table directly across from me.

"Your head is somewhat larger than usual today," said Sills.

"I was brutally attacked on the street last night," I said. "Where were you?"

"Were they after your wallet?" he asked.

"No, just some sport, I'm afraid."

"I was out retrieving another body, a woman whose eyes had turned to blood," he said. Here he lifted the newspaper I had not looked at yet, and turned it over to show me the headline.

"The cat is out of the bag," I said.

"The pressure from the higher-ups to get to the bottom of this thing is crushing," he said. "And listen, I now know what the common denominator was among all these women."

"They all were having affairs with the same sailor?" I said.

"That would be some fellow," he said, "but no. I can't believe they didn't pick up on this sooner, but then they had to be rather hasty in cremating the corpses out of fear the thing would spread."

"Well?" I said.

"This wasn't told to the press. So of course it's still a secret."

"Of course," I said.

"We are fairly sure that each woman was wearing an identical cameo. A pin with the image of a woman with snakes for hair," he said.

I leaned forward in my chair and asked, "What color was the background of the cameo?"

"I believe they said it was a dark blue," he said.

I pushed back my chair and stood. Reaching into my pocket I pulled out a coin and threw it on the table to cover my bill. "Are you checking with jewelers to find out where the cameos came from?" I asked.

"Even as we speak," he said. "Where are you going?"

"I have an errand to run. Are you working tonight?" I asked.

"Yes. Do you know something?" he asked, suddenly suspicious.

"I believe these deaths are murders. Something I can't yet prove, but if you're smart you'll start searching for a fellow by the name of Moret Charbuque."

"Where do we find this Charbuque?" he asked.

"I don't know. Look in the dark. I'll contact you tonight, John. Find Charbuque," I said.

"Piambo," he called after me, but I was on the street in an eye-blink, limping toward the nearest streetcar headed uptown.

AN INSIDIOUS CURSE

EVEN THOUGH I arrived at Mrs. Charbuque's address two hours before my allotted time, I was determined that she would have an audience with me immediately. Women were losing their lives at the rate of three a week. Owing to this tragic fact and the development of my own current situation, the promised commission money no longer held sway over me. In just one day I had gone from self-absorbed, self-interested artist to defender of public safety. Watkin *was* going to open up, and Luciere and I were going to have a lengthy chat about a subject we had not covered as of yet; namely, reality.

It was with a marked determination that I took the path to her front door and with great vigor that I worked the brass knocker. There was no immediate answer. I waited some time and then tried the knocker again. Putting my ear against the door, I tried to discern Watkin's approaching footsteps. I heard nothing. Under normal circumstances I would never have considered entering a home uninvited, but I thought the situation was of sufficient importance to warrant it. I first played the long shot and twisted the doorknob to see if the house was unlocked. Imagine my surprise when the thing turned and the door pushed back with no trouble at all. I stepped inside.

"Hello?" I called in a halfhearted voice. There was no answer, so I tried again, louder. A strange echo returned to me. I could not decide why it didn't sound as I had suspected it should until I stepped into the small room off the foyer and noticed that nearly all the furnishings were gone.

"My God," I said aloud, and walked quickly down the hallway. All those rooms that Watkin always led me through on our twisting journey to reach Mrs. Charbuque had been emptied of most of their furnishings. The pieces that remained were left in haphazard positions as if the place had been hastily sacked. I went quickly through the dining area, through the study, both rooms disconcertingly empty. I was so used to it at this point, I could have made the jaunt to our appointed meeting room blindfolded.

It was only when I flung open the final door and stepped into the high-ceilinged space that I was certain she was gone. The screen was not there. All that remained was my chair, sitting like a lonely atoll amid the sea of polished floor. "Luciere," I yelled, and the name bounced around the empty room for quite a while before dying out. I walked over and sat down, utterly confused and broken.

I have to say that for all the trouble she had caused me, I truly missed her presence. At that very moment one of her stories would have been a comfort. I pulled myself together and decided that since I had already entered the house illegally, I might as well search the premises for any clue to where she had gone or whatever else I was able to discover. Of course, the first place I thought of going was through that doorway and up those stairs at the back of our room. This had always seemed to me to be the ascent to Mrs. Charbuque's private sanctuary. I had no reason to believe my perceptions were correct, but that is where I knew I should start. I got up from my chair and stood still for a moment, looking out the window at the beautiful blue sky, listening to the wind. Then

I headed for the stairs with the same sense of trepidation and excitement as might attend peering behind the screen itself.

The upper floor, I am sorry to report, was not the treasure trove, the bower of secrets, I had envisioned. Merely four large rooms, also emptied of their furniture. As far as clues went, there were none. All I could take away with me was the view of the park Luciere must have enjoyed from time to time. It was dawning upon me that with Watkin's knowledge of the return of Charbuque, Mrs. Charbuque had probably fled into hiding, forgetting my commission and everything else. For her to know he was back must have been like being haunted by a malicious ghost.

On my way from the second floor front of the house to the stairs at the back that led down to our meeting room, I passed in a hallway a door on my left I had not opened. Upon investigating, I found that it gave access to yet another short flight of steps that led up to what appeared to be a small attic not discernible from the street. At first, I was going to forsake the dreary-looking loft but then put my foot on the first creaking step and proceeded.

My head rose above the floor of the attic as I ascended the steps, and the first thing I noticed was that, thankfully, light was coming into the low-ceilinged space from windows at either end. If I had found only darkness, I would no doubt have abandoned my search. The next thing I noticed was a familiar aroma. This I recognized almost instantaneously as the smell of dried oil paint. When I reached the attic floor, I had to bend over slightly, as the room was not tall enough to accommodate my full height. What I found there were rows of painted canvases leaning against either wall. I had only to peruse the first few in each stack to know they were all portraits.

"Incredible," I said as I gazed at each one in turn. The screen with falling leaves figured prominently in many of them, some depicted the monkey arm, one or two the green leaves Mrs. Charbuque used in her act, but all of them were portraits of women. The single female figure in each was, of course, my patron. I knew the signature techniques of the different artists and identified them before reading their names—Pierce, Danto, Felatho, Morgash. These works were marvelous, done in every conceivable style that had been popular throughout the past twenty years. The women represented in them were all beautiful and all remarkably different. Redheads and blondes, raven blacks and chestnut browns, tall, short, slim, full-figured; wearing expressions of lust, contrition, sarcasm, joy, weariness, anguish. They wore kimonos and bathrobes, evening gowns and billowing summer dresses, but none, may I add, was depicted naked, as mine was to have been. There must have been twenty Mrs. Charbuques there, if not more. As with some innocent young lover, my curiosity was tinged with jealousy at the fact that I had not been the first.

I kept digging through the stack, found a Spensher, a Tillson, a very nice Lowell, and then one the sight of which made my knees buckle slightly: Mrs. Charbuque as a kneeling, haloed penitent in a garden, surrounded by crumbling Roman statuary and lit from above by a silvery beam breaking through the clouds. The piece was painted in a Pre-Raphaelite style that could belong to only one artist. I did not have to check the signature to know it was by Shenz. This revelation was enough to floor me, but the canvas behind my friend's was even more devastating, for it had been created by none other than M. Sabott.

I let go of the stack of pictures, and as they banged back against the wall, I turned away and made for the stairs. As I descended at breakneck speed, it came to me that all the work represented in Mrs. Charbuque's private gallery had been done by painters who had either fallen out of the profession, committed suicide, gone mad, or lost their touch and could no longer attract patrons.

I reached the main floor and ran through the house, wanting now only to escape the place. All I could think of was how many artists had been done in by Luciere's game. They had tried their hand at depicting what was impossible to know, and failed. Yes, most likely they were all paid for their interpretations, but their lack of success in the face of the ultimate challenge had left them broken. Perhaps, like me, they thought they would exceed their present circumstances, extend their reach to scrabble up with the great masters, but in the end they realized they could never be any more than what they had originally been. The commission was an insidious curse.

I'm surprised no one noticed me as I fled the place, looking for all the world like a thief leaving the scene of a crime. I hailed the first hansom cab I could get and gave the driver Shenz's address. Once settled inside the conveyance, I began to review what I remembered of the sudden diminution of my friend's and my mentor's talents. It struck me that Sabott's madness descended after a period in which he had taken up portraiture once the galleries were no longer interested in his mythic paintings. I was not staying with him anymore but had struck out on my own with his approval. Just before the insanity took hold of him, I remembered him telling me that he was working on a very important job. He became very scarce for quite a few weeks, and when he emerged, he did so raving.

Likewise with Shenz, a year or so back he had vanished from the scene for a time. I was too busy to inquire what he was up to, and thought I would soon see him standing in my studio, but when he finally did show up after some months of absence, he looked haggard and had begun his affair with the poppy. Now it became clear to me why he was so adamant that I succeed at this commission. Somehow he must have suspected what had happened to Sabott, and after he himself was beaten by the conundrum, he saw me as their agent of revenge. Perhaps I should have been flattered by his belief in my abilities, but I could feel nothing other than remorse for what Mrs. Charbuque had made him believe about his own talent.

The greater question, the ultimate mystery, was whether Luciere was truly hoping the commission would produce a portrait that would in some way discover her as herself or if she knew of its corrosive effects and the power she could wield through it and was using that influence to play God. With her gone, I was left in a less enviable state than my beaten brethren, for I could no longer achieve heaven and had not been officially consigned to hell. In the absurd world of the game, I was now even less substantial than her phantasmal, sinister husband.

FINISH IT

SHENZ APPEARED absolutely decrepit. He left the door open for me to enter and retreated away from the afternoon sunlight. I followed him into his exotic parlor and took my usual seat as he did his. The atmosphere was thick with the scented smoke of the dragon and the exhalations of the drug.

"I had a minor setback yesterday, Piambo," he said, "and it has left me feeling rather weak." His hands clutched the chair arms as if he feared he might float away.

"What was that?" I asked.

"Can you imagine, the Hatstells refused my work. They would not purchase it, saying it was shoddy and no real likeness of their children." He shook his head. "Pigs at the pastry cart," he said. "I've spent the last weeks squandering my time and talent on dolts."

"I've heard Hatstell has had a rather severe financial reversal in recent days. Perhaps that is at the bottom of it," I said.

"Piambo, thank you for your kindness, but I happen to know he was just promoted."

I looked down, ashamed at having been caught in my lie.

"One good thing," said Shenz. "As I was sent packing from their home, the children came out of hiding and accosted me with hugs and kisses. The horrible dumplings and I have become thick as thieves. I will miss them. I gave them the last of the candy before departing."

I did not know how to broach the issue I had come to discuss. It could not have been a worse time, but at the rate Shenz was falling apart I realized there might not be a future opportunity. "I've been to Mrs. Charbuque's," I said.

"How is my favorite enigma?" he asked.

"She's gone."

"The real question concerning her is, Was she ever there to begin with?"

"The house is empty, Shenz. The front door was left unlocked. I walked in and scoured the place for any clues to what had happened."

"And what did you find?" he asked.

"In the attic, portraits of her by some of my favorite painters," I said, and watched as his jaw went slack.

He sat still for a minute and then took a cigarette off the small table next to his chair. Reaching into the pocket of his jacket, he retrieved a box of matches. He lit up and exhaled a perfect ring of blue smoke. "So you know," he said.

"It's a beautiful piece," I said.

"I hated it when I was done and had my meager recompense in my pocket," he said. "I was at first so certain I had accomplished the inconceivable."

"Who is to say you didn't? All we have to go on is the word of a disturbed woman," I said.

"No, Piambo, I knew I had missed the mark once she gave me her assessment. I could feel it, and that feeling continued to grow, like a void slowly consuming my desire to paint again."

I wanted to tell him that the commission had nothing to do with painting, but I was just beginning to know that feeling he had described. "Why did you let me enter upon this doomed escapade without warning me?" I said.

"I regret that I did," he said. "I had such faith in your abilities. I believed so wholeheartedly that you could actually succeed. When I went about it, I played it straight without trying to find any outside sources on which to base my portrait. All I used were my meetings with her and the contents of her wild stories. I thought if I helped you, coaxed you to roam outside the bounds of the game somewhat, and directed your progress as best I could, you would surely trap her."

"Shenz, I'm afraid your opinion of my abilities, though I appreciate the vote of confidence, may be a bit inflated."

"No," he said. He shook his head, and I detected a note of anger in his voice. "It wasn't just me. Sabott had that same faith in you, if not more. That day I met him in the Player's Club, years ago, just before his death, he told me about the strange commission that had addled his mind. So when I was approached by the blind gentleman, I knew what I was getting into. Sabott had advised me to steer clear of the Sibyl, but when the opportunity arose I could not refuse, even though he had warned that it would destroy me. Do you know what else he told me?" asked Shenz.

I said nothing.

"He told me, 'Leave that one to Piambo. He is capable of it.' I thought nothing of it at the time. As a matter of fact, I thought it was just more of his lunacy. But as I said, when the commission was placed before me, it was at a juncture in my life when I wanted a test in order to know that I was not sliding. I wanted to prove to myself that I could accomplish what Sabott believed only you could do. Foolishness, I'll admit."

"Forget it, Shenz," I said. "Let it go, and you will be back on top in no time."

"Believe me, I have tried to forget it. I actively pursued the poppy in an attempt to smoke it out of my mind. What has happened, though, is that the opium has destroyed everything else and left that one haunting notion intact." When he finished speaking, I could see tears welling in his eyes. He looked ancient. After tamping out his cigarette in the ashtray, he covered his face with his hands and gave in to his grief.

"You are not allowed to give up, Shenz," I said. "Pull yourself together. Here is what we will do. I will pay for your medical treatment. We will enlist professionals to rid your system of this cursed drug. There are sanatoriums for this kind of affliction. Then we will proceed from there."

"My God, I don't think I've cried in years," he said. "And now I don't think I can stop." He removed his hands from his face, and the palms were bright red.

It happened at once, my realization that he was crying blood and my recognition of the cameo pinned to his lapel. "Where did you get that piece of jewelry?" I asked. "The cameo."

He tried to wipe his eyes clear but only smeared the gore across his face. "Some pleasant fellow simply gave it to me on the street today. Walked up with a smile and pinned it to my lapel. With my defeat at the Hatstells' yesterday, I was receptive to this small un-warranted kindness."

"You're crying blood," I said, and rose from my chair.

Shenz looked at his hands. "So I am," he said. "Am I having a religious moment here, or have I blown a pipe? Oh, no, that's right, I remember reading about this in the newspaper today. It's all the rage."

I was already running for the door. "Sit still!" I called. "I'll be back with help." My leg was still bad from my beating the previous night, but I ignored its throbbing and raced down the steps and out into the street. Even as I ran, I knew he was going to die. If I reached a doctor, a police officer, what could they do? I knew very well there was no phone nearby in Hell's Kitchen, so I headed for Seventh Avenue.

Twenty minutes had passed before I found a saloon with a telephone and called police headquarters. I gave them Sills's name and told them where Shenz was. When the officer on the desk heard that I was reporting an instance of the newly disclosed illness, he became very attentive and said they would send men to Shenz's address immediately. Before hanging up, he told me not to return to the apartment but to stay where I was. I told him I had to go back, but he said, "If you do, we might very well have two more deaths. Stay put." Then he took the address of the saloon I was calling from, and hung up.

As it turned out, I did not return to Shenz's place. I will regret my decision until the day I die, but the unmitigated truth of the matter was that I did not have the courage to watch my friend die. In the past two days, I had been forced to face the worst of my personal flaws. I had betrayed Samantha, and my betrayal of Sabott had been brought home rather pointedly by young Edward's response to my plea for help when I lay in the street. I slunk over to a corner table and sat down, burying my face in my arms. Having heard my phone conversation and witnessing my tears, the bartender brought me a whiskey. I drank that and many more while waiting for Sills to show up. In my distress, I believed that the quicker I drank, the faster Shenz's blood would flow, and the sooner the gruesome event would come to an end.

Two hours later, Sills appeared in the doorway of the saloon. He walked over, took me by the back of the coat, and pulled me to my feet.

"Come, Piambo, we must walk. You've got to tell me everything."

"Is it over?" I asked.

He nodded. "It was over soon after we got there. At least I got to say good-bye to him."

We walked out of the place into the golden light of the setting sun and headed south. When my step faltered, Sills supported me. He stopped at a coffee stand and bought two cups of the black street swill. But it was hot and brought me around somewhat so that my speech was less slurred. When I was done with it, he bought me another and told me to finish it.

"Now," he said as we started to walk again. "Tell me everything, whatever you know about this Charbuque. I need every last detail."

I held nothing back. We walked down Seventh Avenue a long way, over to Fifth, and then back north. We walked into the night, and I told him the story of my acquaintance with Mrs. Charbuque. I even confessed to him what had happened with Samantha.

I finished with the tale only two blocks from my house, and Sills walked with me to the front steps. We stood there silently for a few minutes, and each had a cigarette.

"I shouldn't tell you this, Piambo. But Shenz gave me a message to give to you. His last words."

"Why shouldn't you tell me?" I asked.

"Because I want you out of this mess now."

"A dying man's last request," I said.

Sills looked away for a moment as if deciding. "Very well," he finally said. "Shenz told me to tell you, 'Finish it.' "

TEARS OF CARTHAGE

*A*s a precaution, Shenz's body was cremated the afternoon he expired. I don't know where I found the strength to arrange it, but I organized and sponsored a small gathering in his honor at the Player's Club two days later. News of his death traveled fast throughout the art world, and I tried to get word of the impromptu memorial affair to all who had known him.

Shenz was one of those people who moved in many circles. In attendance the day of the gathering were fine artists, commercial artists, hansom cab drivers, bartenders, politicians, opium peddlers, ladies of both the drawing room and the night, thieves, and police officers. Quite a number of his wealthy patrons made the trip downtown, and all in all, metaphorically speaking, the lion lay down with the lamb in his honor. There were no speeches given, no prayers intoned. People merely mingled and conversed, and occasionally the crowd fell silent. Tears were shed, and there were many long hard stares into the distance before things would eventually wind themselves back up. There was a little food and a lot of alcohol. I spoke to a few of our closest and oldest colleagues out of respect, but for the most part I stayed to myself and remained silent. I had sent an invitation to Samantha, but she did not attend.

The event lasted well into the evening and did not break up until near midnight. By that time I had stopped drinking and was sitting in a chair wrapped in a daze. Some of my friends said good night to me as they departed, and when I looked up from my trance, I saw a familiar face. Goren, the Man from the Equator, pulled up a chair and sat down across from me.

"Thank you for sending word to me, Piambo," he said.

"Have you been here all along?" I asked.

"For quite a while," he told me. "I've been waiting to have a private word with you."

"Yes," I said, and straightened up in my chair.

"From what I picked up in conversation with others this evening, you were with Shenz when he died. Can you tell me, was it the illness in the newspapers that he succumbed to?"

"Bleeding from the eyes, yes," I said.

"I know a few things about this horror," he said. "Some years back, when I first opened my shop in the Village, I was visited by an odd fellow, pretending to be blind, who offered to pay me for any information I could supply him with concerning this ocular stigmata."

Now I came fully awake. "That would be Watkin," I said. "What did you find?"

"All I had to go on was a description of the symptoms, which I had never encountered mention of before. I told the fellow I would see what I could come up with and that I would get in touch with him if I discovered anything. He said he would return in a few months and that if I had something for him he would pay me well. The image of the disease was a striking one, and I kept it in the forefront of my mind, turning my attention to it as often as possible. This is the manner in which I bring a subject closer to me. Since reality is two thirds a product of consciousness, I began to attract information like a magnet. I had opened myself to it, invited it—"

I didn't mean to be so impatient, but I said, "You can bypass the metaphysics for my sake, Goren. What was it you found?"

He looked momentarily startled, then smiled and continued. "There are a number of references to this affliction in ancient texts. Pliny the Elder, Herodotus, Galen. It had a name in the ancient world, the Tears of Carthage. When that great Phoenician city was sacked by Rome, its fields sown with salt, some of the women who were spirited away by the attacking force carried with them small vials of what was thought to be a rare perfume. They anointed their new masters with it, and lo and behold, tears of blood ran until the men's hearts had nothing left to pump. A parasitical Trojan horse, in so many words.

"The Phoenicians had made deep inroads into the African continent, and my guess is that this was some kind of river parasite, for there are rare diseases that involve this type of drastic exsanguination which have been recorded by explorers of that mysterious continent. It is interesting that the Phoenicians used it as a weapon. The technique must have been learned from the native peoples who had first introduced them to it. From my own travels in Africa I learned a great deal from the shamans of various tribes, who possess a knowledge of natural phenomena that exceeds anything the Western cultures have accumulated. I believe it was the Tears of Carthage that took Shenz."

Goren's disclosure excited me, and I told him in as truncated a manner as possible, not wanting to again recount the whole long saga of Mrs. Charbuque, about the lamp full of liquid that Luciere had stolen from the archaeologist. "Could the stuff still be potent after all these centuries?" I asked.

"It doesn't seem likely, but I suppose it depends on whatever the parasite was mixed with," said Goren. "Perhaps the organism can lie dormant indefinitely and then awake when it comes in contact with the heat of a larger organism. Once it finds itself awake, it invariably moves toward the eyes. The lamp sounds Arabic and is probably much older than its contents. The Phoenicians also traded extensively in the Orient. As a matter of fact, they most likely circumnavigated the entire globe, though I doubt you would find a professor of antiquities who would agree with this statement. But here is a kernel of proof. Along with some of the later descriptions of the Tears, there was also mention of an antidote for it. The spice known to us as nutmeg, when made into a tincture and used to bathe the eyes, repels the vermin that feast on the soft ocular tissue. Specimens of this spice have been found in the ruins of Carthage and other Phoenician sites. The only place they could have procured this was in what we now call the Spice Islands, Zanzibar, in the Indian Ocean, thousands of miles away from their cultural centers."

So much ran through my mind at the moment, I could not respond at first. Finally, "Did you give this information to the man who requested it?" I asked, remembering the small bottle Watkin had given me.

"Yes," said Goren. "He paid me well, as he had promised."

"Someone is using these Tears of Carthage as a murder weapon," I said.

"I suspected this when I read about it in the newspaper," he said. "That is why I wanted to tell you. I was hoping you would relate this to the proper authorities. My personal philosophy prevents me from directly aiding the state."

"It's almost too convoluted to be believed; there's too much circumstance and such vast oceans of time involved," I said.

"An instant to the cosmos," said Goren. "A last piece of information: There was one isolated case of this disease reported in the medical literature. About fifteen years ago, in London, a young woman who worked as a maid in a certain hotel. A mild panic ensued, but when no other cases emerged, the fear of it died, and it was written off as some kind of aberrant condition."

"I'm not sure if what you tell me is more astounding or disturbing," I said.

"It's both," said Goren. "By the way, have you been sticking to the prescription I gave you?"

"Religiously," I assured him.

"Results?" he asked.

"Absolutely explosive," I said.

"If you need anything else, you know where to find me," he said, and rose from his chair. "I will miss Shenz. He was a devilishly fine man."

"I can hardly bear that he is dead," I said.

"Death is a relative term, Piambo. Think of it as a change. There is no death." Goren leaned over and shook my hand, holding it tightly for an instant. Then he walked out into the dark.

Later that night, I lay in bed thinking about Shenz's final plea for me to "finish it." That is precisely what I was determined to do. I would find Charbuque and avenge my friend's death. I did not buy for an instant Goren's belief that there was no death. His exacting equilibrium had left his mind anesthetized to the truth. Life was not about the perfection of balance. That kind of stasis was a death in itself. Life was the chaos that tipped the scales.

What I wanted more than anything at that moment was Samantha next to me. As important as it was for me to find Charbuque, I also had to find a way to regain Samantha's trust. Both these tasks would be at least as difficult as portraying Mrs. Charbuque from her mere words, if not more so. Nonetheless, the successful completion of both was essential for my future happiness. The commission was gone, and I wished it good riddance, pleased to have it cleared from my conscience so I could concentrate on what was now important. That night I slept little, so beset was I by a feeling of loneliness. I had experienced nothing like it since I was a child and my father was killed by his own creation.

THEY ARE ALL HER

*I*N THE days that followed the disappearance of Mrs. Charbuque and the death of Shenz, I roamed the city in the pretense of hunting down a murderer. I wandered on foot, uptown and down, keeping a lookout for anyone fitting his nebulous description. I stayed away from saloons and whiskey, for I knew that path would lead me pell-mell to ruination. As long as I kept moving, I did less thinking, felt less of the anguish that always hovered nearby, and that was all for the good. My daily sojourns also left me exhausted at night and facilitated the welcome oblivion of sleep.

The stories in the newspapers did not cause the widespread panic expected by city officials. Much of the populace had lived through the conflict between North and South and its aftermath, in which the casualties were so monumental that, in comparison, the fewer than one dozen deaths caused by this strange disease hardly seemed something to get excited about. Every day there were hundreds more falling victim to murder, work accidents, consumption, and poverty, and the struggle to avoid those tragedies through the acquisition of wealth took precedence over all else and reinforced the importance of the usual routine. If anything, the tales of victims bleeding to death through their eyes were fascinating as well as horrifying.

Sills was pleased with the information I had passed along from Goren, and the New York Police Department put a strain on the local nutmeg market. The tincture described by the Man from the Equator became regular issue for all men working the case. The police had checked with the Jewelers Association and found the fellow, a Mr. Gerenard, who had created the cameos for Charbuque. Apparently two dozen of the expensive pins had been purchased. They were described as being carved from angel skin coral with a royal blue painted background contrasting with the Medusa head in relief and set in fourteen-karat gold with a two-inch pin attached. These were probably exact replicas of the one Charbuque had given Luciere in London.

Gerenard remarked that he had balked at painting them, but the buyer insisted, saying, "She must be surrounded by darkness." One thing that can be said for Charbuque, he wasn't playing cheap with his victims. The lot had cost him a small fortune. This information was useless, though, for the buyer had given no name or address, paid for them in advance, and picked them up many months earlier. The old artisan could not clearly remember any distinguishing details about him.

In the few minutes of rest I gave myself each day from my pointless meanderings, I could not help but wonder why Charbuque had infected Shenz. All his other victims were women who seemed to be picked at random. My only conclusions were that it was an attempt to hurt me, or that Shenz, having had experience with the commission and having encouraged me to research outside the bounds of what was readily offered by Mrs. Charbuque, represented a wild card in what both Charbuque and Watkin had termed "the game."

I went many nights to the theater, paid, and hid in the back row, simply to see Samantha. There I sat in the shadows, trying to screw up my courage to approach her and beg her forgiveness. I couldn't even tell you what the play was about, so intent was I upon her every movement, each expression of her face, the sound of her voice. When the performance was over, I took up a position in the alley across the street from the playhouse to spy on her briefly as she got into a hansom cab.

Then, on the night on which I had assured myself that I would finally make my move and show myself to her, I was standing in my miserable alley, awaiting her exit from the theater, when I felt something cold press against the back of my head.

"Careful, Piambo, or I'll put a hole in you," Charbuque whispered.

This was the moment I had waited for. So often in the past few days I had told myself that if only I had just one more chance to meet Charbuque, I would throw caution to the wind and wrestle him into submission, perhaps even strangle him with my bare hands. Now the time had come, and I stood there paralyzed, all my imagined courage instantly disintegrating with the first hint of danger. The greatest show of defiance I could muster was to say, "You murderer."

"Are you always this clever?" he asked.

"Why Shenz?" I managed to ask.

"He was rooting around too much, the meddlesome old goat. It is my habit to make only the ladies cry, but I allowed this one exception."

"Very well," I said, thinking that if his intention were to kill me, he would have done so already. "Why those women?"

"Revenge, of course," he said.

"Upon whom?"

"My wife. My witch of a wife."

"Those women were not your wife," I said.

"Where is she? Where has she gone, Piambo? I want her to witness what I am doing," he said. I could hear his anger building and felt the barrel of the gun wobbling slightly against my scalp.

"I don't know," I said.

"You are lying."

"I'm telling the truth. She left no word of where she was going. I've been prevented from finishing my commission."

"If I discover that you know where she is and do not tell me, I'll see to it that your actress friend cries like a baby."

"Why don't you just confront your wife instead of involving innocent people?"

"There is a passionate force that binds us. Call it supernatural if you will. It both attracts us to each other and repels us at the same time. The closest we can get is but a distant orbit. From that frustrating perimeter, we commit acts against surrogates, meant to wound each other. I believe this devotion can only be described as love."

"What has Luciere done?" I asked.

"So you call her Luciere, eh? Don't you know about all the men she has robbed of their creativity through her ruse of that impossible commission? To a man, she has filled them with doubt, made them useless, as she tried to do with me. Which is the more terrible crime, to end a life or to torture the living and leave them empty husks, dried gourds forced to bear witness to their own emptiness?"

"So you feel somewhat righteous about killing those poor women?" I said, and could not help but laugh out loud at the absurdity of his logic.

"You're wrong, Piambo. Those women I killed *are* her. They are *all* her. Every last one of them."

I felt the gun barrel leave my head, and in that instant made my move. I began to turn in order to seize him, but I did not get even a quarter of the way around before a heavy object smashed against the base of my skull. I staggered forward out of the alley, into the street, waiting to hear the shot that would finish me. I was still conscious when my legs buckled and I landed on my knees. I listed to the side and fell into unconsciousness.

I woke with blurred vision and an ogre of a headache, aware at first only of the fact that I'd been beaten and spent a lot of time on the street of late. When my vision had partially cleared I managed to look up, and seeing the vague forms hovering above, I realized a crowd of people was standing around me. I was groggy, and when I tried to speak, my words came forth as incoherent grumblings.

"Is he drunk?" a male voice asked.

"Help me get him to the cab. I know where he lives," said a woman. It was Samantha.

I felt two sets of hands lifting me beneath the arms, pulling me upright. Soon I was moving along, sliding my feet as best I could, but the pain in my head doubled in strength, spreading like a wildfire, and I passed out again.

When I next awoke, sunlight was streaming through the lace curtains of my bedroom window. I tried to sit up, but the mere attempt at movement made me dizzy. Shifting my position, I turned onto my side and found Samantha lying next to me. "Perhaps it was all a dream, the whole bizarre thing—Mrs. Charbuque, my betrayal of Samantha, Shenz's death," I thought. Then I saw that she was fully dressed and lying atop the covers. I reached my hand out to lightly touch her hair, but when my fingers were no more than an inch away from her head, Samantha's eyes opened and she sat up. She saw me reaching for her and got out of the bed.

"What happened to you last night?" she asked.

"I was pistol-whipped on the back of the head by Mrs. Charbuque's husband."

"Serves you right," she said. "And why did it happen in front of the theater I just happened to be performing in? It was embarrassing having to, first, admit that I know you and, second, cart you off the street and bring you here. If Shenz hadn't just died, I would have left you where you lay."

"I was hiding in the alley across the street, hoping to get a glimpse of you, and he sneaked up on me," I said.

"Were you at the show?"

"I have been at every show for the past five nights," I said.

"Why don't you just leave me alone?" she said. "I don't want you anymore."

"Yes, but *I* want *you*. Look, I know I was wrong to have gone along with you when I thought you were Mrs. Charbuque. I was weak. A weak moment. But I swear I've not betrayed you with her. You know as well as I do—I can't lie to you."

"You also told me that she meant nothing to you."

"I was caught up in the commission. I was confused, and my nerves were frayed."

"Your nerves," she spat, and turned away in disgust.

"I thought you would come when Shenz died," I said.

She was silent for a time, her back to me. "I wanted to," she finally said, "but I couldn't see you."

"My life is so incredibly lonely without you," I said. "All I do is walk up and down Broadway and hide in the shadows to catch glimpses of you."

She again turned to look down on me. "I am lonely too, Piambo."

"Forgive me," I said.

"Are you feeling better?"

"I'll live."

"What's happening to you?" she whispered, and I saw tears in her eyes.

I told her as quickly as I could all that had happened since I'd last seen her. She'd read about the murders in the papers.

She stood up, smoothing her sleep-wrinkled dress. "I'm leaving now," she said.

"And about us?" I asked.

She shook her head. "I don't know."

I watched her walk out of the room, but when I tried to get up to follow her the pain in my head returned, bringing with it a grave weariness. The last thing I heard before falling asleep was my parlor door closing.

NIGHT TRAIN TO BABYLON

I BELIEVE I have read somewhere that it is dangerous to sleep with a concussion because of the possibility of slipping into a coma, but sleep I did. In fact, I did not wake until the afternoon of the following day. When I finally got out of bed, the lump at the back of my head was tender, but the internal headache was gone and my vision was clear. I dressed and went out to find something to eat, for I was ravenous.

On the way home from Billy Mould's Delicatessen, I decided to forgo my search for Charbuque for that day. I was filled with a kind of hope: Samantha had said she would think about our getting back together. Her demeanor had been rather bellicose, and her statement was far from a resounding affirmation of our relationship, but even the slim possibility that all was not lost afforded me the only ray of sunlight I had had in weeks. I wanted to relax and revel in that possibility for a few hours.

At home I rummaged around the studio, trying to recall my career before Mrs. Charbuque had interrupted my life. It had only been a matter of weeks, and yet my life as a painter-for-hire seemed far away. It would take some doing to get back to work, since I had reneged on several important commissions. Although it had been only a few weeks, I had been absent from the social scene and left without patrons who would recommend me to their wealthy friends.

From the studio, where I was relocating my lost self and conjuring fitting literary allusions, I heard a knock at my front door. As you can imagine, I was hesitant to answer it. I had had all the beatings I really needed for the time being, and as I said, I wanted nothing to do with the Charbuque case for the day. Still, I thought perhaps it might be Samantha, so I went to answer it.

What I found was not a visitor, desired or otherwise, but an ultramarine-tinted envelope lying on the top step, secured against the autumn wind by a large rock. I hesitated, remembering Samantha's forgery. Of course, eventually I picked it up and brought it inside. Standing in my parlor, I slit open the envelope.

Dear Piambo,

I have not forgotten our arrangement. Please forgive me for temporarily abandoning you, but the sudden reappearance of my husband caused me to flee the city. I hope you will understand. Take the Long Island Railroad to Babylon station. Once there, arrange conveyance to the La Grange Inn. I have reserved a room for you. Further instructions await you at the inn. If you do not check in within the next few days, I will cancel the reservation—and the commission. I look forward to completing our work together.

Fondly,
Luciere

I had no doubt that this missive had been penned by the real Mrs. Charbuque. Only someone as unhinged as she could address me in the tone of a bank manager proffering a loan after all I had suffered at her hands. Now I had a decision to make—tear the letter to shreds, ignore it, and try to reassemble my old life, or as

Shenz had requested, plunk my five thousand down at Hanover, so to speak, and "finish it."

When my suitcases were packed and I had assembled the painting supplies I would need to execute the portrait, I wrote a letter to Sills, asking him to keep a close eye on Samantha. I gave no hint of where I was headed. My supposition was that the minute I made a move, Moret Charbuque would learn of it and follow me. I planned to go quickly so that he would be unable to work his evil beforehand. In this manner I hoped to put as much distance as possible between him and Samantha.

Late that afternoon, I left the house looking like a pack mule, toting my bags, a few rolled-up canvases, my paint box and easel. I went directly to Crenshaw's and asked Mrs. Crenshaw to have a messenger deliver my letter to John. The old woman may have been nosy, but she was devoted to her regular customers, and I could be assured that my message would arrive, even if she had to take it to him herself. Then I caught a hansom cab and pleased the driver with the prospect of a grand fare by requesting that he take me to the Flatbush depot. We traversed the Brooklyn Bridge as the sun was setting, casting a golden glow upon that marvel of engineering. I could not help but contemplate some far future in which the remnants of New York would be unearthed like those of Carthage, and what silver lamps full of horror and wonder it might yield.

I caught the late train to Babylon. There was a change of trains at Jamaica, where most of my fellow riders disembarked, after which I settled back and closed my eyes. My head still ached, but my conscience was at ease; I had decided to act. My thoughts turned to Sabott, and my memories of him followed me into sleep and mingled with my dreams.

I sat with my mentor in his studio at night, two candles lighting the scene. Each of us held a glass of claret. Sabott smoked his Dutch pipe and I a cigarette. I felt comfortable, at ease. The master scratched his beard and yawned. Outside, a horse and carriage rattled by on the cobblestones. Somewhere a cricket chirrupped. I closed my eyes for a moment, and when I opened them Sabott was smiling at me. He took his pipe stem from his lips and whispered something.

"I'm sorry, sir, but what was that?" I asked.

He laughed to himself, whispered again, and then glanced over each shoulder as if searching for spies in the shadows.

I knew that he was trying to tell me a secret. I put my wineglass down, stubbed out my cigarette, and leaned across to him. He motioned for me to come yet closer, so I got out of my chair and kneeled before him. After taking a great draw on his pipe, he leaned forward, and I could feel him blowing the smoke into my ear. As it passed into my head, I heard but one word, "Idiosyncratic." Then he sat back, and I rose to my feet.

When next I looked at him, to my horror, he had melted into a puddle of colors, a swirling cataract of paint. His transformation frightened me, and I tried to call his name, but all that issued from my mouth was a long stream of smoke. I knew it was the smoke he had put into my head. Before my eyes the misty blue exhalation took shape in midair, finally coalescing into the image of Mrs. Charbuque, naked, standing behind her screen. But now I was behind it with her. I meant to regain what I had believed was irretrievably lost, and lunged for it. I slammed my chin against the train seat in front of mine and came awake just in time to hear the conductor yell, "Next stop, Babylon."

It was late when I disembarked from the train. The only ride I could get to the inn was an open horse-drawn wagon with wooden benches lining its sides. The young man who piloted the rig was pleasant, though, helping me store my things on board. I was to be his only passenger for the trip. Early November was not exactly tourist time at the Long Island shore. He gave me a blanket in which to wrap myself against the cold night, and we set off. The moon was full, and the stars were clearly visible. What a relief to be out of the city. I breathed deeply, savoring the fresh air tinged with the scents of acre upon acre of farmland and wood.

I had visited this area a few years earlier for a party at the Willet estate. The Willet family had been the original owners of most of this land, and I had done a portrait of the clan's patriarch the previous summer. There were many large estates in the vicinity, owned by such families as the Udalls, the Gereks, the Magowans, and the Vanderbilts. A bit farther east was the Gardiner estate. What interested me most about the southern shore was the proximity to the bay and, beyond it, the ocean.

Eventually the driver ran out of things to say, and we rolled along in silence. I stared up at the moon, blue-white in the night sky, and its hue reminded me of the phantom Mrs. Charbuque who had returned to me in my dream of Sabott. I concentrated on recovering the image, almost afraid that I would not be able to find it in my thoughts. To my utter joy, it reappeared in my mind, as clear as the portrait Charbuque had destroyed. I decided then and there that *this* was the figure I would paint for my patron. As delusional as it might sound, admittedly no less unbelievable than Luciere's advice from the Twins, I was certain that Sabott had come to me in my dream to say, "Trust yourself." Although he had never spoken those words in life, it struck me that they defined the spirit that animated every lesson he had ever taught.

THE HOUSE ON THE DUNES

WHILE EATING breakfast the next morning in the La Grange dining room, I was approached by the desk clerk and handed a peacock blue envelope.

"Sir, I am to give this to you from the gentleman who arranged for your room," he said.

I thanked him, and once he was gone, I opened the letter. One thing I could say for Mrs. Charbuque, her stationery was first-rate even if her choice of husband was not. The message was written in her familiar looping script: a set of directions to her summer-house. Apparently I was to travel by water whether I liked it or not. Her place was halfway across the Great South Bay, on Captree Island. I was to take the ferry from Babylon, disembark at the island's boat basin, and then strike out eastward over the dunes until I came into view of a two-story yellow wooden house with white trim.

I determined on the spot to make the trip that day. There was just one other matter I had to deal with. The room at the inn was lovely, but it was rather small and would not serve as a studio. I needed to rent a place in which to paint. If the weather had not been so frigid I could have made do outdoors, but as it was, my paints would freeze in the late-season temperatures of morning—and I liked to begin work early in the day.

When the waiter approached to refill my coffee cup, I told him I was a painter and asked if he knew who might rent me a space for a week or two to be used as a studio.

"You might have some luck in Babylon," said the man, "but nothing comes to mind immediately."

I thanked him for his advice and turned back to my meal. After he moved off to attend to other guests, an older gentleman wearing a clerical collar and black priestly garb approached my table and introduced himself as Father Loomis. He was a rather portly little man with round spectacles, a drinker's nose, and a shock of white hair ever so lightly tinged with color as if it had been stained by weak tea. I had never had any great affection for the church, but I always tried to be polite. I gave him my name and held out my hand.

"I could not help but overhear that you are looking for a place to paint," he said.

"Only for a few weeks at most," I said. "I'm from New York but have a commission from a local patron."

"My church is about a half mile down the road from here. Right off the Montauk Highway. Calvary Church," he said. "Out in the back field is an abandoned carriage house. A fireplace was put in a few years ago. Would you like to rent it?"

"It sounds perfect, Father," I said, "but it must meet one criterion. I need light. Are there windows that let in a good amount of light?"

"The structure is like a large box. There is one good-size window on the east wall and another on the west. If you're interested, I would charge you only a dollar a day, and that would include wood for the fireplace."

"It sounds as if we have a deal," I said.

"Also, a path behind the building winds down to the bay-side shore."

"Perfect," I said. "I hope to be ready to paint by tomorrow morning, the day after at the latest. Where can I find you?"

"I live in a small room behind the church sanctuary. The front doors are always unlocked."

"I will pay you a dollar and a half a day if you can promise me that you will tell no one that I am working there," I said.

He agreed to my further stipulation, and we shook hands on the deal.

After breakfast I dressed warmly for a journey by water and arranged a ride to the ferry in Babylon. The day was bright and crisp, and the autumnal country scenes were as beautiful by sunlight as they had been by moonlight. I arrived at the ferry at approximately noon and waited with a small group of people, mostly sightseers from what I could gather.

The boat finally came, and we boarded. There was a small cabin to keep passengers out of the weather, and my fellow passengers took advantage of this shelter. I stayed out on deck and took in the immensity of the Great South Bay, watched the boats in the distance, and felt for all the world like one of Melville's sailors. That day, gliding over the choppy water, I felt a need to paint directly from Nature and promised myself that when I was finished with Mrs. Charbuque I would do just that. My pipe dream of seagoing adventure did not last all that long; the entire trip to the island took no more than forty-five minutes.

I easily found Luciere's summer residence, the lemon yellow house nestled amid tall sand dunes. One had to descend from the path to reach the walkway leading to the door. The front of the house faced toward the remainder of the bay, beyond which lay Fire Island and the Atlantic Ocean. It was much warmer standing there on the white stone walkway, the height of the surrounding dunes breaking the wind. Whereas most of the other dwellings I had passed closer to the dock were shacks and shanties used by fishermen and clammers, this was a real two-story house with a wide porch, a tile roof, a widow's walk at the top, and intricate lacelike gingerbread bordering the eaves. A wind chime consisting of tin monkey figurines hung on the porch and jingled in the breeze. I took this as my cue to proceed.

I had barely had a chance to knock before Watkin was opening the door.

"Mr. Piambo," he said. "Glad you are well."

"No thanks to Charbuque," I said.

"Why, did you run into him again?" the old man whispered.

"He cracked me across the back of the head with a pistol a few nights ago."

Watkin shook his head and sighed. He quickly recovered from his concern and said, "This way, sir."

As we made our way through the house, I recognized some of the furniture from the New York residence, but the place was far more sparsely appointed than the city mansion. I was led to another door, again at the back of the house. Watkin tapped on it and then opened it and ushered me in. I thanked him and stepped forward into a barren room. It was not quite as large as our old meeting place, the ceiling was not as high, but it was sizable. Here, the walls were bare of paper and the gray plank floors were unpolished. There were windows to either side, one looking out toward the bay and one onto the dunes I had just crossed. The screen stood in the center of the room as if waiting for me like an old friend, and I could not help but smile when I saw it. Also present was my chair. I sat down, taking up my familiar position.

"Hello, Luciere," I said.

A floorboard popped, the chime on the porch tinkled, and the wind beyond the dunes whistled. Afternoon light poured in, casting a vague shadow on the screen.

"Piambo," she said, "I am so very pleased you have come. My apologies, but . . ." There were a few moments of silence, and then I heard a muffled sob.

"No trouble," I said. "I understand after having met your husband."

"You have met him?" she asked, her voice giving way to alarm.

"Oh, yes, he seems a rather violent fellow. Very adamant about something, though I am not exactly sure what that is."

"People are dying because of his twisted obsession," she said.

I considered telling her about Shenz but did not want to add to her grief. "I told no one I was coming here," I said. "Does he know of this place? It seems perfectly remote."

"I have always tried to keep it a secret. Even back when I was performing, I used it as an escape when the public became too curious about me."

"I am here to finish the portrait," I said.

"That makes my heart lighter," she said. "Since there has been a disruption in our progress, I was wondering if you would want a few days' compensation."

"I will deliver the painting to you in exactly one week's time, no more. You will tell me how close or far off the mark I have hit, and then you will pay me appropriately. After that, Mrs. Charbuque, we will part company, and I will resume control of my life."

She laughed. "Very well," she said. "Do you think you will succeed?"

"At this point, just finishing the commission will be a great success."

"Do you have any more questions for me?" she asked.

"Why so many portraits by so many artists?" I asked.

"What are you alluding to, Piambo?"

"I went to your house for our last scheduled appointment. No one answered when I knocked. The door was open. I entered and had a look around."

"You were in the attic," she said.

"I knew a good many of the artists," I said. "Strange coincidence. Many of them came to a bad end."

"The artistic sensibility is a delicate one," she said. "What I want to know is how the world sees me, even though I cannot be seen. Ostensibly, I was for a time each of the women those painters conceived—but only on their canvases. The reason the commission is so large—if the artist achieves an exact likeness—is to push the artist to think deeply about his subject, about me. More important, my belief is that if one were to match my secret looks to my personality, my intelligence, my experience, my words, then it would be time for me to shed the screen and emerge into the world."

"Why only then?" I asked.

"In a world ruled by men, a woman's looks are more important than her moral character. Women are to be seen and not heard. That is why my audience was always so enchanted and somewhat afraid of me. I had attained great power as a woman simply because I was invisible yet possessed something men desire: knowledge of their fate, their destiny. I will not join the world until my outer form and inner being can be perceived at once, each equal to the other. So I wait, and test the waters now and then by hiring a man to show me what he sees."

She delivered this explanation in a voice full of heartfelt righteousness, but for the life of me I could not quite grasp what her point was. "Interesting. I see what you mean," I lied.

"Is there anything else?" she asked.

"I can't think of anything more, but since this will be our last session, tell me something just for the sake of it. Whatever *you* like," I said.

A few moments passed in near silence, the only sound the lonely tinkling of the tin wind chimes. Finally she said, "Very well. I will tell you one more story. This is not about me, but it is from a book of fairy tales I read and loved as a young girl, when I lived on top of a mountain, learning the language of snow."

THE BOON COMPANION

I REMEMBER THE name of this tale as being 'The Boon Companion,' and I believe it was Austrian, but it could very well have been Turkish. Not even 'Red Riding Hood' or 'Aladdin and His Wonderful Lamp' fascinated and pleased me as much as this story. It conveyed a sense of terrible loneliness, and for this reason it seemed to befriend me, and I read it again and again.

"There was a young man, Po, living in a foreign city, who dreamed of being a famous singer. Although he worked during the day as a salesman in a shop that sold mirrors, he spent his nights in the cafés, listening to his favorite vocalists. If truth be told, his voice was not very good, and he could not hold a tune. More than anything, what he wanted was to be up on the stage, garnering the admiration of a great crowd.

"He would have grown old believing that he could have been a great singer if only he had been given a chance, but something unexpected happened that turned his life upside down. War broke out, and he and all the other young men were conscripted into the army. After harsh and rudimentary training, he was sent to the frontier to fight. Upon arriving in an inhospitable land of rocky hills and little water, he was attached to a company and issued his weapon. His government was hard-pressed by the war, so instead of a gun to take into battle, he was given nothing but a rusty old sword.

"The first action Po's company was involved in was to be, by all accounts, the deciding battle of the war. The two armies faced off across a wide plateau. Thousands of men on each side waited for the order to charge. Our hero understood when he was put in the first row with only his sword that he was meant to be nothing more than cannon fodder. There came a great shout from his own ranks and from those on the opposite side of the plateau, and then both armies charged at each other. Tears streamed down his face as he ran with his sword held out straight, for he did not know why he was fighting, and did not want to die.

"Po had run forward no more than a hundred yards when a cannonball exploded nearby. Shrapnel flew everywhere, and a piece of it hit him on the head. He fell, and as he lost consciousness he believed he was dying. The battle raged on all day around him, but he did not die. The wound to his head was minor and had merely left him unconscious. He was so deeply asleep that he could not hear the din of the battle and the death cries of soldiers all around him.

"The young man woke the next day to the sound of crows cawing. He was dizzy and his head pained him, but he was alive. When his eyes cleared, he looked around and saw the battlefield littered with dead bodies. As it happened, the warring sides had completely obliterated each other. Po was the only survivor. Or so he thought.

"His first inclination was to flee. The sights surrounding him were horrifying—mutilated corpses being eaten by the carrion crows, smoldering fires giving off the stench of burning flesh, battle animals, elephants and horses, hacked to pieces or blown to shreds by artillery. He started picking his way across the plateau but soon found himself running, trampling on the remains of the battle's victims.

"As he neared the edge of the battlefield and could see a path that led down from the high plain, he heard someone call to him. At first he thought it was a ghost, so anguished was the cry. Then he saw a hand reaching up, fingers groping out of a tangle of bodies. He went hesitantly to it. It was an enemy soldier. The man was gravely wounded and begged for water. Our hero, feeling great empathy for the dying man, took out his canteen and held it to the enemy soldier's lips. When the man had quenched his burning thirst, he then begged Po to kill him. 'Finish me,' he said. 'Please. Do it quickly with your sword.'

"The young man wanted to help the dying soldier and did not want him to suffer, but he did not think he could deal a killing blow. 'If you sever my neck, I can promise you a great reward,' said the enemy soldier. 'What can you possibly give to me once you are dead?' asked the youth. 'My spirit will watch over you when I am gone and make sure you return to your home safely.'

"Po wanted desperately to be on his way, but to leave the enemy soldier there to suffer would be the greatest cruelty. He finally lifted his rusty sword, and swinging it now as he had never done in battle, he brought it down on the dying man's neck. The head rolled away, but no blood came forth. Instead, black smoke issued in a stream from the corpse's neck. It rose up like the smoke from the smoldering fires but did not waft away on the wind. Instead it coalesced into a human form.

"When Po saw what was happening, he was terrified. He dropped the old sword and ran from the battlefield. Once he gained the path that led from the plateau, he traveled at top speed and did not look back. All the time he fled, he wondered if his survival was a stroke of good fortune or a curse.

"That night Po found a cave in which he managed to light a small fire. He had run nearly all day and was exhausted. Leaning back against a rock, he sat shivering, trying to decide which direction he should take in the morning in order to reach the city.

"Just as he was about to doze off he noticed something moving near the cave wall. What he saw there paralyzed him, for it was a shadow creeping closer and closer to his own shadow cast by the fire. The worst part was, the shadow that approached did not belong to anyone or anything. He wanted to run but found he couldn't move. The intruding shadow wrapped its dark hands around the neck of his own shadow. The young man could feel an icy coldness filling his body. His breathing grew labored. When he thought the strange apparition was actually going to kill him and he hovered between life and death, he heard a voice whispering in his ear, 'You don't need this old shadow. Its ignorance allows it only to mimic you like a monkey. I, Shathu, will serve you as your new shadow.'

"Immediately the young man was able to breathe again, and he gasped for air. As his breathing returned to normal, he heard a sweet song coming from all around him. The beautiful tune instilled in him a deep sense of peace. He fell sound asleep and rested in tranquillity for the remainder of the night.

"When he woke the next morning, Po shrugged off the bizarre visit of the alien shadow as a bad dream. He felt otherwise refreshed and resumed his homeward journey. It was only after he had been walking for a few hours that he noticed that, although the sun was to his back, his shadow moved alongside him, not in front of him where it should have. He stopped in his tracks and turned to regard the dark patch on the ground. It flew to him, and he heard in his ear, 'Do not worry, for I am with you.'

"As they traveled many miles on the road together, Po and his new shadow, Shathu, became fast friends. Whenever he needed money for food, our hero would go to a tavern and bet the men drinking there that he could make his shadow do unusual things. No one could pass up the opportunity to win such an easy bet, and many people were coaxed into putting their money down against the seemingly impossible. Then Po's shadow would remain standing while he lay down, or it would turn in profile while he faced forward. Even when the young man's predictions came true, the crowd of onlookers could not believe it. Many a time Po had to run for his life from a village, chased by an angry mob that cursed him for being possessed by the Devil.

"After long hardship and much perseverance, the young man reached the city of his birth to find that the war was now over and had been won by his government. He decided to return to the mirror shop to seek a position, and that is when Shathu whispered to him that they should turn their tavern trickery into a performance.

"They named their act The Boon Companion. With a strong light projecting its beam upon him and casting his silhouette onto a white screen, Po would address the audience and explain to them that his shadow often became impatient with him and had recently decided to do whatever it liked. The first few things the young man did were closely mimicked by the shadow, and then slowly it would start to change its direction and movements slightly. Eventually the two were performing wildly divergent acts. The crowds loved the show. Adults as well as children were enchanted by the idea of a shadow with a mind of its own.

"Our hero's reputation grew far and wide, and he and his boon companion performed constantly and became enormously popular and exceedingly wealthy. Po had finally achieved his goal in life—to have throngs of people admire and respect him. Still, deep inside himself he felt a very small kernel of uneasiness about his situation. He was never alone because as long as there was light, Shathu was with him, and yet he was also very lonely because the shadow was somewhat jealous and did not like the young man getting close to another real person. If Po met someone he liked and wanted to strike up a friendship, the shadow would spy on that person until he discovered some immorality or misdeed. Shathu delighted in divulging the secret, hurtful knowledge to Po, ruining his chance for human friendship.

"One night after a show, a young woman named Ami approached Po and asked him to sign her program. He signed it and struck up a conversation. They went out for dinner together and found they had much in common. She was not strikingly attractive, but Po instantly fell in love with her innocence and charm. As he walked her home through the dark city, where Shathu could only join them beneath the street lamps, she sang a song. Hers was truly a beautiful voice. Po asked her if she would like to sing before his act on the following night. Ami was shy, but Po did everything in his power to convince her, and she finally accepted his invitation.

"The next morning when the sun rose, the shadow was livid that the young man had spent so much time with the girl. All day the dark form whispered into Po's ears reasons why Ami was no good for him. After lunch Shathu went to spy on her but found that she was an even-tempered, loving person to one and all. Still, he flew back to the young man and told him lies about her. Our hero refused to listen, and the shadow went mad with envy.

"That night Ami sang in front of a huge audience and was so admired, the spectators called for another song and another. The girl kept singing, and by the time her voice finally gave out, it was too late to begin The Boon Companion. Po was not concerned, even though Shathu whispered that the singer would ruin them. 'She is real,' said the young man, 'and we are not. It is only right that the crowd appreciate her more.'

"Later that evening after a walk through the city in the dark, the two new lovers came to a halt beneath a street lamp. As Po kissed the girl with the golden voice, he did not notice that projected on the wall behind them his shadow held hers by the throat. The kiss was long, exceedingly long. And it went on too long, for Po felt Ami go limp in his arms. When he pulled her away from him, he discovered she was dead."

CALVARY CHURCH

*P*O TURNED on his own shadow and tried to avenge Ami's death, but how could he? Shathu laughed as the young man smashed his bleeding fists against the brick wall. A passerby saw Po acting violently and the body of the young woman lying dead at his feet and screamed 'Murder!' And our hero fled into the night.

"The only place he could think to go for help that was dark enough to escape his shadow was the confessional booth at the local church. There he sat, waiting for the priest to appear on the other side of the small screen. Finally the priest came in the morning and blessed the young man, asking him what were his sins. Po told the old priest everything. The priest told him, 'I cannot help you, for you are possessed by an evil entity. You must travel up Ossinto Mountain and find the saint who lives in the caves there. It is said that she has the power to face down such wickedness.'

"Po spent the rest of the day hiding in the confessional. When night fell, he gathered supplies quickly and fled the city before daybreak when he would certainly be discovered and arrested for Ami's murder. Whenever he passed through an area of light, he could hear Shathu laughing at him. When the sun rose and Po had reached the base of the mountain, the shadow's laughter and insults raged constantly.

"Although he was weary from lack of sleep, the young man began the ascent. By afternoon he stood in the snow outside the saint's cave and called to her. The saint, whose heart was always open to pleas for help from those who sought her, emerged from the cave. She was radiant, dressed in a blue cloak the color of the sky. Light emanated from and encircled her head of long blond hair.

"While Shathu berated him, Po recounted his tale for the saint. When he had finished speaking, the saint told him, 'Don't you see, my poor friend, that you are troubled? This shadow is merely an invention of your mind. I know you didn't mean to, but it was really you who killed Ami. It was your jealousy of her beautiful voice, a voice you had desired since childhood.'

"Po was horrified to hear the words of the saint. He could not bear the fact that he had strangled Ami. Without another word, he walked to the edge of the precipice and leaped to his death. The saint felt great sorrow at the young man's decision, for she knew she could have saved his soul. Then, as she was about to return to her cave, she noticed that Po's shadow was still standing before her.

"Shathu came forward and wrapped his long dark fingers around the shadow neck of the saint. The saint, feeling her life leaving her, called on her savior and was filled with a great cosmic energy. She glowed like a star, attempting to burn away the existence of the murderous dark form. When Shathu was on the verge of incineration, he called on his savior, and his pervasive gloom increased. A terrible battle between light and dark ensued.

"In the last rays of the setting sun, Shathu was victorious in extinguishing the flame that was the saint. Her body dropped dead upon the ground as darkness prevailed. Only two small sparks of her sacred fire escaped. They flew into the night sky, turning into brilliant snowflakes that fell on the town below."

Here, Mrs. Charbuque went silent. Some minutes passed before I realized she was finished. Although she said nothing more, I bid her a good day and left without having to be told to go by Watkin.

I found it disconcerting when I left the beach house and stepped outside. Where I was used to leaving Mrs. Charbuque and stepping out into a crowded street, with the noise of traffic and the sight of huge buildings crowding out the view of the sky, I found instead sand dunes and sea grass and utter tranquillity. I shook my head to get my bearings as I took the stone path and began to ascend the dunes. By the time I was traveling through the hills of sand back toward the ferry dock, I was laughing out loud.

All I could imagine was some parent reading the tale of "The Boon Companion" to his child at night, using that sweet affected voice grown-ups sometimes use when addressing the young. If that story actually appeared in the book of fairy tales, I swore on the spot I would eat my hat. I made a mental note to check the volume, which was now in my possession, when I returned to the city.

If she had not acquired the story from the book, which was more than likely, then from where? And what was her reason for telling it? Of course, there were bothersome parallels to her own fractured autobiography, but as for absolute connections, they were as elusive as real understanding often is in dreams. For now, I crumpled the thing up in my thoughts and tossed it out onto the sea wind, for I did not need its confusing symbolism mucking up the vision I intended to paint. "A laudable attempt to bewilder me, Luciere," I said to a seagull whizzing by overhead, "but I have transcended your insane shenanigans."

The following morning I woke before the sunrise and left the La Grange, carrying my paint box, my easel, and, rolled up in three swaths of canvas, the pieces needed to construct a stretcher. I didn't want anyone to know where I was going, so I did not bother to arrange for a ride. Luckily even the night clerk had dozed off and was leaning back in his chair, snoring. I made my way to the Montauk Highway and headed east as Father Loomis had instructed. My baggage was cumbersome—the paint box alone, which held everything I would need, weighed at least thirty pounds—but I had lugged just such supplies around so often in my youth that my now much older body finally recalled the task and settled down to it.

Calvary Church was not large, but it was beautifully constructed with a small steeple and tall doors. Panes of stained glass depicting biblical scenes lined the length of the structure, while the pews and altar were made from highly polished cherrywood. As the priest had said, the doors were unlocked. I entered the dim space. The sun was just then rising, and it set the colorful scenes along the right side of the church to glowing. An aroma of incense lingered in the dreary atmosphere. My mother had made me attend services when I was a child, and I remembered that distinctive smell of mystery, of ritual, of death. It was Sabott who turned me away from incorporated religion by saying, "At the heart of the ancient inception of it lie the quintessential questions and answers, but the present-day dogma it comes wrapped in can only weigh an artist down."

I strode up the aisle toward the altar and called out the name of Father Loomis. A few minutes later, he appeared from an inconspicuous doorway to the left of the altar. "Piambo," he said, smiling.

"I'm sorry to come so early, Father, but as I told you, I am trying to retain my privacy and needed to escape the inn before the other guests had risen."

"No problem, my boy. I rise every day with the sun. Come, I'll show you your studio."

The old carriage house out behind the church was an ideal spot, a large empty space with plenty of light. A good blaze in the fireplace would effectively heat the area against the November temperatures, which of late had been rather bitter until late into the morning. Luckily there was also a cot in the corner that I could rest on and a small table. The old man showed me where the woodpile was and told me not to hesitate to call him if I needed anything. He invited me to join him in the church for a glass of wine when I was done working in the evening, and then he left me to my own devices.

After building a nice fire, I set to work immediately, setting up my easel and unrolling the canvas. On the small tabletop, I began constructing a stretcher from the lengths of wood I had carried from New York. This was one aspect of the job I could do in my sleep. Although I carried a small one in my box, I hardly ever even used a square to check the angles. Once the basic frame was completed, I stretched the canvas over it and cut it to fit with a razor. In mere minutes I had the material folded and nailed in place and had hammered the keys into the back corners to keep the painting surface as taut as possible. It was no later than nine o'clock by the time the rectangle was primed and drying on the easel. I sat down on the cot and smoked a cigarette, feeling very pleased with my work and my new studio.

While the canvas dried, I set to remaking a sketch of the figure of Mrs. Charbuque. The image came clearly to me, and the charcoal pencil moved over the paper with the ease of flowing water. The drawing did not take very long to complete. When it was finished, I stared at it for longer than it took to create it. I knew then that I needed some time to consider it more fully. Putting on my coat and hat, I left the studio and took the path that led back through the trees toward the bay.

At the water's edge, I found a section of a tree trunk, driftwood that had long before rolled ashore and dried in the sun. There I sat for hours in the cold, staring out across the bay. I found it surprising that the mystery of Mrs. Charbuque, the constant threat of her husband, and the enigmatic part that Watkin played in the whole charade no longer interested me much. In the sublime presence of Nature, I was able to circumvent that sideshow and find the elements of my life I cared most about. I spent a good bit of time remembering Shenz and Sabott, and even longer thinking about Samantha. Now the commission had become simply a professional arrangement that I would execute in my usual accomplished manner. Damn the money and damn my artistic insecurities. I realized it was not worth bartering away the present for a future no one could foretell.

HER BEWITCHING FORM

FOR THE first time in weeks, I worked with intensity and clarity, approaching the portrait of Mrs. Charbuque with utter poise. I lost myself in the process, executing every painterly technique with the greatest unconsidered facility. With each pale explosion of color on canvas, her bewitching form slowly cohered as it had out of smoke in my dream of Sabott. Even though I followed the same methods I had during my first attempt, it all seemed new to me, startlingly fresh and alive. Nothing was mundane, from the depiction of the fingernails to the pupils of her eyes. Every strand of hair was rendered with a genuine sense of joy and accomplishment.

My days started early, before sunrise. Each morning I struck out in a different direction to throw off any interested onlookers, but I always doubled back and made for the church. After stoking the fire, I would smoke a cigarette and begin work. Usually around ten o'clock Father Loomis would come to visit and see how I was getting on. He brought coffee, and we would sit and chat for a half hour or so. He was thrilled to witness each day's progress and offered just the right amount of praise and speculation. I would work for a few more hours until lunch, when I walked to the bay and ate the sandwiches prepared for me the previous night by the cook at the inn. And when day was done, and the sun was leaving the sky, I would go over to the church, sit in the sacristy with Loomis, and have a glass of wine.

The schedule suited me perfectly and pushed the thought of trouble from my mind. On the third day of the week, though, when I returned to the La Grange in the evening for dinner, the clerk told me that two gentlemen had called that day looking for me. When I asked him to describe them, he said, "The first, this morning, was blind. An older fellow. Very polite."

"Did he leave a message?" I asked.

"He said he would return to speak to you."

"And the second?" I asked, with a feeling of dread.

"A younger man, perhaps your age, with a mustache. He seemed rather annoyed when I told him I could divulge neither your room number nor your whereabouts."

"Listen carefully," I told him. "If the younger man returns, do not accept anything from him. Tell the rest of the staff too. He might be dangerous."

That night I slept uneasily, knowing that Charbuque was in town, expecting him to emerge from the shadows of my room at any minute. I also wondered why Watkin was looking for me and why he had not left a message. My thoughts turned to the portrait, and I resolved to take steps to protect it while I was away from it.

The next morning I left my bed even earlier than usual and went out into the cold predawn air. I cannot describe my relief upon reaching the carriage house studio and finding the painting exactly as I had left it the previous night. That morning, while we shared our morning coffee, I asked Father Loomis if he would store the piece in the church at night.

He was more than happy to comply and told me I could hide it behind the altar each night before taking my leave. That evening as we sat having our wine, he told me he was thinking of having an altarpiece painted depicting stories from the Bible. "A beautiful backdrop to the Mass" was how he put it. We discussed what subject matter would be appropriate. He was leaning toward the story of Jonah, but I told him he should choose a scene from Genesis, because creation was the only proof of God's existence in the world. He shook his head, called me a heathen, and refilled my glass.

That night on my return to the inn there were neither messages nor tales of visitors to distress me. I slept soundly with no interruptions. But the next morning, after starting the fire in the studio, I came to the church to retrieve the portrait and to my horror found that it was missing.

"Loomis!" I yelled.

"Easy, Piambo," I heard behind me.

I turned and saw the priest standing in his robe, holding the picture.

"What are you doing, Father?" I asked.

"Well, my son, last night there was a visitor to your studio. I woke sometime after two and heard a voice coming from the carriage house. I loaded my shotgun and went out back there to see what was about. There was no light other than the moon, but I could make out a shadowy form pacing back and forth in your studio. Whoever this intruder was, he was wild with anger, cursing like the devil. I aimed the shotgun in the air and fired, and he took off into the trees. I yelled that I was going to summon the police. I realized he must be looking for the painting, and so when I returned to the church I took it from behind the altar and hid it under my covers with me to protect it. Of course, the gun lay on the other side of me."

"I can't thank you enough," I said to him.

"It was nothing," he said. "Just don't tell anyone I spent the night with a naked woman in my bed."

"I'll take the painting with me when I leave tonight," I said. "I don't want to put you in any danger."

"Nonsense," said Loomis. "I'll keep it safe here for you. I don't usually like to lock the doors, but once they are secured, one would need a battering ram to force them open. It will be safer here than at the inn."

I reluctantly agreed, knowing Charbuque was as slippery a character as the Boon Companion in his wife's incongruous story, but the priest had made a good point and seemed honestly committed to the task.

The night of the fourth day, upon returning to the inn, I sat down and wrote two letters. One was to Sills, alerting him that Charbuque was no longer in the city but now roaming around Long Island. I wrote the second letter to Samantha and told her where I was and the whole story of my stay on the south shore. I told her I loved her, and asked her to come back to me. I wrote that if I did not hear from her, I might stay on to paint landscapes for a time.

On the morning of the sixth day of my final week in the orbit of Mrs. Charbuque, I finished the painting. One last brush stroke to adjust the expression at the corner of the lips, and then I stood back, realizing it needed nothing more. I lay the brush and palette down on the small table and staggered back to sit on the cot. She was exactly the way I had pictured her in my mind. The sight of it, the sense of completion, brought me to tears. It was by far the best painting I had ever made. Now that it was finished, I felt empty. I had worked so diligently for so long; the abrupt cessation disconcerted me.

I varnished the canvas, only once, to bring out the glow of the solitary figure without making the surface reflective. After completing this last step, I lay down on the cot and slept for the remainder of the day. That night I did not return to the La Grange but stoked the fire in the studio and stayed there, standing guard until morning.

Finally, after a night spent staring into the fireplace, conjuring ghosts and scenes of my past in the flames and watching them

dance about in the hearth like moving figures on a magical painting, I saw the sun show itself. The portrait was dry enough. I put
it in a cheap frame I had bought in town, and wrapped it in paper.
After the paper, I wrapped it again in oilskin to protect it from the
weather and tied the whole package securely with twine.

I then returned to the inn, ate breakfast with the package sitting
next to me in the dining room, and afterward went to my room
to rest for an hour or two. At noon I arose, put on my coat and
hat, and went down to arrange for a carriage to take me to the
docks. While I was standing in the lobby waiting for my ride, I
happened to notice a copy of the late edition of the *Babylon
Gazette* lying on the counter. The headline fairly screamed at me:
LOCAL WOMAN DIES, CRYING TEARS OF BLOOD. Be-
neath that, in slightly smaller type, ran: MYSTERIOUS DISEASE
PLAGUING NEW YORK CITY STRIKES LONG ISLAND.

At that moment my ride pulled up. Before I could get into the
conveyance and be on my way, I was shivering uncontrollably with
the realization that Charbuque had begun his game again. What
was more distressing was the thought that it was I who had forced
his hand.

PHANTASM IN THE FLESH

W HEN I arrived at the dock the ferry was there, but I was told that there was some engine trouble and it would be a while before they got it up to snuff. I was directed to a nearby establishment, a shack whose sign said The Copper Kettle. It was only a two-minute walk back up the road to the bay, and I was assured that someone would fetch me when things were in order. I was peeved, to say the least, anxious to put an end to the affair, but I had no choice. As I walked to the tavern, I noticed that the sky was growing overcast and the air smelled of impending snow.

I spent much of the afternoon nursing a whiskey in that hovel. To be fair, the old fishermen and clammers who were the place's regular patrons were a good bunch. They looked and sounded like a gaggle of pirates, bearing scars and tattoos and using foul language, but they treated me kindly and told me many tales about the history and lore of the bay. When I informed them I was a painter and on my way to deliver a portrait to a patron, they laughed as if this was the funniest thing in the world. Finally a lad came to the Kettle to fetch me. I shook hands all around and thanked them for their hospitality.

I hadn't realized how late it was until I stepped out of the tavern and saw that the sun was already well on the wane. I hurried along the dock and boarded the boat. There were no other passengers, but the ferry captain seemed more than happy to take me across. The water was choppy, and the skies were heavy with dark clouds save for a sliver of red at the horizon. I stood on the deck with the mate as we made the crossing. He took out a small spyglass with which he showed me the different sights back onshore. "It's blowing up pretty good now," he said to me above the wind. "You can see the clammers heading in."

I took the glass from him and turned it on the boats making for the dock at Babylon. I noticed a small skiff with only two people in it. I could barely believe my eyes, but I was looking at Watkin. A young man was rowing, and the old fellow was sitting facing the pilot. "Perhaps he is coming to fetch me or tell me that if I am not finished, the commission is canceled," I thought.

Although the sun had not yet set, the sky was so overcast it might as well have. It was early night as I left the basin at Captree Island and, portrait under my arm, headed east over the dunes toward the summerhouse of Mrs. Charbuque. As I crested the last dune and looked down into the valley of sand that hid the house, I was struck by how different the same place could feel depending upon the circumstances. Gone was the warm feeling of tranquillity I had felt when visiting during the daylight hours, for now the house appeared dark and forbidding. I saw no light from where I stood, and the tin chimes on the porch were ringing with an insistence that might wake the dead. I descended the dune and made my way up the stone path to the porch. Drawing closer, I saw that the door had been left somewhat ajar.

The dark house and the open door made me nervous, reminding me of my discovery when Luciere had fled the city. I prayed she was not gone again. Although the situation alarmed me, my desire to deliver the portrait was even greater. I would not be denied my opportunity to fulfill the commission. I went up the steps and knocked on the doorframe. No one came, and I heard no sound from inside the house. The wind was blowing rather wildly now outside the valley of dunes, and it was difficult to hear above its keening.

"Oh, hell," I said, and stepped into the house. The floorboards creaked mercilessly as I advanced one step at a time, trying to remember the layout of the place from my previous visit. The rooms were draped in thick shadow. I called out, "Luciere." When I got no response, I felt my way along the walls and around furniture to our meeting room at the back of the house. By the time I reached the door, I was quaking like a child, not even completely aware of what it was that had me so frightened.

I breathed a great sigh of relief when I saw a sliver of light coming from beneath the door. "She is waiting for me," I comforted myself, "but cannot hear my call because of the wind." Standing for a moment outside her den, I gathered myself together and then opened the door and stepped inside. The scene I had grown so used to—the screen, the solitary chair—was made lurid by the addition of an oil lamp on the floor beneath the left-hand window. Its guttering glow cast long shadows upon the wall and ceiling.

"I've come with the portrait," I said.

I heard rustling behind the screen and the sound of her chair creaking.

"I hope you will be pleased," I said, and set to undoing, with my penknife, the wraps that held the painting. When it was free, I walked forward and lifted it up over the top of the screen. I was reassured when I felt another pair of hands take the weight from mine. With a tempest of butterflies swarming in my solar plexus, a sense of anticipation that could have cut a diamond, I sat down in my chair and waited.

"I saw Watkin making the crossing to town," I said, unable to contain my nervousness.

She sighed.

I did not know whether to take this as a response to my state-

ment or a critique of my work. My answer came a few long minutes later when something flew over the top of the screen and
landed on the floor at my feet. I looked at it before retrieving it;
a monumental stack of cash tied up with string. I grabbed it up
and began counting. Not only was it a huge number of bills, but
the denominations were staggering. My thumb flipped their corners three times, and I gloated with each pass.

"Luciere," I said, "does this mean I have done it?"

I waited, and then saw a black-gloved hand grab the side of the
screen. The seemingly immovable barrier was violently cast aside
with the ease of a leaf being buffeted by a November gale. It happened so quickly, I could barely follow. But before the thing had
crashed to the floor, I knew I was looking directly at Moret Charbuque.

"Yes, Piambo," he said. "You've certainly done it and done it for
the last time." He held a gun in his gloved hand. I could not move,
but still I was curious to see this phantasm in the flesh. He was a
man of somewhat younger years than myself, with refined features,
a mustache, and long locks that fell to his collar in back. He was
dressed in a black jacket and black trousers, and his white shirt was
opened at the top.

"What have you done with your wife?" I managed to ask.

"Let us just say, she will not be returning," he said, and smiled.

"I'll be going, then," I said.

He leveled the gun at me and laughed. "I'm afraid you will not
be returning either," he said.

"I thought you were unable to approach your wife," I said.
"How did the game change?"

"I knew all along that you were seeing her. You were making
love to her. And the painting proves it. She broke the rules. She
gave in to infidelity, and that, my friend, gives me license to seek
revenge."

"But you haven't seen the painting until now," I said.

"Sorry, Piambo. I saw it in the church. When that old fool of a priest came out to fire his shotgun, I doubled back and went inside. I'd seen you place it behind the altar earlier. All I needed was a quick look at it, and I was off before the priest returned to the church. And that showed me the truth."

"I swear to you, I have never laid eyes upon your wife," I said.

"Come, come," he said. "In any event, you have your commission, and a little something extra along with it."

"A bullet?" I asked.

"Those bills have been doused with the Tears of Carthage. Before too long your remorse at having treated me so shoddily will give way to tears. You will cry blood for me, Piambo."

This revelation made me instantly frantic, and in rapid succession I saw in my mind's eye the victim I had discovered in the alleyway and Shenz, weeping his life away. I lashed out in fear and anger. Throwing the hefty stack of money at Charbuque's head, I lunged for him. He was taken by surprise but managed to fire the gun. I felt the bullet whiz past my ear, but that did not deter me. I was on him in a flash. Grabbing the bottom rung of his chair, I tipped it backward, and he sprawled onto the floor, the gun falling from his grasp. Before he could retrieve it, I booted him in the head as viciously as I could.

He was not unconscious, but he was groggy. Wasting no time, I searched my coat pocket for the small bottle of tincture of nutmeg that Watkin had given me. I found and opened it. Tilting my head back I poured a liberal dosage into both eyes. It was immediately evident why the parasite that brought the tears found this solution inhospitable. My eyes stung as if being attacked by wasps. There was an infernal burning sensation, and no matter how much I rubbed them my sight would not clear. For all intents and purposes, I was totally blind.

I turned and ran for the door, but my sense of direction had abandoned me, sending me headlong into the wall, knocking me off my feet. I was stunned and scrabbling to my knees when I felt a boot force me back to the floor. Before I could make another move, the gun barrel was pressed against my cheek. I could see nothing but could feel my hands being tied behind my back, my ankles being bound together. Struggle was now useless.

Charbuque was winded. I could hear him heaving. "Your painting will burn with you, Piambo," he said, but there was something wrong with the voice. It modulated with the pronouncement of the words and ended in a higher register. My eyes cleared then, and I blinked them repeatedly to gain more focus. What I saw was Charbuque across the room, leaning over to pick up the lantern. His glove was off, and the hand that reached down was most assuredly feminine, and when the locket swung out on its chain from inside the open collar of his shirt, I knew it was Luciere.

"I know who you are," I said.

"You know nothing," came the reply, but this time the voice was missing its gruff affectation. It was most assuredly the voice of Mrs. Charbuque.

The next thing I saw was the lantern smash and shatter against the back wall. Fiery oil flew outward, and each of the little puddles of flame took hold on the dry unvarnished wood. Strangely, before departing, Luciere leaned over, lifted the screen, and set it up in its usual position. "I don't want to have to watch you die," she said, and, with this, stepped over my body and left the room.

BLIND DEVOTION

HE FLAMES spread quickly as I struggled against my bonds. Smoke billowed up, gathering against the ceiling like a storm cloud, and I knew that the entire house would soon be engulfed. I found it difficult to breathe, the heat from the fire making the air incredibly heavy. My plan was to roll onto my back and then bend my legs at the knees, bringing my ankles up within reach of my bound hands. I managed to get onto my back, and that was about all I could manage. That simple movement left me drained, and I stared up at the ceiling and screamed for help with the little strength I had left.

My throat was soon parched from the heat, and my cries were little more than hoarse, whispered pleas. Eventually only my lips moved, producing no sound at all. I was disappearing. My money, infected as it was, was burning, my painting was being incinerated, I had stepped away from my daily life, lost my friend and my lover. I was, in all, now no more substantial than Charbuque. I imagined the fire consuming me and the combustion of my being offering little more than a dull burp. My original reason for having taken on the commission was to test my art, but as it turned out, much more had been tested and found sadly wanting. Then I thought I was hallucinating, for I saw Sabott standing over me, staring down, holding what looked like a palette knife.

"Master," I said.

"Good evening, Mr. Piambo," he said, but now I could see it was not Sabott. I blinked my eyes once and then once again, and the form above metamorphosed into Watkin. He was not holding a palette knife but a long hunting knife. He grabbed me hard by the left shoulder and flipped my body over. In a moment, my wrists were free. Another pass with the knife and my ankles came apart. He put the knife in a scabbard on his belt and helped me to my feet.

The fire was nearly everywhere in the room. It had crawled along the walls and now blocked the exit. Watkin was searching frantically with those pure white orbs for an avenue of escape. "Follow me," he said, stepping forward and lifting my chair from the floor. "When I clear the window," he called over the roar of the flames, "you've got to move fast because the incoming draft will fan the fire." I didn't have time to so much as nod. He ran at the window to the right, the only passage not choked off by the blaze, and tossed the chair. The glass shattered, and he yelled, "Now!"

Yet I stood helplessly dazed until I felt his hand on my back, shoving me. When I reached the opening I dove, my arms out in front of me. It seemed as if I flew for a few seconds before coming down hard on the sand outside the house. I had only enough time to roll clear before Watkin followed, landing only a few inches from me. After helping me to my feet, he supported me with an arm around my shoulder, and we made our way to the top of the dunes.

There we sat, watching the inferno below us.

"Thank you, Watkin," I said.

"My apologies, Piambo. I was on my way to town to try to find you and warn you to be on your guard. I knew things were coming to a head. As soon as I got over to the dock, I asked if anyone had seen you and they told me you had taken the ferry. I told the oarsman I would double his pay if he would take me back immediately." He put his hand to his eyes and, one after the other, plucked out the white prosthetics that had been the false proof of his blindness. "I won't be needing these anymore," he said, and tossed them away.

"Can you explain any of this?" I asked.

"I'll try," he said, and turned to look at me, his face lit by the fire from below. I couldn't believe it, and still can't upon recollecting it, but I swear, Watkin was cross-eyed.

"I loved her, Piambo. I loved her as if she was my daughter, but by the time she hired me to help her, she was already damaged, I'm afraid."

"Damaged?" I asked.

"Troubled," he said. "She was already more at home behind the screen than in the everyday world. There, she had a sense of power and confidence, and her performances reinforced that feeling. Still, I could tell she was not right and was moving always closer to a crisis."

"London?" I asked.

"Yes," he said. "She was weakened by the tour. I thought the travel would do her good, but it only exacerbated her mania. She took physically ill, and in that time had a breakdown."

"And was Charbuque a lover who left her?" I asked.

"There never was any Charbuque save in her mind," said Watkin. "She concocted Charbuque, not as a lover. She did not want a lover, she wanted a persona she thought would give her the same power and confidence in the world that she had behind the screen. From what she knew of the world, one had to be a ruthless, manipulative man to be safe.

"What brought it to a head was that one day a cleaning woman at the hotel we were staying in came to her room. The maid did not know she was behind the screen, and Luciere watched through her secret pinprick as the woman pulled the stopper from the ancient silver lamp, something Luciere had never dared do, and sniffed the opening. The maid most likely thought it held expensive perfume and dabbed it on her neck before going about her chores.

"Twenty minutes later, the woman sat down in the chair facing the screen and began to cry, and you know what happened next. Luciere watched the woman expire before her eyes. She wanted desperately to help her but could not venture out from behind the screen. The police ruled the death the result of disease but were still skeptical about it. We had to leave London quickly.

"Luciere did not want to accept responsibility for the death of the woman, so she invented Charbuque and a whole story to go along with him. From time to time, he would surface. Since I had worked in the theater, she begged me to tell her about costume and disguise, and I did. She made herself up to be a man. Eventually, in 1886, she settled upon the guise of the writer Robert Louis Stevenson because she read his novel *The Strange Case of Dr. Jekyll and Mr. Hyde,* which came out that year. Charbuque was her Mr. Hyde. You see, they were the Twins.

"Sometimes she would go months without a visit from him. But each time he came, he had more power. She would go out at night in that getup and do terrible things to surrogates as a way of hurting her feminine self. In order to regain her power behind the screen, she would hire painters, all men, and play with their minds. 'They are so egotistical, they make perfect subjects,' she told me. The best that can be said is that she suffered a grotesque sickness. It is truly beyond explanation."

"Was this recent spate of murders the first time she used the Tears of Carthage as a weapon?" I asked.

"I think so," he said. "When we returned to the States, she had me research what the substance in the lamp could be. A young fellow from Greenwich Village, a scholar of such things, told me of its origin and how it had been used in antiquity as a weapon. And fool that I was, I could refuse her nothing. I told her, which makes me as guilty as she."

"Where will she go now?" I said. "She seems to have made a full break, leaving her screen behind to burn."

"I don't know, but now I owe it to the world to stop her. I can't let this go on. Too many have suffered; too many have lost their lives."

I had a thousand more questions for Watkin, but he rose and swept the sand off his trousers. "I will find her before she kills again, Piambo," he said, his determination punctuated by the partial collapse of the roof. There was a loud groan, a crash, and then a million sparks flew into the air and were carried away on the wind.

He looked as if he was making ready to leave, so I asked him one last thing. "Did you ever see her?"

"Of course," he said, and took my hand and shook it. "Good-bye, Piambo. Forgive me." He turned and walked out eastward across the dunes where there was nothing but beach. I watched him until he was swallowed by the night.

Then I was alone. It started to snow, and I could not help but wonder if what had just transpired was also not just an enormous red herring. I had nothing left save my life, but I deemed this the perfect condition for an artist seeking to create something beautiful. As I headed back through the snow toward the shacks to look for shelter for the night, it seemed to me that the flakes were falling two by two, in perfect pairs.

MY SELF-PORTRAIT

HE NEXT day, after making my way back to the La Grange, I telephoned the local police and told them everything I knew. They told me that just the previous evening they had heard from Detective Sills in New York. Two days later, John and a few other men from the force came out to Babylon to search for Mrs. Charbuque and Watkin. It was good to see my old friend, and we spent a night drinking whiskey at the Copper Kettle before he had to be off in search of his quarry. I asked after Samantha, and he told me she was fine. I had hoped perhaps she had sent a message with him, but none was forthcoming.

When all the hullabaloo associated with the strange case had finally died down, I made a decision to stay on instead of returning to the city. It was my desire to paint for a few months the natural scenes I had become so enamored of during my time at the carriage house. Father Loomis made me a deal. He offered to let me stay in the studio free of charge if I would paint an altarpiece for him. I told him I would, but the theme must be from Genesis.

"Very well," he said. "You can do me a favor, though."

"And what is that?" I asked.

"When you paint Eve, give her the face of the woman in your other painting, whoever she was," he said.

I made the priest this promise but did him one better, because I painted both Adam and Eve so that they bore the visages of Mrs. Charbuque.

Except for missing Samantha so terribly, I had what was really quite an idyllic life. After moving my things from the La Grange to the carriage house studio, I set up a daily routine. In the mornings I walked through the woods and down by the bay carrying my sketchbook, making preliminary drawings for landscapes I would later execute. The weather was colder than ever, and I could not take the easel outside. In the afternoons I worked on the church altarpiece. After eating dinner and having a glass of wine with Loomis, I returned to the studio to light another fire and two oil lamps and create, from my sketches and my memory, those scenes I had witnessed on my morning walks.

Landscape painting was new to me. Gone were the figures and the need to render an expression precisely. In the manner in which I approached them, these pieces were more fluid in nature, offering greater room for interpretation. I was not working in the classical style or the Pre-Raphaelite or the Impressionist. There wasn't a moment's thought about where I might sell them or to whom. I was simply painting what I felt and what I saw. The experience was most liberating. After a few weeks I lined them all up against the walls of the studio and was amazed to see that they represented my thoughts and emotions more vividly than any portrait might have. They were, in a sense, all together, my self-portrait.

It was near the end of November, and I was in the church one afternoon laboring on the image of Satan as the serpent. My snake had a human face, and in honor of Shenz, I used him as the model. I had just finished his beard when the doors of the church opened wide and two men from the local funeral parlor entered pushing a wheeled cart upon which sat a coffin. Usually such a delivery was attended by the deceased's loved ones. Today, however, the casket was accompanied only by the two deliverymen and the priest.

He approached the altar and said to me, "You can keep working, Piambo. I don't think anyone will be attending this Mass. From what I've been told, the man who brought this poor woman's body to the funeral parlor said she passed away from a broken heart, although the official certificate says consumption. Do you find that odd?" He looked at me sideways, as if wanting to say more. When I didn't respond, he continued. "The stranger left a request with the undertaker that I say a Mass for her before she is buried, but he was not able to stay for it. He left quite a nice sum as payment, though."

"What was his name?" I asked, afraid to hear the answer.

"He didn't say," said Loomis softly. "But the deceased's name is Sibyl."

All I could manage was a nod.

"Well," he said briskly as I placed my hand on the smooth wood of the coffin, "I have to go to town for an hour or so. When I return, I'll say the Mass. I suppose I'll be praying to the rafters. Unless, of course, you want to stand in as a mourner."

"Perhaps," I said.

"That would be good of you, but either way is fine, my son," said Father Loomis. He turned, walked down the aisle, and then left the church accompanied by the two workers.

I held my hand over my mouth as if stifling a scream. The wood of the coffin gleamed with the colored light that streamed in through the stained glass windows. I moved my fingers across its smooth surface. "Luciere," I said. "Luciere."

Here she lay behind her screen. I was no longer in her power, no longer striving to fulfill a commission. I knew that what I should do was complete my work for the day and leave. "Don't give in," I said aloud. I wondered how Watkin had actually done her in and made it look like consumption. Did this too fall into the category of his expertise in disguise and costume?

As I told myself it was time to go, my hand moved along the edge of the casket to find the latch. I slowly pulled it back. The lid popped open a sliver, free now from its clasp. I took two deep breaths and then whispered, "I am here, Mrs. Charbuque."

There is no reason to believe me, I know. What were the chances? But I tell you that the figure in my portrait and the woman in the coffin were one and the same. Yes, they were twins. I cried upon seeing her. Perhaps it was for her and her tortured existence, perhaps for me and all I'd been through. Whatever the reason, I felt as if I were weeping blood. She was dressed in a white gown, and around her neck was the locket that held the future. Very carefully I reached in and undid the chain from her neck. Holding the heart-shaped pendant before my eyes, I pictured the two snowflakes inside, unmelting, constantly swirling around each other in endless predictions of tomorrow. I slipped it into my pocket and closed the lid, making sure that it was latched.

I stayed for the Mass that afternoon, and I was the sole mourner at the funeral of Mrs. Charbuque.

EPILOGUE:
THE ANGEL ON THE BEACH

*T*wo days later I took a late-afternoon walk along the beach. I could not concentrate on work, and Father Loomis was away for the day. I strolled down to the shore and sat on my driftwood log. The sun was setting on the horizon, and the air was frigid, the water of the bay nearly frozen over in icy wavelets. I smoked a cigarette and thought about the city and how much I missed it just then. With only a few minutes of light left in the day, I rose and was about to start back to the studio when I saw a figure in the distance, approaching along the shore. At first glance, the person seemed to possess white wings like an angel. They beat wildly and glowed in the last rays of sunlight. A tremor of fear ran through me. Perhaps it was the spirit of Luciere returning to claim her locket. When finally those wings revealed themselves to be the wide ends of a long white scarf, I recognized who it was and went to meet her.

ACKNOWLEDGMENTS

I HOPE THAT the reader will not consider *The Portrait of Mrs. Charbuque* a historical novel in the strict sense of the term. Many of the locations, characters, phenomena, and events described herein were actualities of 1893 and can be validated by textual sources, but at the end of the day I am a fiction writer and not a historian. Occasionally I played it fast and loose with the facts, both out of necessity and desire, so that I could bring you the story of Piambo's strange commission. Still, there were many works I relied upon in my endeavor.

For a view of New York during this time period, I found the following books very helpful: *King's Handbook of New York City 1893* by Moses King; *Gramercy Park: An American Bloomsbury* by Carole Klein; *Walt Whitman's New York*, edited by Henry M. Christman; and *Victorian America: Transformation in Everyday Life 1876–1915* by Thomas J. Schlereth.

Some of the texts that helped to expand my limited knowledge of the art of painting, and especially Victorian-era painting, were *What Painting Is* by James Elkins, *The Art of Arts* by Anita Albus, *What Is Painting?* by Julian Bell, *Oil Painting Portraits* by Ray Smith,

Acknowledgments

Victorian Painting by Christopher Wood, *Whistler: A Biography* by Stanley Weintraub, and *John Singer Sargent: His Portrait* by Stanley Olson. The quote from Albert Pinkham Ryder that appears in the novel was found at Rickie Lee Jones's Albert Pinkham Ryder website.

For insight into the use of opium during the nineteenth century I am indebted to *The Seven Sisters of Sleep* by Mordicai C. Cooke and *Opium* by Martin Booth.

End Product: The First Taboo by Dan Sabbath and Mandel Hall is a truly amazing and delightful work on the history, philosophy, politics, and power of evacuants. It's a real shame this book is out of print.

For information concerning the Phoenicians, I turned to Glenn Markoe's *Phoenicians*.

Many individuals helped me as I worked on this project. First and foremost, I must thank my agent, Howard Morhaim, whose guidance and skill made it possible for me to write this book. I would also like to thank: Kevin Quigley for sharing with me his firsthand knowledge of the art of painting, Michael Gallagher and Bill Watkins for reading and commenting on the manuscript while in progress, Devi Pillai for her role as assistant editor, and Jennifer Brehl, editor, whose encouragement and expertise helped me make this story the best it could possibly be.